Edge of Sundown

Jennifer Worrell

"Compelling! Vivid, enigmatic characters struggling against a system rife with secrets."

Robin Quackenbush,Contributing Author, Writings to Stem Your Existential Dread

www.darkstroke.com

D1248617

Discover us online:
www.darkstroke.com

Join us on instagram:
www.instagram.com/darkstrokebooks/

Include **#darkstroke** in a photo of yourself
holding this book on Instagram and
something nice will happen.

Acknowledgements

First I must apologize in advance. As soon as you start naming people, someone inadvertently gets overlooked. And I'm going to lose some cred by saying that there aren't enough words to express my gratitude. Know that your support and time means the world to me.

Thank you to:
My parents, for encouraging me as a wee one and not making a deal with the Morlocks to take me ahead of schedule.

My husband Joel Wicklund, my biggest cheerleader. Putting up with 21+ years of my neuroses is admirable. Thank you for getting me through the rough spots and giving me the courage to submit my stories. I love you more than pie.

Laurence and Stephanie Patterson—who took a chance on a newb with a difficult concept—and my friends at Darkstroke Books. You welcomed me into the fold and made my dream come true.

Without my SU family, I don't think I'd have come this far. So many of you read bits and pieces of this book, and I owe you one.

Extra tip of the hat to Elias McClellan, Trond Hildahl, Robin Quackenbush, June Low, Myna Chang, Cayce Osborne, Carrie Houghton, Andrew Wentzell, Steve Judah, Devin Overman, Leslie Muzingo, and Mick Northam. Y'all are the Valrhona truffles on the sweet tables of life.

Emily Clark Victorson: your advice, I'm certain, helped make publication a reality.

Deborah Balogun, Glenda and Cregg Thompson, P. J. Mayhair, Courtney Maguire, Cassiopeia Mulholland, Beth Perry, Nancy Dinsmore, and my Query Trenches pals: thank you for putting up with my endless questions, having my back, and cheering me on.

Everyone who helped with research, especially my sensitivity readers: your input was invaluable. I learned a lot and hope I was respectful in my execution.

And finally, thank you to the teachers who encouraged me: from Ignatius Valentine Aloysius, who kicked me into high gear, to my kindergarten teacher Marilyn Davenport, who was sure I'd be a writer someday.

About the Author

If Jennifer were to make a deal with the Devil, she'd ask to live—in good health—just until she's finished reading all the books. She figures that's pretty square.

In case other bibliophiles attempt the same scheme, she's working hard to get all her ideas on paper. She writes multi-genre fiction and the occasional essay, and is currently working on a collection of shorts and two picture books that may or may not be suitable for children.

Edge of Sundown is her first novel. She's always been drawn to "what-ifs" and flawed characters, and has never quite mastered the happy ending.

Jennifer is a member of Chicago Writers Association and Independent Writers of Chicago, and works at a private university library.

To connect with her and find links to published works:
Check out her website - jenniferworrellwrites.com/
Twitter - www.twitter.com/JWorrellWrites, or
Facebook page - www.facebook.com/JWorrellWrites, and
Sign up to her newsletter - www.subscribepage.com/o7d4i7

Edge of
Sundown

Chapter One

Twilight was settling.

Val Haverford exhumed an ancient cardboard tube from his writing studio closet and smoothed the roll of floor plans onto his sketch table. They still smelled faintly of pencil lead and wood shavings and dime-store aftershave. But the sharp, precise lines were now fuzzy, paper tinged the color of weak tea. He couldn't fathom how his brother had found the time to draft them, much less hide such vast sheets right under his nose.

He immediately recognized the one he was searching for, a sketch based on incessant dreaming: twin houses angled northeast on the bank of the Gulf of Mexico. Years after Michael's death, imagining what might have been gnawed a hollowness straight to his bones, unearthing guilt once buried deep. As long as their neighbors could deliver vengeance, they could go back to living in their perfect world.

Now those old scandals felt like déjà vu, the source of inspiration he'd blown half a century avoiding.

Careful to handle the paper with a soft touch, he affixed it to a mat board, measuring once, twice, confirming it was perfect. He set it into an ebony frame and hung it where it was visible from his writing desk, to remind him why he sat there every dawn, every night, typing until his fingers were raw.

Crimson spilled across Lake Michigan where the water met the horizon, its shimmer telling the time. Grabbing his partial manuscript off the desk, Val considered another quick read-through. After so many years of block, the bravado that led to calling his agent now felt rash. He should have stuck to his forte, a classic sci-fi adventure, and avoided last-minute doubt.

Ten minutes. He could skim in ten minutes.

He stopped short halfway through the first page. One letter —always one letter—flickered like a figment of imagination, an apparition from a nightmare that lingers after you wake. His fist curled around the pages until his knuckles threatened to pop at the joints. He squeezed his eyes tight, counted to ten. When he opened them again, everything was still.

That should grant some reprieve. At least for a while.

Stuffing the pages in a manila envelope, he chucked it into his portfolio along with a copy of the *Tribune* and headed into the city, gray clouds distorting the sunset.

***

Submerged in dusky light and the revenant spice of cigarettes, Calvyn's was the last unpretentious dive on Chicago's Gold Coast: no menu, no frills, and no name. Calvyn himself brought the usual double Macallan on the rocks to Val's permanently reserved table. Val slipped a roll of quarters in the wall-mounted jukebox and cobbled together a playlist of sultry R&B. He sank into a chair, enveloping himself with the smooth sound of Sarah Vaughn while the scotch melted down his throat. His favorite form of meditation.

Detecting an excited chitter in the booth along the opposite wall, he opened one eye just enough to see two women, both having seen the bottoms of too many rocks glasses, giggling and throwing sidelong looks in his direction. He whipped out the *Trib* and fanned it open, busying himself with finding an article. At the sound of "I'm going to talk to him," he ducked low and sped up the search, crumpling the pages as though that would deliver some great air of urgency and importance.

"You really need to get out more."

Val jolted at the disembodied male voice and rubbed a floater from his eye.

Graham Van Ellis, gray overcoat bulleted with rain, leaned his umbrella against the jukebox.

"I will never get used to that," Val said. He raised his glass

4

to Calvyn—ice rattling without his permission—and stuck out two fingers: another scotch, and a beer for my friend.

Calvyn nodded. He'd already popped the cap on a Bud.

Graham hung his coat on a wall hook and willowed into a chair. Smoothing down his tie, he regarded the pair of women. "They were just being friendly! And two of 'em, not bad."

"No thanks. I don't think my life can handle that sort of thing."

Graham's laugh was hoarse and strident after years of supporting the tobacco industry. "Your life, please. How busy are you?"

Val slid the fat manila envelope across the table. "Don't give up on me yet."

Graham slapped the tabletop. "I hoped that's why you called me out here on such a shitty night! You writing again?"

"Started Monday, yes."

"Another Battaglia?"

"I'm done with that series. Time to go in a new direction."

"Again?" Graham scooted his chair forward. "All right. What's this one about?"

"That," Val said, pointing up at the muted TV screen flashing a photo of a redheaded teen boy, another victim of violence on the Southwest Side. "And this." He closed the newspaper and spun it to show Graham the front page, a photo of an old man in tattered clothes. Neighboring district, same grisly end.

"I don't follow."

"Every day more people are killed for no good reason. Look at this," he said, opening the paper to an inner spread where the front page story continued. "Seventy years old, harassing tourists for money. He was unarmed, yet half a dozen people jumped in to subdue him. And that guy." Val scowled at the TV. "What is he, fifteen? Looks like he weighed a hundred pounds soaking wet. Can you imagine, coming home and hearing that your son…"

All the moisture vacuumed out of his mouth along with

5

the rest of the sentence. Val tugged at his temple, cleared his throat. More than fifty years and bitter reminders still brought the same reaction.

"Anyway."

Graham tipped up his bottle. They emptied their drinks in silence. Val signaled for another round.

"How do these guys figure into your story?" Graham asked.

"All the perps have gotten off easy. How does that keep happening? That gave me an idea." Val held a measure of scotch in his mouth, welcoming the burn. "A tangential universe with covert invaders quietly cleaning things up. Only they're specific about who they target. Drug pushers. Gangbangers. Vagrants. Troublemakers not likely to be missed. With a rigged judicial system, each member of the syndicate gets a minor sentence and is free to kill again. When the undesirables of one territory are eliminated, they move on to the next, until the planet is gentrified. But where the line is drawn, and where it ends—what happens when you reach the goalposts?"

"That's…an incredibly frightening concept." Graham tapped the envelope. "What's this, the first chapter?"

"The first three. And a synopsis and outline."

"Outline! Can't remember the last time you bothered with one of those."

Calvyn swapped out the empties, smiling down at the manuscript.

"What, you've been writing this here?" Graham asked.

"Calvyn's getting sick of me."

"I'm not getting sick of your money," Calvyn called over his shoulder. "You come write whatever you like."

"Well, no wonder those two were after you." Graham skimmed the pages. "They want a piece of the action."

"Maybe I can get them a walk-on role when Hollywood comes calling again." Val snapped his cuffs.

"That means you'd have to talk to 'em, get their numbers," Graham mumbled, without looking up. "This is a damn good opening. Is this my copy? I assume you have the original napkins?"

"Very funny. It's all yours."

"Glad you're back."

"Me too. I hope I'm not deluding myself, getting back into it after all this time."

"Don't be silly. It's like riding a bike."

"How do you know?"

"I don't, I'm talking out of my ass."

The news broadcast gave way to a late-night talk show. Shots of the featured guests materialized for an instant before shrinking off to a column along the left side of the screen. Andre Wallace, an emerging young author in a brown pinstripe suit, tan shirt, and paisley tie the color of ripe pumpkins appeared last, his toothy smile cocksure and beatific. The man was a tail Val couldn't shake.

He snorted. "Have you heard about this guy? One at the top."

"Course I have."

"Best-seller, right out of the gate."

"Well, that's no indication of skill, could be clever marketing. Have you read him?"

"Yes, and unfortunately it's not just marketing. It's an impressive debut. And he's already working on the follow-up."

"Not wasting any time."

"No. Have you seen the *New York Times* review? '…Full of the color and vibrancy reminiscent of Haverford's mid-career brilliance.'"

"Hey, don't let it get to you. Ignore the bullshit and keep at it. You have a gift. And I'm not just saying that because you made me rich." Graham slipped on his coat and raised the envelope in farewell.

Val lounged back, clinging to the last of a Julie London ballad. Per tradition, he stayed until the ten dollars ran out and silence settled over the bar. By then the women had gone and the place was empty except for the token drunk at a spectator table near the door. Val swallowed the dregs and waved goodbye to Calvyn, who was pouring himself some gin.

7

Fine mist glittered in the dim glow of the street lamps. Tires shushed against wet asphalt. Meandering back to his car, Val pictured Graham walking home, swinging the envelope with each stride. The rain could've soaked right through, smudged the ink. Softened a weak spot in the glue, causing it all to slide out. Or worse, drift away page by page without him noticing, littering the street like a ticker-tape parade. Val cursed himself for not clipping them together. He stroked the leather handle of his portfolio with his thumb, pinched the prominent seam, counted the heavy stitches. He should've given the entire thing to Graham. By concentrating on the phantom weight, tensing his arm with the effort of lugging it, he could imagine the manuscript were still in it, and all of a piece.

Under the delightful surrender of scotch, noises muted and tangible things danced out of reach. Gothic stone houses loomed over the sidewalks, giving the impression of strolling through a tunnel. People retreated into their high-rise condos by dusk in lousy weather, leaving the streets dark and bare. Flipped collar obscuring his face, preventing the rare passerby from stopping for a double-take, imparted a delicious sensation of invisibility. The only soul awake in a sleeping city.

As he reached his coveted parking spot in front of a long-shuttered hardware store, silence tapped him on the shoulder. A cluster of old men used to hunker into the recesses of the doorway, forcing Val to step over legs stretched drunkenly across the pavement, bypass chewed-up cardboard signs begging for change. The early cold snap must have driven them to a shelter. He shuddered at the possibility of men being dragged forever into the shadows.

***

Lingering thunderheads had swallowed the moon, their gray bellies glowing yellow-white. Val sank into a blanket of grass and spongy earth as he walked across his rear courtyard, the dense air draping around his shoulders. He held a mug of tea against his chest to stave off the chill.

Once the advances from his novels and film options had offered the opportunity to burst out from the scruffy, overcrowded apartments of his early years, he'd whipped out one of Michael's floor plans and researched North Shore acreage before the next check cleared. He'd counted the days until his escape from the crowds and the craziness and the never-ending noise, where he could stretch out his arms and not touch plaster. Breathing in the smell of sweet cedar, gazing down the length of the breezy, open hall to his studio, hearing nothing but the birds chirping in the grove and the refrain of water on sand, he'd been amazed at the incredible weight that eased off his shoulders. But now the tension returned, screwing his muscles into solid knots.

Catching snatches of illuminated whitecaps where Lake Michigan ought to be, he had an impulse to head to the beach and surround himself with the crash of waves. As he started down the limestone steps, one of the wood rail posts wobbled under his grasp. He'd need to get that repaired. Navigating his way down the embankment, however shallow, would be a fatal mistake in the dark.

He settled for perching on the stone wall that bordered his property. Too bad his neighbor's porch light was a constant, ugly distraction even at this distance. Swinging his legs up, using a limestone slab as a pillow, Val tried to lose himself in the burnishing stars as he replayed the conversation at Calvyn's.

Brooding over every word, he tried unsuccessfully to interpret Graham's reaction to the new project. On one hand he'd seemed intrigued, but on the other, disappointed that Val wasn't writing another installment in the Battaglia series. They both knew fans would eat it up. If history was any indicator, another film deal was inevitable. Though the last entry sold in the hundreds of thousands, its hasty second printing overshadowed the stand-alone bombs that came between. Though largely buried in the industry's collective memory, inside they sprawled and festered, taking up residence like stale air after a long illness. Those few

9

awkward minutes at the bar were bittersweet; he still had fans who remembered the glory days.

It was hard to pinpoint when the elephant had invited itself to their shit-shootings at Calvyn's. Val had always prickled at Graham's teasing curiosity about his next project, yet when it dawned on him how long it had been since the last prodding, it hurt like nothing else. Stories used to pile up in Val's head, colliding into each other as they multiplied. Legal pad after legal pad littering his floor with madcap scribbles, just enough detail to remind him of one plot before moving on to the next. Now someone else's calendar filled up with interviews and speaking engagements, their hard drive spilling into the Cloud, while Val's floor remained spotless.

Shame concentrated into a singularity, and it took every effort to pretend nothing had changed. He'd practiced a smile until it came almost naturally. But the idea of dragging that world-weary science officer out of the dust was against all principle; an admission of failure and a shrug of the shoulders. He might as well take a back cover shot with his palms up and pockets turned out.

A barricade had sprung up whenever he'd headed toward the open laptop, obligation turning his passion into a chore. The cursor blinked in time with the ticking of the clock and it was all downhill with the brakes out: one day gone, then two, then thousands, twilight looming larger and urgency hissing louder. Trying to make a comeback with more of the same would be humiliating to both of them, whether Graham wanted to admit it or not. An allegory mirroring the current gravity in the news, packaged in his signature brand of dystopia, was bound to rekindle the allure that used to follow every release.

He returned to the studio and paced, massaging his hands. Unknotting the kinks in his back and limbs was an incremental, percussive event. Foolish, lying out on a stone wall in this weather. His right eye adjusted more slowly to the indoor light, the stars not quite faded.

History spread before him in the bookcase. He fingered the glossy spines, his embossed name that demanded increasingly shorter titles. The days when language rolled like poetry, mellifluous and robust, a rich broth you could savor on your tongue. At the end of the last row, a block of space waited for one more hardback. After that, he'd have to clear the half-empty notebooks and outdated travel pamphlets off the bottom shelf.

Westerns were his novice's fast-track to publication. That old 'write what you know' chestnut was gold. But after a few years, a miasma of romanticism pervaded the reviews, people whitewashing the past with little more than picnics and parades. Spending so much time writing in one era projected a false sentimentality that he had no trouble ditching. Declining interest in the genre didn't hurt, either. The challenge to reinvent himself led to a full reversal. If he couldn't escape the primitive mindsets of real life, he would write them into existence. Evolution under the guise of cutting-edge technology and rocket science.

He knew exactly how the narrative rhythm, the drawl of his protagonists, the cadence of every line, should sound in readers' heads. But until he could figure out how to pin the words down on paper the way he used to, it was all music and no lyrics.

When he'd moved in with little more than the tube of floorplans and a massive box of notes, the cardboard handles cutting off the circulation in his fingers, he had nothing but time. No clock ticking backwards. The future stretched before him in an endless, laggard expanse.

Imagining Graham reading this draft, then seeing his expression sink, was something Val couldn't handle. He needed to nail a pivotal scene, compose one little snippet of biting prose, anything to combat any possible criticism, before he could sleep.

He fired up the wood-burning stove in the corner and set a pot of coffee on to percolate. While waiting for the telltale rumble, he polished the sketch's frame, rubbing away the smudge on the glass obscuring 'MH, Kano IL, 1967' in the bottom right corner.

This time I won't let you down.

11

Chapter Two

All night long, plots intersected into a maze as characters fought for position, shouting compelling dialogue that seemed perfectly clear until Val opened his eyes. An apocalyptic future where characters had to constantly prove their worth to creatures both otherworldly yet eerily recognizable didn't make for restful sleep.

He stumbled into the bathroom bleary-eyed, scratching his head until his hair poked out in all directions. A dark smudge danced in the mirror. *Goddamn spiders.* He wadded a handful of toilet paper and spun, lunging toward the spot on the wall. When he lifted the paper away, the paint was unmarked. No satisfying smear of carcass to signify a successful hit. Yet the spot remained, floating along with the tilt of his head. He ground the heels of his hands into his eyes and splashed water on his face. Just the sudden light after a shitty night's sleep. Old peepers getting slow to adjust. Nothing to dwell on.

His word count, however, was another matter.

Val's ritual had gone nearly unaltered since the cabin was built, woven tightly into a safety net. Read the newspaper over as big a breakfast as his pantry allowed. Raise the bamboo shades so the entire east wall flooded the studio with natural light, or in good weather, set up camp at the picnic table facing the lake. Coffee, notepad, and pen on the right, water on the left. A few reps with weights between chapters; jogging along the beach to work through block. When he needed a change of scenery, off to Calvyn's.

These days he swapped the newspaper for the mindlessness of social media. It was quicker to scroll through snippets of color and bullshit than to shuffle oversized pages.

Breakfast was all but forgotten. Life had an urgency to it, a grinding, noisy shift. Punch the clock, the boss was watching.

He had to smile at his Twitter feed. Tweets ranged from passing interest to ravenous celebration to quoted text, his precious words followed by ellipses to leave readers hanging. *Ah, Graham, early at work even after a couple of beers.* Val switched to Facebook where the messages repeated, paired with old photos of himself at various signings and events. The posts had been up for only a couple hours, but the responses and shares ran into the thousands. *Guess those hackneyed bits weren't so bad after all.*

Graham knew him all too well, hedging his bets behind a wall of faith and conviction. Val couldn't resist the opportunity to give him a hard time. One quick phone call, then on with it.

"Van Ellis and Associates, Graham speaking."

"'Triumphant return?' This is what I'm paying your marketing team for?"

"That wasn't us. Some celebrity gossip site wrote that and it's been forwarded everywhere. You can't control these things."

"I have a good idea of how it got started. It was that cousin of yours, wasn't it?"

"Good ol' Kenny? No comment."

"Some of those lines might not even make it into the final draft. It's false advertising."

"Haven't you ever watched a trailer for a movie and when you see it, some of the dialogue isn't in it? Maybe an entire scene is deleted? Think of it as a teaser. People eat that shit up."

"Puts a lot of pressure on me."

"Relax. I'm just getting a little head start with the publicity. Speaking of trailers, we should discuss 'em."

"Trailers?"

"Yes, Val. Things have changed in the new millennium. People make 'em for books now, same as movies."

"I know what they *are*, but—"

"Give it some thought, will you? This book is going to put

you back on top."

"It was pretty nice up there. But after this stunt you can forget about a jacket photo."

"Now, wait a minute—"

"I'm not sitting for any more mugshots. The world can do without another picture of me advertising an invisible watch. We'll have a *trailer!*"

"Val—"

"Sorry, need to start on those next chapters. Self-imposed deadlines are a bitch."

Val grinned and cradled the receiver, picturing Graham cursing the dial tone. He'd smooth things over later with a round of Graham's favorite shitty beer.

While another pot of coffee brewed and a half-eaten takeout lasagna reheated in the oven, Val searched online for details on the most recent violence. In the few weeks since he started writing, several new cases had popped up across the country. It seemed like most of the local incidences happened in the most impoverished South- and West Side neighborhoods, where heavy crime had been a problem for decades. Yet few reports made it to the front pages. Was that a way to try and cover them up? Or maybe get them out of the public eye quicker? He was ashamed to admit he'd forgotten a number of them as well. Would the average Joe even be able to tell a random killing or gang shooting from something more sinister, more personal?

He riffled through the pile of travel pamphlets until he found a sun-bleached foldout map of Chicago. Marking the location of each incident with a red china marker, it quickly resembled a rash. Although the trail seemed to have started in the South and West, it trended upwards, scooping toward O'Hare airport and the surrounding 'burbs, outnumbering his estimates twice over.

That fifteen-year-old's picture kept popping into every rabbit hole Val burrowed down. Why *that* kid? What made him more tragic than the rest? Digging through articles from smaller publications helped piece together the story. Sean Davis: a rebellious kid throughout grade school, constantly in trouble with cops, in and out of foster care. Until he found that special person, a retired music teacher, who taught him about better things than drugs and gangs. Who maybe was a little too old to take on the responsibilities of a young man on the cusp of adolescence, not quite detached from the old life. The boy slipped, pilfered some cheap liquor with some friends after band practice.

For a second Val's thoughts drifted to Michael, but he shoved the past back in the closet.

Sean was the only one who didn't run, couldn't run, after drinking more than he could handle. Only after the boy hit the ground did anyone realize the chrome in his hand was a mouthpiece, not a semi-automatic.

The hint of a scene sparked into Val's brain. A fragment of an antagonist who sought to eradicate every trace of delinquency, making the world a better place even as he made it worse. The first line of a new chapter formed, in wavy letters under—

A siren blasted through the cabin, as though an ambulance had parked in his front room. Smoke and the scent of burnt cheese billowed through the hall.

Shuffling through the haze, he hacked and sneezed his way into the kitchen and threw open the window. Found the oven knob and turned, ignoring the searing heat. Stood on a chair and snapped the alarm off the ceiling. Residual screeching echoed in his ears. A full minute passed before he realized someone was banging on his front door. Only one person refused to ring the doorbell like a civilized person and instead knocked like a drunken moose.

Through vision like swimming pools, he poked his way to the front of the house and peered through the peephole.

Yep. Raymond. *Christ.*

And how was it evening already?

The man was speaking before Val fully opened the door.

"…alarm go off, so I thought I'd come by and check on ya…" His neighbor bobbed his head to glimpse inside. Like always. As if he was on a tour of *Lifestyles of the Rich and Famous*, looking to bask in a secret world lurking beyond the foyer.

"Raymond—"

"Mr. Haverford, I know—"

"Val. No need for formality."

More nodding. "You've said that, yep. Don't know why I keep—"

"I just burned something in the oven, so…"

"I figured you was all right but I had to check, you know, that's what good neighbors do. I was walking by, it was no trouble. I mean, I know you'd do the same for me…"

Watching Raymond bounce on the balls of his feet was making Val seasick. Another headache started up, spiraling from the base of his skull. Along with it, another black patch appeared before his eyes.

"I haven't seen you jogging for days. I was starting to worry."

"It's been raining a lot."

"That's so, but you could go runnin' along the main road. I've seen you do it." He gestured behind him as if Val didn't know where it was.

"I've been *busy*, Raymond."

"Still workin' on the new one, are ya? Thought you'd never have to work again."

"It's not about having to—"

"I know, I know, you artists got the creative bug. I gotcha. I'm just lookin' out for ya, Mr. Hav—Val." Yet he stayed rooted to the stairs.

"Appreciate that. Really need to get back to it. I'll be sure to wave next time I jog past." *Which would be never.*

"Gotcha, gotcha. I can take a hint. Good luck with your writing, there. When will you let me read it?"

"When it's published, Raymond."

"I bet that'll be real soon…"

Val hung a smile from his grizzled cheekbones, narrowing the gap as Raymond continued to bounce, hoping the onslaught of questions would stop the less space he had to throw them.

Eventually Raymond turned, looking over his shoulder as

16

he descended the steps, and Val was alone again. Even then, he felt naked on a stage. Concentration flagged until he was sure the old coot wasn't still tracking along his property, peeking into the windows. The essence of the scene forming in his head had dissipated along with Raymond's loping figure. The charred lump of his former meal smelled both tantalizing and nauseating.

Hell with it. Nothing more done than a lot of useless reading; procrastination under the guise of research. And the last thing Val wanted was a reminder of more dead children.

***

After grabbing dinner out, Val headed to Calvyn's to restart his process with the *Trib* and burnt coffee. Right there on page three was an op-ed by none other than Andre Wallace, lecturing on the influx of violence. Hauntingly written, the moralistic opener quickly disintegrated under waves of emotion. Val muttered little passages out loud, huffing at every eloquent turn of phrase.

The closing burned in his belly. While Andre continued to write his debut's sequel, he was concurrently working on a second novel, a passion project, interpreting the indiscriminate loss of life from a fresh perspective.

"Son of a bitch!" Val banged his mug down so forcefully that a third of the coffee sloshed out. He tried to soak up the mess with cocktail napkins but instead spread it everywhere. Calvyn brought a fresh mug and mopped away the spill.

"Sorry, Calvyn."

Calvyn tapped the article. "You worrying too much about this boy here."

"He's basically writing the same thing I am, for Christ's sake. Except his has 'fresh perspective.'"

"Plenty of room for the both of you. People can buy more than one book! Lord Jesus, you writers'll be the death of me."

"Don't tell me he drinks here too."

"Go home, Mr. H." Calvyn patted him on the back. "You need a vacation."

***

Wired and trembling with nervous energy, Val regretted taking the long way home. A waste of precious time, an entire day lost, when Andre was probably congratulating himself for another extraordinary word count. New worries threatened, replacing those that emerged overnight. The stopwatch had been set, the pistol fired.

Val poured a scotch, ritual be damned. He paced, clutching the tumbler to his chest. He couldn't simply bang something out and leave nothing but the editing to look forward to, couldn't rely on his familiar cadence and flow and guaranteed set of devotees. Especially with Andre threatening to eclipse his career's revival. A debut novel with such power only promised a strong future. And from the sound of things, he was plowing through the next one. Next *two*.

His headache returned like it had a deadline to keep. Val's knuckles ached and his drink was soon warm, heated by his paralyzed grip. He tossed it back and then another. Was it safe to drown aspirin in liquor?

One quick check of Twitter and he'd get right back to it. More masturbatory scrolling would get the juices flowing again. Flicking a finger along a mouse wheel practically counted as exercise at that hour.

Then, graphic details of his novel's climax. Everywhere. Passages taken directly from the synopsis. The first plot twist, given to Graham just days earlier, up and down the feed. Spoilers headed the trending news. Facebook, same thing. *No no no no...*

Maybe this was the result of some horrible virus. Something from his hard drive had repeated itself all over his screen, that was all, they couldn't really be everywhere.

Each quote attributed the source as Van Ellis & Associates. Val checked their site and platforms and there they were again, loud and clear, as well as on his own website: spoiler after spoiler, fresh off the press and into the stratosphere.

Barely able to focus enough to dial the phone, he paused between each number, pressing until the tones drove him mad. If Graham hadn't seen this, he might not even be in his office.

"Van Ellis and—"

"What the fuck am I seeing?"

"Oh, Jesus. Let me give you my sincerest apologies—"

"Don't give me that customer service bullshit. What happened here?"

"We—I gave our new Marketing intern responsibility for keeping all the platforms updated. He got carried away…"

"No shit."

"He's gone. We fired him as soon as we noticed. Ken's working on damage control."

"Damage control? That's rich. What's he going to do, hit rewind?"

"Val, I'm so sorry, truly—"

"You have any idea how impossible this has been for me?" He cringed at the Southern twang, however faint, that always resurfaced when his blood pressure surged. Dead air compounded the pulse beating in his jugular. Before he could demand a response, Graham's choked voice came over the line.

"No. What—"

"What's the name of the incompetent you hired?"

"I can't tell you that. Val…please…calm down."

"I have to go in a completely different direction now. Do you have any clue the extent of work I need to do to fix this?" A phantom floated in and out of his periphery.

"I—you're a brilliant writer, I have full confidence…"

Val slammed the phone down with such force that the plastic cracked, and yet he leaned his full weight on it, steadying himself. Every muscle vibrated as though trying to shake loose. Then he saw it again—along the rim of his glass —a refraction like blazing asphalt in a summer haze. Rage detonated through him and he hurled the glass across the studio. It exploded against the north windows, scotch trickling down in golden rivulets.

***

19

After a week of sleepless nights, pissing away the time stress-pumping weights and plucking glass fragments out of the wall and running—away from Raymond's—Val fretted over a different set of words. He wasn't sure which he was avoiding more.

In the mailbox, stuffed within the heap of bills and bullshit, was a bright red envelope, delivered with such shitty timing it was like the postal service and the Van Ellises had joined forces to deliver a guilt trip.

He'd gone to Graham and Anna's holiday gathering every year since they'd gotten married, yet it always slipped his mind until the festive invite vomited red and gold confetti over his coffee table. The plan to stay out of Graham's way for a few months until time patched things up wasn't going to work.

As much as he hated to admit it, he owed Graham the truth. He must've sounded completely deranged. If he hadn't been such a damned fool, he wouldn't be trying to figure out how to have this conversation in the first place.

Working too long...too much self-induced pressure...the albatross Andre. They turned the world cockeyed by sundown, and at daybreak everything weighed half as much. But when the light disappeared, it was impossible to see.

He had about an hour to catch Graham, assuming he was in the office. If he agreed to see Val without an appointment. Only one way to find out.

***

The elevator to Van Ellis & Associates crawled at an imperceptible pace. Lucy smiled from behind the receptionist desk, sure Graham would be glad to meet with him, as always. He must not have shared the details with her, and she didn't seem to pick up on Val's mood from his forcibly chipper small talk. She waved him down the hall and went back to her work.

Val hesitated outside Graham's office, clenching his fists inside his pockets.

Graham flipped through pages of financial spreadsheets and contracts, twirling a green pen between his index and middle fingers. Since he'd inherited the business from his father, he refused to allow mark-ups in red; turning hard work into a crime scene was a detail he'd been glad to amend. For a second he stopped spinning to rub the clip. Then started up again, faster, like a pinwheel in a storm.

Not a good sign.

He must've sensed Val hovering in the doorway and looked up. His frown melted into a grin and he swept a giant hand toward the guest chairs.

"Hey! Have a seat. Again, about the other day—"

"No. Please. I was way out of line," Val said. Graham leaned forward and cupped his ear as Val spoke.

"Completely understandable. You had every right."

Val had been inside this office more times than he could count, yet this time the ice blue walls were uninviting and claustrophobic, like he'd wandered into a similar suite on the wrong floor.

"Hey, are you okay?"

"No." Val chewed the inside of his cheek, clicked the door shut gently. "We need to talk."

Chapter Three

Second Christmas.

Christ.

Graham and Anna's observation of the Dutch tradition was more about celebrating their freedom from prying family than extending a beloved holiday. Although this time, relief accompanied the chore. Only Graham could brush away an intense conversation with one hand and welcome you to his home with the other. And promising to keep Val's secret from Anna was icing he didn't deserve. Chalk it up to Christmas miracles.

Every year Anna put Val in charge of the wine, and succeeded, every year, in weakening his resolve. Having about as much interest in wine as holidays in general, he let the local liquor store clerk cobble together two cases of random bottles. Basic statistics had to yield at least a couple of winners.

He rolled his latest chapters around a particularly narrow bottle and dragged the lot to their condo. The building's portly, panting doorman assisted with the load, setting his case down with a grunt and retreating into the elevator before Val could attempt a tip.

Anna opened the door, brushing invisible crumbs from her skirt. "Val, you made it!" Smoothing her hands down her thighs, she stood on tiptoes to plant the customary kiss on his cheek. "Thanks for remembering the wine, we're down to three bottles. Did you have trouble finding a spot?"

A couple feet of snow had accumulated overnight, adding to the festive aura and bringing with it another seasonal highlight: the notorious sport of aggressive parking. Val couldn't resist the opportunity and neutralized his expression.

"None at all. I just threw some guy's folding chairs out of the way."

Anna grabbed his arm, eyes wide. "Oh no. You *didn't*."

She was too easy. A smile fought its way through and gave him away. Anna visibly relaxed and swatted his arm, hoisting the other box on one hip as though it were empty.

"You can carry that?" Val kicked the door closed with his heel.

"Sure, these are fine baby-makin' hips, didn't you know? Leave it unlocked," she said over her shoulder. She led him down the narrow hallway, past the galley kitchen, and into the main room stuffed with tipsy partygoers. The walls dripped with pine swag, velvet bows and sparkling gold baubles. Creatively repurposed leftovers filled the buffet table from end to end.

"Sounds like you had a good time yesterday."

"You bet. Always good to tune out the family for eight hours at a stretch. You can drop that here." She placed her box on the floor near the sideboard, which was so overloaded it resembled a barman's fire sale. Anna dug some ice from a bucket teetering on the edge, then fished around in the cabinet underneath for a bottle of Macallan.

"My dear mother-in-law insists I only have a couple more years to give her grandchildren before I dry up," she added, cocking an eyebrow. She handed him the double. "Her words. My tongue aches from all the biting I had to—"

"Val! How the hell are you?"

Val choked at the hard slap to the back, dribbling scotch down his chin.

Graham, wearing Anna's ruffled pink apron and matching oven mitt, held out a steaming tray. Lopsided cups of twice-baked stuffing were filled with his infamously hacked-to-bits turkey and topped with cranberries that had deflated into little berets. "Here, have a turkey thing. Can I get you s'mething t'drink?"

Val grinned and jiggled his glass.

"Say, are those new pages?" Graham vibrated a finger in the general direction of the open wine box.

"They are."

"Wonderful! I'll take 'em."

Val turned Graham's limp hand over and closed it around the roll. Graham immediately started reading, then walked off into his study, wavering slightly, still holding the tray.

Anna smiled. "He's had a few."

"No kidding."

"How's the writing going?"

"Great, actually. That fool intern did me a favor. It's almost like I never stopped." His grin widened at this simple admission. Having to revise so early cleared the murk, and words had stampeded onto the page. The way his eyes were fading, there wasn't any time left for holding back.

"Wonderful, honey. Maybe this time you'll write me in?" Anna squeezed his forearm.

Val chuckled at their shared joke, more from nostalgia than enjoyment. "Maybe you'll get lucky."

A group of fur-clad women appeared in the hallway, looking dazedly around for the hosts. "Oh, hang on," Anna said. "Hold that thought."

Val backed against the wall. He didn't like the look of the wink she shot him as she passed.

These gatherings were often full of other industry types: clients of Graham's, publishers, illustrators, critics; a few of Anna's colleagues and volunteers and donors from that hospital foundation she headed. Their motley collection of friends, which included a number of musicians, provided much of the entertainment. The music and food were the only unpredictable aspects. But this time she had something up her sleeve. Maybe if he tried blending into the offbeat artwork she'd forget about him.

A bluegrass quartet tuned up to riffs from "Blue Moon of Kentucky" beneath the condo's massive picture window. Skyscrapers lay black against an inky purple canvas, their bright windows a spatter of stars. Thin tendrils of fog curled around the vertices. Content to play the wallflower for every tune, he claimed a post near the buffet to give the illusion of mingling.

Anna led the newcomers in. Val raised his glass and nodded at the throng, all of whom he recognized but couldn't name.

A youngish guy waved and headed over as if beckoned. "Great to see you again!"

Shit. He looked like someone Val should know. Chad? Stewart? He had an unctuous Southern accent and one of those ridiculous Civil War bartender moustaches. With a handshake tighter than an iron maiden, the stranger leaned in like he was going to divulge a secret. Maybe it would be his name.

"You don't remember me, do you? Meh, it's been almost a year. Anthony Marczek. My wife and I attended the ribbon-cutting to the Leg-Up Foundation, then we went to dinner, the five of us..."

It was coming back to him now, though more an impression than solid fact. Marczek had been exceedingly thrilled over Anna's dreams being realized after much stress and financial red tape. He had some tie to the community—alderman? cop?—and threw a bunch of money her way to jumpstart the Foundation. Although he didn't seem to know much about medicine, accounting, or running a charity, his fascination with the cause made Anna offer his wife a job. If memory served, she was quite a few years older with silver-white hair.

Val glanced around to try and spot her. Unfortunately Mrs. Marczek was nowhere to be found. Instead, a flash of bright purple within the sea of black caught his eye. A tall brown woman with a puff of chestnut curls swept toward a group sitting across the buffet. Her long nails glided along the edge of the table and drummed on the wood, fingertips barely touching the surface.

Marczek's voice rose as he droned on. Seated at that fancy restaurant, Val'd never realized the man was such a close-talker.

"...Leg-Up Foundation is well under way. We'd love to have you speak to the kids. Writing is a great way to improve their communication skills. They should have access to only the best. I mean, the right *kind* of kids, not everyone's a natural—"

"Yes, yes."

"Perfect! They can't learn about medicine without expanding their…"

The woman in purple weaved among the crowd, leaning in for embraces and speaking with her hands. The flimsy fabric of her dress slinked around her waist as her right hip dropped on each downbeat. Her pace modulated with the changing tempos, transforming her entire figure into a percussive instrument.

Anna crossed his line of vision. Her grin was nothing if not devious. Val blinked and averted his eyes back to what's-his-name's rambling, but Anna zoomed up for the kill with the stunning brunette at her side.

"Val, this is Sandra Bayliss, co-producer of *On the Record*. Sandra, Val Haverford. Come help me in the kitchen," she said to Marczek. She winked again and skipped off, pulling the poor bastard after her.

"Oh, hello! It's great to meet you finally." Sandra lit up with instant recognition and eased her hand into Val's. A hint of mischief shimmied behind the melody of her words.

"They've mentioned me?"

"Graham's told me *all* about you."

"He has?"

"Mm-hm. Enjoying the music so far?"

"Hey, Sandra." The banjoist, a wrinkled man in a vintage brown suit and round glasses, tuned his instrument for the next set. "You gonna play with us, darlin'?"

"Not tonight, Till," she said.

"What do you play?" Val asked.

"She plays ever'thang," said Till. "Ever'thang." He grinned and plucked an indistinct intro.

"That's not quite true," said Sandra.

"She plays the *guit*ar, the bass, the mandolin, the harmonica, and the fiddle," Till said as proudly as if she were his child.

"Impressive!"

"And she sings, too."

"But tonight I'm here just for kicks."

"You're teasing us, Sandra," said a thin, younger man in the back, adjusting the endpin on the bass for her height. "It's all ready for you, if you want."

The band started to strum, softly chanting her name in time.

"Okay, okay, Jimmy. One number, guys, that's it. 'Broken Bottle?'"

The band murmured in agreement.

Sandra turned to Val. "Do you like bluegrass?"

"It's not really my style, no."

"And here you are living in America's heartland. Tsk tsk. A shame."

"Well, I admit I don't know much about it. I don't cotton to the drinkin' songs or the cheatin' songs…are there others?" Val asked, a smirk curling at the corner of his mouth at Sandra's puckered expression.

"We'll have to show him how it's done, Sandra," Jimmy said.

"Now listen here," she warned, poking a finger into Val's chest. "I've had two glasses of wine already so my cords are dry. Go easy on me."

She twisted her way to the rear and tilted the massive instrument against her pelvis like a dance partner, adjusting her weight toward the upper bout. The deep strum of the bass flowed around him, her caress of the strings like an illusionist channeling dark magic. Sultry phrasing filtered in purrs and whispers, smoke and smolder unraveling in long strands of silk.

The room dissolved, transporting Val to a long-ago nightclub, as the tune's haunting lyrics leveled the din and softened it. This was a lullaby, but it kept Val alert to every syllable that passed through her lips, stirring something low in him he hadn't known in years. Her eyes were downcast though her face remained upturned, as though serenading the headstock.

The song ended much too soon. She gave a theatrical bow

to the crowd, extending a hand in a grand curlicue. Jimmy reclaimed his bass and she strode back to Val, planting a foot between them, hands on her hips, challenging him.

"Well? Did I turn you?"

"Not a bit." That earned a devilish glint from Sandra. "But it was a pleasure listening to you."

"I guess that'll have to do. For now. But only because I'm starving. Join me?" She nodded toward the buffet.

They filled small plates with appetizers and took opposite ends of the loveseat.

"What is it you do again?" Val asked. "Co-producer of—"

"*On the Record.* I handle the indie book scene, for the most part, but we cover music, film…"

Ah, there it was, Anna's angle.

But why didn't she stick around with Marczek? It's not like either of them operated under pen names. Val felt a twinge of guilt. Graham must have told Anna about their last conversation and this was her way of helping smooth things over. The neutral party to bridge the divide. Dragging Marczek out of the way allowed Val to keep his pride.

Sandra laughed. "Listen to me go on—"

She must have segued into a tangent. He pushed away this particular conspiracy theory for another time. "Nonsense. Takes the pressure off me. How did you get started in the business?"

"I blame my cousins."

"Your cousins?"

"When we were babies, they insisted we play celebrities, dressing up in overblown costumes and sunglasses and acting the fool. They loved mugging for an invisible camera. But eventually they needed to be interviewed, and since I was the youngest, they dumped that job on me. It was either that or be left behind." She devoured a square of baklava, tossing the question back to him with a flourish of her free hand.

Val shrugged. "I just did it for the money."

"Ha! Good one. Now I pass my obsession down to—" She flipped one leg under her and set the mini plate on her thigh, then reached into her purse for her phone. "Sorry, I can't help

28

bragging every chance I get. Hang on—"

After a few taps and swipes, she handed him the phone. A video of a skinny boy with a mischievous grin much like Sandra's was already in progress. He was talking to a sweaty girl with a long ponytail, fanning the neck of her hot pink soccer uniform.

"Yours?"

"My grandson. Lewis. He wants to be a sportscaster. I was a bad influence."

The party drowned out what was being said, but it was clear Lewis was mid-interview, posture showing the utmost professionalism, but the glint in his eye giving away his excitement. The moment seemed much too intimate to share with a near stranger, yet here he was, invited into Sandra's family life without warning. And no idea what to do about the audio volume.

Between bites of a roast beef slider, she asked, "Do you have any family nearby to corrupt?"

He pretended not to hear, too involved with the video. But the picture blurred when she'd lowered the phone, the camera snapping to a halt.

Before he could respond, the band's break ended with the first few bars of—

"'Wayfaring Stranger,'" Val said.

Sandra slapped the back of the sofa. "So you do like bluegrass!"

"I can name one song that's passable. Well, I guess two, now."

"Pfft. Passable. What about 'Rolling in My Sweet Baby's Arms?' 'Mule Skinner Blues?' 'Cripple Creek?'"

"That song by The Band? Sure, that's not too painful." Val sipped his scotch to tamp down his smile.

"No—that's not—" Sandra rubbed her temple.

"Not a Band fan?"

"You're fucking with me, aren't you?"

"Maybe a little."

"Okay, well…The Band is roots rock, we're getting closer. 'The Night They Drove Ol' Dixie Down?'"

"Was a Tuesday, I reckon. Rainy."

She threw back her head and laughed, a hearty, honest sound like a welcome home. Loud enough to catch the attention of a few guests, she doled out joy with every peal, infecting all those within earshot.

This much attention would only result in a wider social circle, the dreaded small talk and getting-to-know-you crap that spelled the death of any legitimate conversation. He fought the urge to pull Sandra out of this crowd and take her somewhere, anywhere, they could be alone. He was about to make that suggestion when Graham, for the moment somewhat sober, clanged a wine glass for attention. He raised himself onto a folding chair in the center of the room, stooping to avoid beaning himself on the ceiling. Anna swiftly grasped his belt to steady him. He looked down at her, running a finger along the edge of her diamond-studded ear. He radiated pure joy that had nothing to do with the wine.

"Everyone raise their glasses for a toast!" The crowd gathered around, forcing Sandra and Val to stand for a better view. She shrugged, hoisting a plastic cup of liver mousse the color of charcoal.

"Here we are, another Tweede Kerstdag, when we realize our greatest gift and blessing is coming back home."

"Praise Jesus," came a disembodied voice from the back.

"And we have an announcement. Or at least I do on behalf of my modest wifey here." Graham and Anna made faces at each other. "Thanks to many of your donations—especially yours, Anthony, you wonderful sonofabitch—The Leg-Up Foundation collected more in one month than it had its entire maiden year. Due to that and Anna's extra hours cooking the books—*ow*." He swatted away Anna's pinching fingers. "—keeping the books—she's getting a plaque on the Foundation's Wall of Fame."

The room erupted in applause as Anna tucked her face into Graham's hip. "To our friends!" he said, lifting his glass higher.

An emphatic "Cheers!" rose from the crowd.

"To Mary Ellen's pumpkin pie shooters!"
"Better than friends!" someone called out.
"And continued success to all of us. Proost!"
"Proost!"

***

The crowd dispersed, most drifting to the buffet.

Graham descended and wrapped his arms around Anna's shoulders, dipping her slightly. He planted a long kiss on her lips, drawing her to him, ending with a faint peck on the tip of her freckled nose. When he sat, they were almost the same height, and he maneuvered his hands around her waist just above the firm curve of her backside. She leaned in to cup his head in her hands and kiss his widow's peak. Graham smiled, infatuated like a newlywed, and lay his head on her chest. They spotted Val immersed in conversation with Sandra, who was doubled over at some story. Val dug into his pocket for a handkerchief to dab at the tears streaming down her cheeks.

Anna's mouth set into a firm line. "Looks like your scheme's working."

"Told you, babe. You owe me fifty bucks." Graham twisted her hips back and forth like the agitator of a washing machine. It would've taken an explosion to get her attention. Instead of responding, she kissed the air in the vicinity of Graham's head and shoved off.

They shouldn't have stayed out so late last night. She'd clearly had enough socializing for the weekend. Graham watched her make the rounds through the condo, calculating how many more hours until he had her to himself, and what he'd do with her once all the coats had been whisked off the bed. A nice wind-down massage would make the stress go away. A little more and—

He needed something to scramble his thoughts.

Sandra held her phone up for Val to see, scrolling and gesturing at something on the screen. Val cocked his head in that odd way he had now, giving the impression he was going deaf.

There's the way to get Anna off your mind: focus on business. Buried under all the commotion and confusion of planning, not to mention the usual end-of-year wind-down at the agency, he'd forgotten why he was so excited about this year's party to begin with. Val was going to kill him, but it would be worth it. Sandra rose suddenly, tapping her phone, and excused herself. Graham grabbed his chance, calling out to Val and hooking a finger toward his study.

Val closed the door against the din and hovered with his hand on the knob, as if he needed an invitation to sit. Twisting open the window blinds, Graham glanced over his shoulder until Val nodded his approval. Overcrowded rooms, even in good company, never failed to close him off. Discomfort tended to weigh down every word, when he chose to speak at all. A little quiet and a view of the stars went a long way.

"I have some exciting news for you," Graham said, bouncing on his heels. He sat behind the massive desk that used to choke his father's office. "Guess what I got you."

Val sank into a tufted leather chair. "I hate when conversations start like that."

"An interview with *On the Record*, for a segment called 'Six Minutes.' I saw you chatting it up with Sandra Bayliss just now."

"Indeed. Seems nice." Val's face bloomed red and he dipped behind his glass for a drink. "I'm a terrible interview, though."

"You did fine on the last one, didn't you?"

"That was years ago! And the book was already published, not half written."

"Well, since you're not doing a jacket photo people will want to re-familiarize themselves with your face."

"What, is this payback?" Val laughed. "Please tell me this isn't live."

"No, no, I wouldn't do that to you. The whole session will be taped, but they're only using six minutes' worth of clips on the show and e-mag, thus the name. After editing, of course."

"Six minutes? That's it?"

"You're complaining?"

"No, it's just...odd. The last interview lasted an hour, more."

"That's all anybody seems to have time for. A minute here, two minutes there. Be glad it's not a Snapchat."

"The hell's a Snapchat?"

"Ten seconds, I think."

"Why bother? 'So, Mr. Haverford, tell us about your new book.' 'Well, it's about...' 'Cut!'" Val slashed an invisible line across his neck. "'We're out of time. It's a book, it's about something...'bye!'"

"People these days can't keep their minds on anything." Graham lit a cigarette and reclined as far as the chair allowed. "God, I sound old."

"What does that make me, then? I might as well record an eight-track tape. Maybe I should write a string of tweets instead. How many would it take for a novel-length feed?"

Graham squirmed and ducked his head. Val's outburst confronted him every morning with the alarm clock, his confession about his failing sight worrying new bite marks in Graham's pen caps.

"Sorry, let me rephrase—"

Graham waved him off. "About four thousand. I think. And it's been done. Not a bad idea, though...no editing, instant publishing...of course, you'd have to type it all at once, and backwards."

"Maybe next time."

"Hey, remember what Dad used to say?"

Val pulled his fountain pen from his shirt pocket and clenched the end between his teeth. "When's that Haverford kid going to write about the future of the American attention span?" He growled out the corner of his mouth in a perfect imitation of Ed Van Ellis.

"Christ, those cheap cigars. Was he smoking them when you first came on?"

"I think they were a permanent fixture to his dental work. I was so thrilled to be signed I didn't care that I couldn't

33

understand a word of the contract. I had to become rapidly proficient in Stogese."

"Good ol' Dad. God bless his sooty lungs." They toasted. "So I can set something up with Sandra?"

"Ah, what the hell." Another sip. "I should be able to give them a decent six minutes without making an ass of myself. Especially if they're non-consecutive."

"There you go, confidence! This will be great. You'll do the spot, say, end of January?"

"A little early, isn't it?"

"Considering the rate you're going, let's aim for a deadline of June first. Sound...doable? How's..." Graham waggled a finger in the direction of his head.

Val glanced at the door, as though checking to make sure no one had snuck in to eavesdrop. "June first sounds reasonable. I'm glad you didn't tell me about this before I met her." He exhaled through pursed lips and swirled the scotch, knocking the cubes around like dice, before tossing it back.

Graham pulled on his cigarette, studying Val a long while before answering. After so many years of watching this man skyrocket from newb to respected artist, sparring—on somewhat friendly terms—with Dad, he'd come to know his every trick, every nuance, leaving nothing for him to hide behind. Not even that glass, held like a mask against anyone attempting to glean his truth.

On leaving this room, Val was his buddy, no question. This minute, until the heels of Val's shoes set down outside this office, he was a business partner and nothing more.

"You'll be fine. The whole thing will maybe last thirty minutes."

Val slipped the most recent issue of *Chicago Lit Review* off the edge of the desk. It was rolled open to an article about Andre Wallace and his yet unrivaled debut.

"Oh—don't read that now. You'll lose my place," Graham said.

"I think I can remember a page number."

"No, really—"

34

"What, is there something about me in here?" Val skimmed the article. "'Andre Wallace has written an impressive debut...' Yeah, yeah. Bastard. '...masterful handling of emotional complexities—' Wow, that's pretentious even for them," Val said, stealing a quick glance upwards.

"Yeah..."

"'Devoid of material to suggest the contrary, Wallace may very well become the Haverford for this generation.' Son of a bitch! The old Haverford never went anywhere!"

"Well, you did sort of disappear into the woods."

"Maybe. But that doesn't mean I've lost my touch."

"Why don't you forget about that and we'll get back to—"

"Wait a minute...'Wallace is indeed proving himself to be the successor to the—" Val cleared his throat. "'—late... great...Val Haverford.' Well." He tossed the magazine back on the desk where it immediately flipped closed. "At least they called me great."

"I wrote a letter to the editor calling the writer out on poor research. They said they'd print a correction, but claim it was less a case of lousy fact-checking than a dig at your lack of recent output."

"Ha! That's quite a dig!"

"I told you not to read it."

"When did I die?"

"We're not sure. Anna and I were so upset. We weren't even notified. That hurts, man."

"You're blaming the corpse? Classy."

"You know what your problem is, Val? Perspective. You should be flattered! You've been Twain'ed!"

"Right, right. Nothing shoots you to the top of a bestseller list like a posthumous release."

"Speaking of which, I read your new pages." What Graham derived between the subtext had nothing to do with science fiction, but an old axe long in need of grinding. "Tell me about 'em."

"Do you have any idea how many vigilante killings there've been the last couple years?"

Graham flicked a long cylinder of ash into an Altoids tin.

"Hundreds. Most of them never made the news. Average people, for things like smoking pot, petty theft, panhandling —"

"How do you know it was vigilantes? As opposed to self-defense."

"They weren't forcing crack on children. What were they defending? Why not call the cops?"

"Well." Graham grimaced, hating himself for the glib attitude. The relationship between cops and civilians have been on shaky ground for years. Too much corruption of the former led to rampant distrust by the latter, and both came out the loser.

"Some of them had their businesses destroyed, Graham. Delivery vans smashed to pieces on suspicion of selling drugs out the back. Arson—" Slamming his glass on the table, he paced in tight circles, knees snapping into place like a tin soldier's. "Sounds oddly familiar, don't you think?"

Graham's heart skipped. "To...?"

"Some of these cases were so low-profile I needed a backhoe to dig them out. What if police are turning away on purpose? The idea of a local mob orchestrating this kind of violence under a guise of decency and virtue is—"

Graham lit another cigarette, flicking the chrome lighter sharply closed. "Too close."

"What was that?"

He blew hard streams of smoke through his nostrils. "It's *speculation*, Val. Not a dissertation. Don't forget that."

Val stared at him as though he'd lost the ability to blink. Probably hadn't heard 'no' since Dad ran the agency.

"This isn't what your fans are expecting."

Val kneaded his thumb against his knuckles. "I *know* that."

"Just watch what you're doing here," Graham said, softening his tone. "That's all I'm saying."

***

With her coat half on, Sandra gave Anna a one-armed hug. "Oh no, you're leaving?"

"I wish I could stay, I'm having a ball. I'm glad I made it this year. Unfortunately, the boss is being a tyrant." Sandra's scowl eased into a grin, and she patted her reddening cheeks.

Anna never took her for much of a blusher.

"Who am I kidding? It's nice to be needed, even though it's the worst possible time to ping me. I guess the holiday is technically over, but—"

"Oh, they can wait a few more minutes, can't they? Just tell them you had a train delay."

"Well…"

"We didn't even get time to catch up," Anna said, sticking out her bottom lip.

"Okay. A few minutes."

Sandra always caved to a bit of theatrics. But the whole time they talked, she kept leaning on the counter then quickly straightening, squeezing against the doorframe as if allowing someone to pass, even though no one was there. She tugged the dangling half of her coat across her body instead of taking it off, leaving it at an odd angle. She hummed and laughed in all the right places but her answers were short, her side of the conversation lagging.

Val slipped out of Graham's study, alone, frowning at his shoes. Anna tried to ignore him, but wished she'd had the nerve to eavesdrop on their meeting. What was Graham still doing in there? Did they have another fight?

Sandra's words dropped off and she swiveled her head in the direction Anna stared. "Oh! It was lovely meeting you," she said, pulling on her coat and fluffing her corkscrew curls from under the collar.

Anna swatted her bangs away from her face. *Darn it!* Why did Sandra have to be so easily distracted? Who knew when they'd get to meet up next, with their crazy schedules. And she had the nerve to use Val as an out!

"Leaving already?" Val asked.

"'Fraid so. Duty calls."

"It's a shame you have to go so soon." She bounced up on

her toes like she was going in for a hug.

Anna's heart quickened, but Sandra was only readjusting her coat.

"Maybe we could get together again," Sandra said. "A drink? Say, Saturday evening?"

"I'd like that." Val smiled, his face brightening, erasing the doubtful expression he wore seconds ago.

Sandra tore herself away long enough to give Anna a simple nod and mutter "thanks again" before breezing out the door. There went their chance at girl talk.

Anna cleared her throat. Val's smile flickered as though surprised, even a little annoyed, that she was still there. The spark in his eyes disappeared as quickly as it came. She jutted her chin toward Graham's study. "Everything go okay in there?"

"Sure. Just some things I need to figure on," Val said softly, attention drifting.

Stop staring at the door, you twit. She's not coming back.

Then he launched into an unusually wordy monologue about manuscript problems and inner-city violence and the never-ending plague that was Andre Wallace.

Anna'd heard enough about this Andre person, and barely avoided rolling her eyes. Why spend so much time worrying over him anyway? He wouldn't be getting so much attention if he wasn't some ripped hottie who rose up from poverty. Andre had one novel out, not thirty-nine. So what was the big deal?

Val worked his butt off non-stop these days. She rarely even saw him anymore unless Graham invited him. And why he wasn't done writing this thing already? He used to have a new book out every year, sometimes two. Now he was talking like he barely passed English Lit. Maybe if he could keep his mind on more than one thing instead of being a typical man. Anna scooted over to draw his attention from that blasted door.

But he wasn't staring at it after all.

He had this weird head-tilt thing going on, like he was trying hard not to acknowledge a distraction in the distance.

The only thing in front of him were two Motherwell knockoffs, a housewarming gift from the in-laws. Big impressionistic things with thick black ovals on bland yellow backgrounds. But he wasn't studying the paintings so much as the space between them. His sudden, bright laugh contradicted the frown.

"Listen to me babbling on like a fool," Val said. "I hope I don't take a detour during my interview. Why are you looking at me like that?"

"No reason, honey." She forced a smile. "Good luck."

Chapter Four

Val's response had been largely automatic. Already in the mindset of spending more time with Sandra, he'd answered in the affirmative, not thinking. The week passed like any other, until 'Saturday evening' became 'tomorrow,' and all the implications of the invitation crashed down around him. Whether she meant this as a date, or two burgeoning friends going Dutch, or simply a brainstorming session or interview dry run, he never bothered to ask. She emailed the location of a meeting place in his neighborhood with the sign-off, 'See you there!' and left no concrete opportunity to reply with silly (in hindsight, *useful*) questions.

Dodging dogs and strollers maneuvered by young upstarts in puffy coats and ironic hats, Val slipped into an overheated café with mismatched tables and chairs and overstuffed loungers. Free jazz played through the speakers, at a volume unobtrusive to the writers sitting along the picture windows, yet loud enough to dull intense conversations. A vase of long-stemmed roses topped the espresso machine and tickled the shelf of wine bottles above it. A softly lit bakery case beckoned with chocolate-scented fingers. Was this place some kind of hint, or…what?

Sandra hadn't arrived yet to offer direction.

While trying to decide what balance of repartee would equal 'professional' as well as 'open to possibilities'—eyebrows lifted to the perfect subtle degree—a band of yuppies jostled in from behind and swept ahead as though he weren't standing within arm's reach of the counter.

As they loudly declared their preferences of vegan-friendly milk and pumpkin spice flavor profiles, he felt another breath of cold air against his back and legs. Without a sound to prove it, he turned, knowing Sandra had arrived. She smiled, dropping the hand preparing to tap him on the shoulder.

"Get the Boston cream pie," she said.

"Hello to you too."

"There's only one slice left, they better not snatch the last piece."

"No wonder Graham likes you so much."

"I used to cover the restaurant beat. When I moved to books and interviewed indie publishers, he suggested we meet at Carmine's."

Val snorted at the image of Graham sitting awkwardly beneath a white tablecloth and fairy lights. "The hell was he doing at Carmine's? Must have been Ed's idea."

She grinned and shook her head. "He's apeshit over their giant chocolate cake. He's also a lousy tipper, so we don't go there anymore."

"What are you having?" Val asked, not realizing he implied treating, thus initiating an official date. So much for passivity.

Possibly worse, the pie was gone.

Sandra gave the side-eye to the yuppies carrying their plates to the back and out of sight. "Espresso. And one of those giant cookies," she said, a little ruefully, pointing to a glass jar a good six inches in circumference.

The server placed the cookie on a dinner plate and slid it over. Val ordered two espressos and carried the plate to a table with a view, tucked into a little alcove created by two columns circled with silk vines.

Sandra folded her hands on the tabletop. "I wanted to discover everything about you for this interview, but it was tougher than usual. Your website has precious little meat to it. You're quite the mystery man."

"I don't have anything to hide."

"Mm...you're full of secrets, I can tell by your web page. 'Val M. Haverford grew up in a small town in Illinois... '" She pronounced the silent s as a string of z's, then dissolved into a dramatic pantomime of sleep.

"Blame Graham's intern. Leaving it blank would've been more interesting."

"Oh, so you came from Dullsville too. It couldn't have been worse than Carbondale. Population: sixteen thousand people and one horse."

"When did you escape?"

"Let's see." Sandra ticked off her life on her fingers. "Went to SIU, married stupid young, had my daughter…and finally wised up and ran screaming. You?"

"Not ten minutes after my high school graduation."

"Wow, you didn't waste any time. Were you on the lam?"

"Something like that."

"I'm *all* ears."

Every table now claimed by fellow caffeine addicts, tiny screens and steaming drinks sealing them into private bubbles, no one would hear if he lowered his voice. He tried to work out the best way to start, only to discard every prelude as deficient.

He'd seen this coming yet somehow stepped into it up to his knees. Worse, he didn't know how to get out. Explaining the way he'd grown up, about Michael, how both shaped him and sparked an idea for a conspiracy theory fifty years later, would likely sound shallow. Instead, he'd rely on the ol' tried-and-true Haverford Special: avoid the question at all costs, then dive into a topic rife with tangents.

"I lived in a town full of inbred hicks. Until I didn't have to." He broke off a chunk of cookie and ran with the first detour to pop into his head. "Pretty good party, eh?" Stuffing his mouth effectively lobbed the conversation across the net.

She raised an eyebrow but let it go. "The band's schedule and mine never worked out during the holidays, for various reasons. When I found out Graham knew them in college I nearly fell over."

"How's that?"

"Ed hired them to play at a release party for a novel about a bluegrass singer ages ago. I missed that gig, unfortunately."

"Small world."

"Truth."

The server brought their drinks, barely avoiding a stroller nudging into the aisle. Sandra moved the plate out of the way and kept it on her side of the table, as though she was on to Val's trick already.

"According to Till and Jimmy you're a one-woman band."

"I used to play in clubs before I had my daughter, and after she went off to college, I begged them to let me back in. I'm lucky they did."

"Nonsense, you're incredible."

"Well." A heavy curtain of lashes brushed her cheekbones.

"But anyone can play five instruments and sing."

"Oh, I see! Okay, let's hear you."

"My cords are dry."

Sandra mimicked flinging her saucer at his head like a Frisbee.

"You wouldn't be interested anyway. I only yodel in Sanskrit. Come on, there must be something memorable about you."

"I do make a fine boeuf bourguignon if I follow the recipe exactly and don't sample the wine until after," she said, downing the espresso like a shot. Her accent was perfect.

"Now you have my full attention. You were boring me to tears until you mentioned stew."

"Why, no man's ever said that to me before."

"You're kidding!"

"No, my ex-husband used to say that all the time. 'At least she can make stew.'" Her eyes widened. "Oh God. I can't believe I brought that up. I have such a big—forget I said that," she said, waving her hand around frantically before tapping her fingers against her lips. "Back to music. Have you heard of Stephanie Giroux?"

So she was good at dodging subjects too. "Not that I recall."

Sandra bounced a little in her seat, as though debating whether to divulge a secret.

"I guess I've been missing out."

From beneath the hood of a stroller, an uncomfortable whine rose like a drone of angry bees. Val gestured at his

43

demitasse cup, nearly as empty as hers.

"Maybe we could continue this conversation at my place?"

"Perfect timing." Sandra grabbed her giant purse from the floor. "Where did you park? I'll follow you."

"I walked."

The grin widened. "Even better."

Outside, she unlocked the doors to a retro yellow Cadillac with her fob. Before starting the engine, she fished a CD from a stack in the dashboard pocket.

One glance at the cover told Val all he needed to know. A chubby-cheeked woman of no more than twenty, wearing a corduroy jacket decorated with lace, peeked beneath long bangs. Along with the square, pink font, it reeked of alt-country.

"Looks can be deceiving." Sandra nudged him with her shoulder.

"Let's hope."

"Give it a chance," she teased, revving the gas. "Tell me what you think."

***

Val lit a fire in the front room hearth, leaving Sandra to jot notes for the camera crew while he hunted up a snack. He shook out a sleeve of water crackers and upended a package of prefab cubed cheese onto mismatched plates, arranging them on a walnut tray with two glasses and a white of indeterminate age.

Between sips of wine, Sandra moved from the couch to the adjacent sofa and wing-back chair, scribbling from each new spot. Meandering through the room, she set her glass on the mantel and squinted like she was casing the joint. A devilish grin inched up one side of her face.

"What are you up to?"

"Just a little extra research, sensory details…" She slipped her pen into the spiral of the notebook and dropped them both into the purse dangling from her shoulder.

"About?"

"Shelves, fireplace, lovely little sitting area…"

"And?"

"No desk."

"I'll be damned! You're right!"

"I'd love to see where you write. I can't picture you out here with a notebook balanced on one knee."

"It's nothing unusual, I'm afraid. A studio like any other, really."

"I doubt it, in a house as beautiful as this." She raised her eyes and pointed to the vaulted ceiling, smiling as though appreciating a work of art. That minor gesture was worth ten times in pride.

Spinning through a rolodex of excuses in his head, he landed on nothing of substance. He didn't usually bring people back there? Lame. After those spoilers were leaked, trust didn't come easy? Not a good tactic to take with an interviewer, a colleague. He had nothing, despite the feeling that the walls were expanding. He set his glass on the mantel next to hers and tipped his head toward the studio.

"Come with me."

Moonlight reflected off the snow in the courtyard, illuminating the entire east wall. Their footsteps whispered against the floor as Val led Sandra through, the windows—and Raymond's damn porch light—like beacons in the darkness.

"You can't see it from here but at the edge of the property there's a stone wall—"

"I can see it. It goes on forever—"

"—and just beyond is the lake."

The deepening twilight transformed the crests to lace and silver. A chill sighed off the glass. Sandra leaned in closer, the curve of her hip sidling against his.

"I sit out there often, watching the waves." Val cleared his throat and stepped back. "Give me your hand. This is part of the tour. Come forward, just a bit more." He guided her along the length of a narrow daybed until she was bathed in a pool of white. Shadows of fat snowflakes dotted her hands and vanished.

"Oh!" A massive skylight provided an unobstructed view of the stars.

He felt the need to speak in a hush, as though they were in a deserted chapel he didn't care to disturb. "Much of my inspiration comes from this. I keep a telescope in the drawer under the mattress. When I can't stay outside anymore, I lie here, beneath this skylight."

She dipped her head and her hair swept over her face, concealing her reaction. That comment was too forward, too suggestive, so loaded with unconscious innuendo that he felt, superficially, that he should apologize.

"I'd identify an asterism for you, but there aren't any visible from this vantage point right now," he said. "Though it doesn't seem like it, the universe is forever expanding, moving astonishingly fast, actually, and we have no equipment to take us to the end; we have no idea whether it even has an end. According to the Big Bang Theory, celestial bodies continue to move outward due to an explosion that happened billions of years ago. Once they run out of energy, everything will collapse in on itself. Other theories suggest outer space is contained. But by what? If so, there may be another side, a whole other universe, we don't know about. Science fiction and horror aren't that far removed."

Sandra's smile froze as she scanned the room, most likely for all available exits.

Val laughed in spite of himself, anxiety switching to empathy. "The possibilities make me giddy. Here, I'll lighten the mood. Don't move. I mean—hang on."

He hustled to the light switch, infusing the room with warmth and color. Sandra stretched her arms and took in the room inch by inch. She seemed to be memorizing everything she lingered on: the gentle slope of the skylights, small wood-burning stove topped with an antique coffee pot in one corner, three walls lined with a modest library of books.

"Looks like someone's a fan," she said, stooping to check out a shelf with twin copies of Marilynne Robinson's works. Every book she'd written: one copy for reading; the others, spines heavily creased, tagged with sticky notes.

"Have you read her?" He placed a hand on the small of her back, quickly savoring the red trim of her dress that disappeared into the crossover at her breasts.

"I don't think so."

"You'd remember. This is her first, but it's still my favorite." He pulled *Housekeeping* from the row. "She has a mastery of prose, so distinct that I haven't found an equal. She captures raw emotion like no one else."

"A recommendation from you means a lot. What do you love about it?"

Val grinned, widening his palm. The book fell open to a page dog-eared by repeated viewing. "It's this, this one passage, that kills me every time."

She started at the top of the paragraph instead of jumping right to that point. He closed his eyes as she read, absorbing the haunting lyricism as a musician would a classic composition.

Dwarfed in the darkness between worlds, Ruth and Sylvie waited in a little rowboat for a train to pass overhead, while another, decades in its grave, hovered just beneath the hull. Two lost souls adrift on a lake littered with the bodies of the dead, finding solace in their isolation. Val anticipated the hollow thud in his chest that accompanied the end of the passage. So many travelers were never seen again, some no one ever knew were on that train in the first place. In a matter of seconds, they were there and not there, disappearing as a drop of rain slides through water.

After a beat, he raised his head, aware of the silence. Sandra watched him with an amused expression.

"What?"

She gave a little shrug and shake of her head. "You're right, that's impressive."

"And the end is outstanding." He nestled the book back into place.

"You won't even let me take a peek after a tease like that?"

"I can't spoil the end, that's blasphemy! I'd lose all my cred. Besides, you're press. How do I know you won't tarnish my reputation?"

"I guess you don't. You'll have to wait and see."

"I'll tell you what. I'll lend it to you as long as you don't cheat." He handed the book back to her, and after faking a flip to the last page, she tucked it into her bag.

"You're still carrying that around! Come on back to the front room, set it down," Val said, glad to have an excuse to kill the lights.

"Nice try."

She continued her route back towards the windows, pausing at the butternut desk in the center of the room with a laptop, a pencil case, and an inbox full of loose-leaf notes weighted with a single fountain pen. Sandra circled the desk, doodling her finger along the ornate edges, gaze drifting toward the shelf above the sketch table. She squinted as she wandered over, tucking a stray bit of hair behind her ear.

He watched her liquid gait, following a few steps before leaning against the desk. Certain she was fascinated by the row of miniature wood creatures, dwellings, and spacecraft, he flipped the top sheaf of notes, hiding a mass of scribblings forming a giant O, the center blank. Sandra rubbed her arms again, squeezing tightly.

Val decided against lighting a fire. He was acutely aware of his posture, his hands, the position of his feet—was he always so pigeon-toed? He couldn't remember the last time he'd had anyone in this room. It was akin to having someone read his thoughts, and for a moment, as her eyes twinkled under a sideways glance, he suspected she might. Perhaps with an ebb of hospitality she'd get her fill and return to the front room and the wine.

She pointed to a diagram on the sketch table. "Guess you better stick to writing."

He never looked at his sketches with a critical eye before, but it was worthy of a first-grade classroom. "No question." He flipped to a plan of a seven-room Martian residence. "There's an upside. I start with an outline, but until I sketch the scene, I can't plot it fully. See here?" He tapped a crude, humanoid figure splayed in the center of room labeled

LDRY. "Jane Doe would've escaped had she been nimbler. But she's the inert sort. This is an argument for regular exercise: do your squats or die doing laundry."

"That's an unusual technique, isn't it? Sketching as part of the first draft? Something tells me there's a backstory."

"My original pursuit of interior design didn't take. I couldn't get excited about a lifeless set of rooms. Quit after a year. Lost my scholarship. I don't think my father ever forgave me for failing to follow in his footsteps." *Too much too soon.* He brushed off some stray eraser shavings and started out of the room.

"I'm sure he was proud of all you've accomplished."

"I like to think he would be. I wouldn't know."

"Why's that?"

"We weren't close, unfortunately. I was not the best son."

"That's so sad."

"If I had it to do all over—" Val paused in the doorway and let out a gush of air around the unbudging knot in his stomach. "I seem to have gone off on a tangent. Where were we?" He ran his palms over his thighs as though he'd hidden a fresh topic in his pockets.

"Hang on. There's still the question of your name."

At least she was following him out. He clicked off the light. "What about it?"

"It sounds like it's short for something."

He headed to the fireplace. "Damn logs don't seem to be catching," he mumbled, stabbing at the wood with the iron poker until sparks danced their way up the flue.

"Aha! There's even more to you than I thought. You don't intend to disappoint a fan, do you?"

"I'm afraid you'll laugh. It wasn't a very masculine choice on my mother's part."

"Go on." She held up two fingers. "I promise."

Val hesitated, screwing up the corner of his mouth and rolling his eyes to the ceiling. "Valery."

"Hm."

"There, you see. I should've known. Scout's Honor is three fingers."

"I wasn't laughing! It's just different. Is there a story behind it?"

"My father was stationed overseas when I was born. Mom thought if she gave his son a gallant name, it would bring him luck. He came home in one piece, so perhaps she was right."

"Did it bring you anything?"

"A lot of bloody noses."

She cooed sympathetically. "Now how about that M?"

"Just M." He diverted his full attention to the fire, shoving another log in, squatting close so the flames could color his cheeks.

"No one has a single letter for a middle name."

"My publisher started printing covers with my name larger than the titles. They could only fit 'Haverford' on one line. They needed to fill out the extra space, so I picked the letter with the widest typeset."

Her eyes crinkled. "Now I am laughing at you. You could've just as easily gone with a W."

"That's a mouthful. 'Val M. Haverford' has a nice ring to it."

"Okay, don't tell me. I'll figure this one out for myself."

He froze as Sandra traced the stained walnut bow stem displayed on ebony stands in the center of the mantel. Elaborate scrollwork evolved into the face of a snarling dragon; a childish representation of a Viking figurehead. The curve of its neck was blackened, the base splintered and violent. He relaxed only when she moved her fingers away, leaving each particle of soot intact.

"This is an interesting piece. What happened to it?"

The wine glasses sang as she picked them up. As he reached out, the back of his hand collided with hers. He paused, then grazed her skin until he sensed the coolness of the glass and cradled the bowl, never breaking eye contact. *Brilliant.*

"It was inexpertly removed from a boat. Please, have a seat."

Her eyes drifted downward as she curled into the sofa,

studying the smooth lines of the mantel and the decorative carvings along the trim. These were exactly the same, though stained rusty brown and refined, tighter, the work of an accomplished artist.

"You made these!"

"It's a hobby of mine. I learned to carve as a boy."

"They're beautiful! And your desk, the figures in the studio—"

"Helps me with setting. You know, I've been talking about myself all night, how about we—"

Sandra rested one hand so delicately on Val's chest that her touch was barely more than a passing whim. She bent his head toward hers, fanning her fingers through his hair.

Her lips nuzzled his, tracing their outline, then parted just enough to taste his bottom lip before drawing it in. The kiss was so modest, so maddeningly indefinite, that he pressed his hand against her back to lock her in place. Val hastily considered where to set his glass.

Instead, he eased away and dipped two fingers in the wine, painting a deliberate stripe down the length of her neck, spreading the vee of her dress open just the width of his hand. He ran his tongue down the trail to the divot between her collarbones. She murmured all three syllables of his first name, and he was surprised at how much he enjoyed hearing it. No woman had ever expressed it that way before, all the negative connotations turning to vapor. For a second he feared it was less a moment of ecstasy than admonition until she walked her fingers down his shirtfront, unfastening the buttons, taking her time with each. Four down, her hand like fire on his bare skin, when a disembodied warble from the answering machine cut through the air.

"Val, it's Frances. We need to talk."

"Damn, I thought I unhooked that thing." He dropped his brow against Sandra's shoulder.

"I've been going over your manuscript and there are significant problems here..."

Val darted into the bedroom to shut off the volume. He crouched next to the bed, swiping his fingers along the base of the ancient machine. After a pause, his editor's nagging increased in pitch.

"*Val!*" She nearly knocked him off balance. "I know you're hiding in your studio—"

Finally finding the notched wheel, he muted her to a whisper. He used the mattress as leverage, stretching into standing position before sauntering out with his hands in his pockets.

"Nothing is a bigger buzzkill than having another woman call and tell you you've failed."

"I should get going anyway. Early start tomorrow, yadda yadda—"

"I'd love the chance to see you again. Make up for this interruption," Val said.

"Sounds fantastic. Come to my place next time, I'll cook you my specialty." Sandra grabbed her coat off the back of the sofa. "I'll be here an hour before the interview." She swept out the door, leaving him sagging into the cushions.

Chapter Five

"Wow. That is *bright*." Val squinted at the sudden assault of light.

"Can we dim those a bit?"

"No, Sandra, I need to get a decent shot. You did insist on sitting by a window." Kevin, the cameraman, had thrown a sheet of gauze over Val's front room curtain rod to reduce glare while still affording a minor view.

"I'll get used to it," Val said.

"Graham told me you're a bit camera-shy," Sandra said.

"Thank you, Graham."

"Don't worry about it. Most people are." She squeezed his bicep. "Talk to me like we're back at their place and ignore everything else. Just let me know if you need a break. That's what editors are for."

"Ready when you are," Kevin said, tapping the viewfinder.

Val draped an arm over the back of the couch in an attempt to look casual. Sandra balanced note cards on her knee. The first questions were soft, perfunctory, by way of introduction. Sweat beaded along his hairline and threatened to drip down his temples. The heavy tweed sports coat started to feel like a terrible mistake.

"Has writing fiction become second nature, or are there still challenges you face?"

"Oh, writing's easy as pie. You just have to organize the perfect assemblage of words so no fewer than one million strangers think you're worth their time, preferably within the first three pages."

At Sandra's chuckle, he relaxed a bit, one minor hurdle conquered. *Like riding a bike.*

"Can you tell us what it was like growing up in a small town, and how that influences your craft?"

Shit.

He'd assumed the interview would be virtually all about his current manuscript. He analyzed the question, tried to invent some eloquent response to coalesce the sentiments eddying in the pit of his stomach, something to break through the familiar gridlock of memories and time. Distracted momentarily by faint streaks of headlights beyond the scrim, he turned back to answer. Sandra's mouth contorted in tiny increments, the corner of her top lip folding into a dimple before reappearing. She reached back and caressed his hand creeping toward the window, fingers fluttering like insects.

"They're popping up in the shot," she said.

"I'm a little rusty."

"Relax, you're doing fine." She smiled and pulled his hand into the open space between them, massaging his fingertips. "This is out of frame, isn't it, Kev?"

"Yep."

She leaned in close to Val and whispered, "Don't worry, I won't bite."

"We're still rolling," Kevin said. Then, under his breath, "Production's gonna have a blast with this one."

"Your first novel was published when you were in your twenties," Sandra continued. "Can you pinpoint a time in your youth that suggested you'd become an author?"

"Only in retrospect."

"Can you elaborate on that?"

"I don't think I can."

"Let's go in a different direction," Sandra shifted some cards around. "You have an impressive résumé with over three dozen novels, a number of which were adapted for the screen. In your early career, you wrote Westerns, then made a one-eighty to science fiction. Yet despite your success in both genres, you've left your fans hanging for some time. Can you tell us why you've taken such an extended leave?"

After asking himself that same question for years, he recited the answer he kept in his pocket. "In college, I wrote book reviews so I could eat on a regular basis. After a while, it all became repetitive. I started to feel that way about my novels; I got bored with my own style. That's the first sign of trouble. So I just...quit."

"And now your latest, *606/88*, borrows quite a bit from current events. What can you tell us about it?"

"It takes place in a dystopian universe from the point of view of a conspiracy theorist. He's convinced a group of covert vigilantes aim to cleanse society of anyone they deem valueless."

"That's a very provocative subject. Are you prepared for the backlash you may receive from those who read into it the wrong way?"

"I thought about that a lot. My hope is, it will get people talking. An allegory filtered through humanoids..." Aliens were less an allegory than a metaphor. A twinge of melancholy fluttered in his chest. "Sometimes absurdity sheds light on the commonplace."

"You're no stranger to controversy; supremacy was the central theme in your 1974 satirical essay, 'Green Skies and Blue Fields,' correct?"

Wow. Nothing like a curveball to destroy what little poise you'd put in place. Drafted in his post-college writing frenzy, it was a shock that Swiftian piece was ever published, even with the Third Reich relegated to history books. Yet that anthology was long out of print, the publishing house shuttered. How did she dredge up a copy?

"Right." He cleared his throat to diminish the creak. "So much of my later work involved the usual sci-fi tropes, so I wanted to put a different spin on things. Hitler was a monster, a madman. Yet he unified thousands toward wiping millions of people off the face of the earth. That's what's truly terrifying: not only can an army of people be so easily talked into genocide, but that it could happen again."

A flash of panic registered in Sandra's eyes. She pulled the cards closer, but not to consult them. The energy drained from her voice, as though she wished she hadn't gone down this road but it was the only way home. "Can you name a specific incident that was the catalyst for this project?"

He swallowed hard, twice. Reached for his water. Condensation trickled through his fingers as he drained it, the crackling plastic drowning out every other sound. He wanted to press the cold bottle against his face.

Sandra grazed his forearm. "Mr. Haverford?"

"Sometimes you just need to get your ideas down on paper," he said, his laugh hollow. "Otherwise horrible things keep rattling around in your head!"

Her mouth opened and closed, a wrinkle of confusion crossing her face before she replaced the question. "When can we expect to read *606/88?*"

"We're hoping for release next fall."

Sandra's voice returned to its previous brightness as she leaned back and smiled. "Wonderful! Well, we at *On the Record* wish you great success. Thank you for meeting with me."

"Thank you."

"All right, Kev, did we get it all?"

Kevin grunted a positive response.

"That's it?" Val asked, rolling his shoulders.

"That wasn't so bad, was it?" Sandra shoved the cards into the giant purse at her feet.

"You made me a lot more comfortable. After a while I almost forgot about the camera."

Kevin snorted. "God."

"I...didn't mean to get so nervous at the end..."

Sandra raised her voice a decibel. "Don't give it another thought. Quite a project you're working on."

"Now I have to make it good. And fast. This thing is due in four months. What did I get myself into?"

"I for one am looking forward to it. I may have to ask for an autographed copy."

"Consider it done."

"I need to get behind here and unhook the lights, do you mind, please?" Kevin lurched around the couch, snatching at bits of cord.

Sandra's nostrils flared, pupils dilating into inky black

pools.

"We'll just sit over here," Val suggested, pointing to the sofa and wing-back chair. Kevin slammed out the front door with the first load of paraphernalia. "Why don't you stick around for a while, join me for a celebratory glass of wine?"

"Sure. Why not. That sounds great."

Val disappeared into the kitchen and stalled, brushing the dust off a bottle of red dug out from under the sink and polishing the spots off the wine glasses left in the strainer from last time. When the front door banged twice more in quick succession, he assumed it was safe to come back.

Sandra's back was ramrod straight, jawline thrust inches from Kevin's face as she delivered a clipped diatribe. Each time she shot down Kevin's responses, his posture dipped a bit lower. Pure hatred oozed through narrowed lids, but he jerked his chin up in a sort of affirmation and slunk out the door with the remaining equipment. Sandra turned at the sound of glass tinkling and spread her hands in an offering of remorse.

"I apologize. He's usually not such a little prick. I'll talk to his supervisor about his behavior; that was mortifying."

"Don't worry about it. You can't make fans out of everybody."

She helped unload his burden onto the coffee table. "You're very forgiving. I don't understand where it could've come from."

"After all the hate mail I've received over the years, a little attitude is nothing."

"Please, you don't get hate mail."

"Oh yes I do. Especially after that essay. And some of it's pretty inventive."

"Really? Like how?"

"My favorite is rather nasty."

"Try me."

"You sure?"

She raised an eyebrow and smirked. "I've gotten blasted for interviewing gay actors. A couple four-letter words won't kill me."

"Okay…" Val searched for an email on his phone. "See for yourself."

"'You are worse than the maggot-infested fecum of mole rats.' Oh, this guy's pissed. '…second-rate shit-peddler'—you weren't kidding. Why would you keep such a hateful thing?"

"It's so creative. And it has impeccable grammar and punctuation. And look…" he giggled and enlarged a choice passage.

"'Take this book and stuff it, you ass-licking, avaricious puddle of pond scum.' Wow!"

"Who uses a word like 'avaricious' in hate mail? And spells it correctly, too?" He winked.

Her mouth formed an O before dissolving into a grin. "Another writer."

"Bingo. Here's my favorite bit."

"'I hope God zaps your ovaries with a bolt of lightning!' He thought 'Val' was a woman. *Un*believable."

"He may be intelligent but not enough to look at a book jacket. Mostly, I'm concerned this will confuse poor God. I mean, what to do? I should've written this guy back. 'Dear So-and-So. Thank you for your interest in my latest novel. Have you considered a vocation in writing? This type of fierce emotion is what we authors are constantly striving to perfect. All my love…'"

Sandra's brassy laugh bubbled up and in short order tears rolled down her cheeks. She pulled a handkerchief out of her purse and Val recognized it as his own.

"I should probably keep this," she said.

"I need to stop making you cry every time we meet."

"In this business I don't encounter many people with such a warm sense of humor. There are a lot of self-important artists who insist we owe them something."

Val sliced the foil off the wine and twisted the corkscrew in. "It should be the other way around. These days it's hard to get noticed without posting, tweeting, pinning…whatever else…I remember when you simply placed an ad in the paper." The cork slipped from the bottle neck with a pop. "I think I'm showing my age."

"I'm sure you're having a tough time."

"You don't write for ten years, people start to forget."

"Not everyone's forgotten. Sometimes the spotlight has a way of finding you."

"I don't know if that's a good thing or not." He nodded toward the door. Before she could offer another apology, he waved her off. "Thank you for the interview."

Sandra seemed to be studying the wine, the glass to the light, watching the legs.

"Now you're holding something back."

"It's already getting negative attention." She held up a hand, dismissing Val's shrug. "No. Trolls like that are different. That was vague. What if there's an angle to this you haven't considered?"

Her phone buzzed from the depths of her purse. Instead of answering, she stared hard into him, as though trying to read something in the mix of exhaustion and fluster that would soon leave him in a lump on the futon in the studio. Her eyes flickered shades of fear and fever in equal measure, to the point he couldn't see much else.

"I don't know what's riled up the masses exactly, but I suggest you take a much closer look."

"Sandra—it's just a lot of noise."

"Must be nice to live a life that easy." She handed him her glass but paused before letting go. A strangled syllable and a pat on the cheek was all she was willing to give. She walked out without a backwards glance.

Chapter Six

Ridiculous.

Val flipped through Frances' edits, still hot off his printer. She'd developed a penchant for the dramatic, perhaps from years of reading his manuscripts. The markups weren't that extensive, despite her rambling commentary. A few minor suggestions here and there. He tossed them in the desk drawer to fiddle with later and taped the red-splotched map over the closed shades.

Following a spreadsheet listing every incident and alleged motive by date, he traced each greasy dot to the next. Even when a few lined up in a straight line or perfect circle, the pattern would disappear, returning to a haphazard mess.

In the last few months, the suburbs—especially the North Shore—collected more cases than anywhere else in that same time frame. He'd immediately honed in on the stereotypical and overlooked an embarrassing amount of detail. How many others have done the same, making excuses for what they didn't want to see, failing to look beyond into the greater scope? If he had the time, a map of the nation might look the same. As many red splotches as cities, a festering scourge of violence with no beginning or end, no tie and no purpose.

A crunch as he stepped forward, a snap in his left hand: narrow slivers of beige paper littered the floor around his feet. He'd pulled the white string clear off the china marker, now leaving waxy red waves in the creases of his hands. He wrapped the marker in a tissue and secured it with a rubber band.

Forgetting the dates, he concentrated solely on motive. What about the 'burbs held such a magnetic pull for murder?

That, too, was a dead end: no pattern erupted from the

markings here but chronology, as if the killers completed a job within a specified time frame and moved on to the next.

Spending years rewriting the old frontier was a metaphor; switching to sci-fi was prediction. Readers were glad when you guessed wrong. The world didn't come to an end, the aliens were defeated. The world went back to normal when you closed the cover.

The concept no longer held a delicious fascination, the thought of playing god a sick game. Present-day humans destroying human life haphazardly, with no credible provocation. Where did they get the urge to eliminate their own, and why? It was the Wild West out there, a barrage of bullets from a posse of modern desperadoes.

Satirizing Hitler years after the war was easy with so many books and articles to pull from, so much speculation about the man, his mental state, his reasoning or lack of. When reason didn't exist, there was nothing to dissect. He should have spent more time reading true crime and serial killer novels.

A chill spread through his limbs. Could all this be traced to one person?

No one person could cause so much strife without ever having been caught. One syndicate? How many members? In either case, Val had circled back to the motive question.

Mind spinning, deviations whirling out of control with no answers in sight, he dropped the map project in favor of revisions. For once it felt like relief instead of drudgery.

***

After a week of overthinking the slightest word changes, he called Graham for a meeting. Headaches erupted and spread in all directions like an outstretched hand. He needed a second set of eyes. Preferably ones that worked.

Their meeting was in less than an hour, and he'd be back on the road before the incoming snowstorm filled in all the footprints from the last onslaught. Center console stuffed with enough CDs for a road trip, he popped in the top one.

An unfamiliar soprano triggered memories of his coffee date with Sandra, how their conversation had again turned to music. She was somehow able to draw a precise bead on him, guessing he'd balk at this disc purely by judging the cover, eventually delighting in the elegant jazz within. How was that possible after such a short time knowing each other? Listening to it for the second—third?—time, he wondered if she had an angle not unlike Anna's. At some point, he'd have to meet with her to return it. He grinned. Just like he did with *Housekeeping*.

He allowed the bare minimum of brain cells to drive while the rest played a movie in his head: Sandra's rich voice; her quick, playful humor; all the little idiosyncrasies he hadn't noticed when they met at the party, like the way she held a bite of food just inside her lips before she bit into it, teasing her own taste buds. How her eyes widened before she said anything revelatory or exciting. The dip of her lids, cheek turned to an invisible sun like a person dreaming, when she spoke of her career as other women gushed about their children. Her fascination with life, the way she pulled him into after it like a collaborator, bridging a gap of mistrust that had grown wider every year tucked away in his bubble. How she rounded out all the things he was missing.

Something chafed at his heart, a sour little bitterness, that they'd never been introduced before. Like Anna and Graham had done him a disservice by keeping her a secret for so long. Even her gibes were welcome, each one causing a twitch in his fingers; he wanted to seize her up and demonstrate that he may be flawed, sure, but he'd give her something to remember him by.

The lush voice filling the car loped into a bluesy, Southern waltz. The gentle twang no longer grated like the scrape of a ferrule against a thin sheet of paper, but a magnet rousing metal filings. Nerve endings sparked at every flex of muscle, the fine hairs on the nape of his neck shivered at the sweep of his collar. He could almost taste her, the flavor of wine on her lips, indulging the possibility of how it might transform with the influence of heat and location.

Familiar landmarks broke his reverie. He had long ago exited Lake Shore Drive and rounded the curve toward Graham's tower. Traffic usually passed like a breeze midday, but never had it felt like slipping through a wormhole. He hadn't remembered even turning the wheel. As he pulled up, his phone vibrated against his belly.

"Hey, I'm running late," Graham said. "My lunch meeting went long and I didn't realize. How about two, can you find something to do until then?"

"Sure, I'll grab a bite myself." Val couldn't keep the smile out of his voice.

"What are you laughing at? Me?"

"I'm not sure."

"Okay…"

The phone made an odd clicking sound. The battery was low, but the icon promised twenty percent power. "See you at the office. Two."

Brain still running on conserve, Val wended around the city looking for a place to eat. The mention of food turned his stomach into a den of lions. The first snowflakes, hours ahead of schedule, collected into a feathery mass along the tops of his wipers. Potholes large enough to hide a body in, cracked cornhole platforms and plastic cones claiming dibs on his patience, suggested it was pointless to keep searching for street parking. But when he saw the prices posted outside public garages he thought he was hallucinating again. *Double digits for two hours? Bullshit.* Early bird discounts laughed in his face. He grit his teeth and pulled in to the next one he came to. At least the choice of restaurants stretched for blocks in every direction.

***

Service took longer than he expected, but he paid no attention to the hour until he saw it printed on the bill: five to two.

"I guess this one's on me," Val said. Graham had answered his phone immediately, as if waiting for the call. "Can we push it to three?"

"I have a three I can't break. It will be a long one, too. Damn." Val swore he heard Graham pull on a cigarette. "I hate to have you wait 'til five…"

"I'll check out a museum or something. Make like a tourist."

"Are you sure?"

"I'm here already, why not?"

"Okay, well…see you at five. Sorry for this inconvenience. Where'd you park? We'll reimburse—"

"Don't worry about it, we're even." Seconds before the call ended, the phone clicked again. Faint but detectable.

When was the last time he'd wandered around downtown? Museums were the first thing that came to mind, but their locations were a mystery. Somewhere off the lakefront, but south. Anywhere between one mile and twenty.

Shoppers and businessmen on cell phones knocked into him and kept walking. Towers heaved upwards from cracked concrete and seemed to tilt inwards, caving over his head. Cars emerging from garages honked as much for safety as ego before barreling into the street, dodging yellow steel girders shoring up a set of L tracks. If memory served, Sears Tower was a few miles southwest.

Spying the Red Line entrance across the street, he descended the lopsided, chipped staircase to the platform. A southbound pulled in as he emerged from the turnstiles. After a quick ride, he got off at Jackson to transfer to Blue. The tunnel between the two lines smelled of urine, an invisible fog that filled his mouth and throat and built a home in the folds of his clothes. The scent lived forever in the glazed brick walls, the crisscrossing red and blue stripes overhead, and hitchhiked in the soles of commuters' shoes.

Val emerged into a horde of people clustered in the doorway and down the block from a storefront popcorn shop, its wide-open door releasing the aroma of imitation butter, powdered cheese, and burnt sugar.

Time bound a rope around his legs as he paced from one end of the street to the next, hoping he'd recognize Sears' famous stair-step architecture. Or anything else. Kids drumming on upturned plastic buckets used to squat on every corner, beating the rhythm of a parade into everyday life, but at some point they'd been replaced with canned jazz buried in parkway gardens. The skyline seemed to retreat with every step he took, taunting the fool who didn't bother to check a map. Soon he was lost in a desolate stretch of pawn shops and dank bars and leather-bound men with careful looks.

Cursing himself, Val caught the next northbound bus. At least he could take in the sights as they rolled past. The driver slowed, teased forward, and lurched. Bodies teetered and swayed, powerless to stay rooted in one spot. They sank into their knees, cinched the swinging loops overhead, widened their stances. A few passengers grumbled in foreign languages with each jostle. Faces tensed with suppressed screams of frustration.

One voice broke through the constant rustle of human sound, clear and droning as though he'd given the same speech for years, his dejected tone revealing his success. At his dead yet insistent "I am not asking for money," Val shut his ears, looking between heads for a patch of window. Anything counted as beat poetry if you romanticized it enough.

"While standing on the corner waiting for a friend, I was brutalized by three…"

Outside, a garish, graffiti-covered booth mounted to a bike leaned against a lamppost. A cluster of tourists gathered around a man in a dusty gray wig, dressed entirely in trash bags with "Open Your Eyes" scrawled across the front in the same greasy stage make-up that creased his face. He bowed to his audience and flicked a switch, filling the air with a yowling, ancient recording of "Sweet Home Chicago." The man tapped his toe to the beat, but at the first shrill note of a harmonica, he sprang forward, dancing with bent limbs like a dislocated puppet.

The broken notes weakened as the bus pushed on, returning the orator to center stage.

"…nobody believes me. See?"

Female passengers gasped and recoiled; some of the men growled insults. Val craned his neck to catch another glimpse. Face unlined, skin a dry paste, blond hair wild and unruly: he could have been thirty or sixty.

"I only want to educate."

Though shuffling, his clear speech gave no question to his sobriety. The reason for the horrified reactions was lost in the stricken faces of those he'd passed. Though the city council's infrastructure upgrades and neighborhood beautification projects cut down on the number of beggars and transients, surely they'd seen a homeless person before. The design of Millennium Park, the city's front lawn brimming with gardens and footbridges, gave them more places to burrow into, not less.

"I was only waiting on the corner for my friend, and this is what I got. I have no money, any little bit helps. I cannot walk well, as you can see…"

As he mounted the stairs at the back of the bus, Val turned away as the others had, swallowing hard. The man had raised his jogging pants around his knees, the elastic pulled to capacity. Leathery skin stretched over both legs, engorged to the width of small tree trunks. His feet bulged from red sneakers with tongues that had never known laces. One leg looked as though a blast had ripped through it. A gaping ulceration had bitten away his flesh, exposing streaks of sinew glistening with pus. The surrounding skin pulled when he shifted his weight.

"…took me down and beat me. One of them tased me and left me with this. Again, I do not want money. I do not want pity. I want to spread the word about what is happening in our great city. I did not deserve this for standing on a street corner."

The words ricocheted around Val's brain and he pushed out at the next stop, long before his intended destination. His foot wedged in the door, the rubber seal locking his ankle in place.

Strangers waiting to cross banged at the folding door. A squeal of hydraulics buried their shouts. A gasp raked Val's lungs as someone grabbed his pant leg and tugged. He twisted, freeing himself, and fell forward, scraping both palms on the coarse pavement.

Someone hoisted him up by the elbows. "You all right, man?"

Arms wobbling, Val rested his hands on his knees. Nodded in the direction of the voice. Its owner patted him on the back.

"You take care, man, be safe."

He watched a pair of red shoes disappear into the crowd.

Straightening slowly, he concentrated on landmarks and street signs to regain his bearings. Everyone passed him by, oblivious.

Eyes up. Too many seductions demanded attention. Posh boutiques. Bike couriers whipping in between cars. A red sightseer's trolley kiosk with a dozen fanny-packed tourists lining up halfway down the block.

He stalked off to Graham's tower, waddling like a stiff penguin and slipping anyway, ankle gnawing like a promise half remembered. One more block.

Orchestral music poured from a speaker outside a 7-Eleven.

Val pulled up short at the contrast of exhausted looking men with chips and Cokes pushing through revolving doors under the strains of Bach's "Minuet in G." At least the sound was in tune, unlike—

With that little bit of distance, the street performer outside the bus came clearer. He was wearing polished wing tips under the rags. Yet he couldn't he afford a coherent recording? Val tried to decipher the meaning of a broken man in trash bags when the phone vibrated again. At this point— lost in space, wet, palms still raw and stinging—he didn't pull it out in time. Graham's phone number flashed on the home screen.

Val waited to listen to the voicemail until he was riding up the elevator, shaking snow off his coat.

"Hey, I'm so sorry. I know I said that before, but I'm running behind again. The weather made my associates late, so—I'll be out before six, I swear. Make yourself

67

comfortable in the atrium. There's coffee, 'natch. I owe you dinner and many, many drinks. Oh, the code's 4-8-1-2 if Lucy's not at the desk. On the positive side, Chicago museums. Fantastic, am I right?"

Lucy buzzed him in, perky and sweet as usual. He dropped the folder of revisions on her desk and headed back out, leaving as pleasant a message with her as he could muster. He left another on Graham's cell, not knowing which he'd check first.

"Hell with this, Graham. I'm heading home before traffic gets worse and I get in about March o'clock. Can we meet Monday at five instead? I'll accept your dinner offer. My phone's running low and making odd noises. Email me, would you?"

***

After an hour of inching through a bluster of snowflakes and ice pellets, Lake Shore Drive resembled a parking lot more than a roadway. Val hated no one more at that moment than Punxsutawney Phil. The little shit predicted an early spring but as usual, Chicago made its own rules. This kind of storm could easily down power lines, block roads, and fuck over a man living alone in a virtual forest. Glaring whiteness burned into his retinas.

After exiting the Drive, he stopped at the first place that promised food and hard liquor. Three hours, one meal, four cheap scotches and about a dozen dirty looks later, Val gave up for home. The storm still howled, but at least the traffic had decreased to a less maddening concretion.

He coaxed the car up to the cabin and was, after a few extra tugs on the box handle, able to retrieve the mail. Chucking the pile on the entry table, more than half of them missed the target and cascaded onto the floor. Tossing his coat toward the general direction of the couch, he cursed himself for having lowered the thermostat ten degrees before heading out.

He flicked on the lamp, and in the shadows at the rear of

the house he saw the silhouette of a male figure bolt upright and dodge behind the desk.

"Hey!"

One of the studio doors banged shut. Running feet ground a path through the snow. Val turned toward the bedroom to call the police but was yanked backwards by the throat. He fumbled at a thick, textured wire looped just tight enough to stifle his breath and hold him still. Any attempt to stand upright would instantly suffocate him. Pressure imploded his ribs as he tried to force air into his lungs. *One breath, that's all I need, just one.* He could make it last a while.

The wire slackened a fraction of an inch and he drew in a huge gulp of air. Knuckles dug into Val's neck. *This is just a robbery. They'll be gone in a minute. Just play along. You'll be fine.*

The thief wrenched Val's left arm behind his back. A voice growled in his ear. "You're going to stop—"

"Take what you want. The safe—" The response was a quick jerk of the wire, causing a corresponding twinge in Val's temple.

"Listen. Talk to that agent of yours and call off this book. Do it and you'll have no further trouble. Understand? We have to secure our future."

"You—what? Who are you?"

"I'm your biggest fan. I don't know how you found out about us, but this ends here, got it?"

"I don't know what you're—"

"Don't act stupid, just take care of it!"

"Go to hell," Val said, marveling at his own bravado.

His arm was released, and for a second he thought he gained an advantage. He tried to wrestle away, but his ankle buckled with a pop and he fell hard on one knee. The wire twanged as the intruder snapped the ends taut and twisted, scraping away flesh. Val grappled with it, failing to find a gap.

Sparks of pain ignited behind his eyes as the throbbing in his skull intensified. His fingers refused to obey any further commands. The warm metal slipped from his grasp. Motes of dim light danced across the room.

His last breath was too long ago.

A hooded figure eclipsed his vision. Val squinted to focus on the face: crooked, fibrous nose that seemed molded from wax. Cheekbones like discs of flint, pulling white skin into concave hollows. "It's not supposed to take this long." He had the tone of a man ripe with experience.

Val was wrong. He was going to die right there.

He heaved a lead fist behind him, hoping to at least jar his attacker's grip. The hooded man's knee hurtled upward long before Val could connect. The floor dissolved into quicksand, pulling him down, down, until he was drowning in it.

Chapter Seven

Consciousness collided with Val like he'd been blasted toward it. Stiffness bloomed in his back. He realized dimly that he lay on the floor of his cabin. The phone in his pocket dug into his hip.

The battery blinked red; hopefully there was enough juice to make one call.

"911 Emergency."

Val tried to speak but his voice perished in the rawness of his throat.

"Hello? Is anyone there?"

One more second and she'd hang up. A croak sliced a path through the ether.

"Can you repeat that?"

"*Help me—*"

"Say again? Where is your emergency?"

The phone bleeped and died. Pain flayed his vision. Frigid air blasted through the wide open door, blowing drifts of snow over the sill. He'd have to crawl to the bedroom phone. Rolling to one side, his throat became a cocktail straw, allowing the slightest wisp of air to pass. The room listed sharply. He reached for the arm of the couch to keep from sliding out the door.

A man's voice called his name. Heavy footsteps echoed off every surface.

Move! Val squeezed his eyes and pulled up. Footsteps thundered toward him. His heel slipped, contorting his ankle and banging it against the floorboards. The quicksand returned and swallowed him whole.

***

Creaking leather and the gentle tap of rubber paced in tedious circles, back and forth, like bored patrons in a gallery. As Val rolled his eyes upwards, the room transformed into a field of stars. Flashes of white light popped and the walls glowed alternately red and blue. Muffled voices spoke a language full of meaningless numbers: Glasgow six. Zone two. He shivered under itchy blankets, tingling with the numbness of having been in one position too long. Two paramedics eased his ankle, deep crimson and twice its normal size, into an air splint lined with ice packs. He tried to ignore the jagged pain radiating everywhere.

This vantage point gave him an uncommon view of the vaulted ceiling. One of the beams had a huge crack in it, a good eight inches long. He'd need to get that repaired.

A young EMT tucked the blanket closer to expose one arm. "Mr. Haverford, my name is Kassie. Squeeze my hand if you can hear me."

Val tightened his fingers in spasmodic increments.

"Have you been prescribed any medications?"

Squeeze.

A man in a dark suit and tie dragged a folding chair to Val's opposite side and sat, leaning over to press a hand against his shoulder.

"Detective Marczek, remember me? I need to ask you a few questions."

"One second, sir." Kassie waved him away. "I need to finish assessing the patient."

"Not right now you don't." Marczek tugged down Val's oxygen mask. "Do you know what happened here?"

Val attempted to shake his head, but something locked him in place. He was glued to the floor, upper arms pinned to his sides. His whole body went rigid as he tried to tear himself free.

"Don't try to move, you're strapped to a board. Did the person who attacked you identify himself?"

"No." Val reached for his throat, dry fingertips stinging ragged welts. Someone was trying to wring his throat shut from the inside.

The detective spat out questions faster than Val could process. "Do you remember anything at all?"

He recalled the arc he was forced into, then dropping to his knees. "Two men. One shorter than me."

The last two words were soundless. Marczek scowled and leaned closer.

"One...in the studio." The strain of squeezing out this statement added to the crushing pressure in his chest. A galaxy of unfamiliar faces swirled above him and pressed in tighter. *Who are these people? How many are there?* The studio. *What are they doing back there?*

Air siphoned away and he drifted in space. Sound funneled and dissipated, sealing him off.

Kassie raised a mask over Val's face. "Take a deep breath and hold it, Mr. Haverford. Count to three."

Val made a shallow, ragged attempt. Like waves in a conch. Moisture built under the plastic and warmed his face.

"Exhale. That's right. Do it again. Come on."

Air never tasted so sweet.

"Oxygen getting to you okay?"

Squeeze. Shakier this time. God, he was tired. Ice crept under his fingernails and bore into his teeth.

Kassie nodded at her teammates. "We need to go. Now." She fastened the lower arm restraints.

Marczek bounced his hand up and down: chill out. He got up slowly and swung the chair out of the way, his sneer revealing a dagger-like tooth.

"Okay, sir, we're gonna move you on out of here. Detective Marczek will keep an eye on you in back."

Paramedics lifted Val onto a gurney and whisked him into an ambulance. The gentle hiss of oxygen melded with the piercing trill of sirens, and the world slipped away into dizzying blackness.

Chapter Eight

The black curtain melted into an orange blaze, followed by an invasion of harsh white light. Disembodied hands roamed over Val's body and prevented escape. Someone had taken a blade to his lungs and scraped them raw, snuffing out his shouts for help before they reached anyone's ears.

The room came into focus in stages; first by color, then by shape. Sea green and powder blue walls had the nerve to provoke placidity where none existed. The technological anonymity of equipment stirred up images of alien probes and mind control devices. Doctors and nurses, marked with rings of fatigue and the mad stare of dispassion, stabbed with fingers and needles, every touch a bolt of pain severing all sound and explanation.

"Can we raise the head of the bed a little, please?"

A plump nurse with heavy-lidded eyes rose into view. Not an ounce of fear or worry effused the fine lines of her face. The name 'Hannah' decorated her scrubs.

"You're at Good Samaritan, Mr. Haverford. Do you understand why you're here?" she asked more loudly than necessary.

The powerlessness, the sensation of falling, the molten, futile attempt to save himself seeped into his memory. But they flickered like clips from a film: detached, random pictures devoid of emotion or context. He hoped someone could fill in the missing scenes. The last thing he remembered clearly was driving through the snowstorm and the cold that bit through his skin.

Doctors tried to cull more information but there was none to give. The din muffled again, but he forced himself awake. His eyes darted, searching, but for what he didn't know.

Nurse Hannah, The Voice of Reason, narrated every task of her rounds, every procedure he'd have to endure. She talked nonstop on the way to radiology, insisting that the CT was quick and painless.

"Why…can't remember—"

"Short-term memory loss is expected after trauma like yours," she said, checking his chart. "It will come back in its own time. The tests will tell us more."

He barely registered the blood draw, the IV. But lying on the CT bed without head support cleaved his throat in half. From the other side of the wall, a tech guided the bed through the revolving scanner, its incessant whirring and buzzing like the blades of a saw. A bitterness flooded his tongue. A reverberation pinged and he felt a wire tighten—

A voice breathed through the ether. "Breathe normally, Mr. Haverford. I'll make this quick as I can. Are you getting any odd sensations?"

Whatever was in that IV flushed through him, one vein at a time. "Metal. I taste—"

"Oh, yep. Just the dye in the IV. It's nasty, no lie. It should go away in a minute."

Through the persuasive effects of exhaustion and morphine, the scene gradually reversed itself: the blinding lights, at first as shocking as an unexpected dousing with ice water, eliminated even the slightest hint of shadow. Even at that late hour, the hospital bustled with organized chaos. Doctors and nurses scuttled between beds, dancing in and out of supply rooms, never breaking a sweat or losing concentration. Recognition flashed on some of their faces. Val's heart slowed, stomach and legs unclenching. They'd never let anything happen to a patient of prominence in a hospital this prestigious, this immaculate; the press would have a field day. As long as he was there he'd be fine. He needed to get over the threshold, find enough serenity to sleep. But he couldn't quite step off that ledge.

As the only reclusive celebrity in the immediate area, a nursing assistant joked, Val had been upgraded to a private room with a view of the parking lot. They'd keep an eye on him for the next forty-eight hours due to his maturity and the risk of rapid, uncontrollable swelling. She slowed down to enunciate that last remark, fucking beaming at her thoughtfulness.

The door gaped from the terminal end of the room with the bed against the opposite wall, making it impossible to see anyone coming down the corridor. Unsure whether the isolating layout or the drugs were making him jumpy, he'd gladly give them both back, stay awake for days behind the thin curtain in the ER, over feeling like bait in a shark's cage.

Flat, black rooftops studded with HVAC units stretched for miles outside the window, scarves of exhaust the only thing moving in the frigid air. He sucked on a chunk of ice and switched on the TV for a better distraction than tar and pollution but nothing held his attention. Daytime television was a garish amalgamation of talk shows and reality courtroom histrionics. A snatch of news, a shot of Val's cabin, startled him into pausing.

When the canopy of trees was in full leaf, the cabin vanished from the walking paths. With one long pull of fresh air, tension, worry—even the world in general—evaporated, allowing him to bask in blissful solitude. Under any other circumstance, he'd be desperate to return. But thanks to this report and a steady, tight shot, his home, his sanctuary—the vining scrollwork of the door and decorating the eaves instantly recognizable—stood spotlighted against the stark snow, neon yellow caution tape highlighting the property.

A pretty young reporter offered direct reassurance: "Nothing of value was taken."

Great.

The phone's clamor disturbed the deathly stillness of the room.

Graham was the only emergency contact he had in his phone. Would the hospital have called overnight before he had a chance to give permission? More likely, it was some amateur suburban press. Regardless of who was on the line, he needed to find the right balance of candor and levity. Sugarcoated responses always pacified reporters. He'd tolerate no speculation, no pity. Not after that crack about his age. He spat out the ice and cleared his throat. A mistake.

"Hello?"

"Oh—I was trying to reach—"

Sandra. She sounded like music. "It's me," Val said.

"Oh my God! Your voice!"

"Am I turning you on?"

"How can you make a joke like that? You sound like—"

"A cement mixer. I know."

"You must've been terrified."

"I didn't have much time to be anything."

"I came to work this morning and you're all they're talking about. I've been calling all morning." Flustered voices threatened to drown her out, but they gradually dissipated, her voice echoing as though she were walking down an empty hall. "Are you okay? I guess that's a stupid question."

"Sounds worse than it is."

"Are you in the mood for visitors?" Val heard a door bang shut, her voice coming clearer. "I can come up there—"

"No! I mean, not right now."

"But—"

"Please. They're releasing me Monday. Anyway, you need to prepare."

"My God—"

"You owe me a concert. And I believe you mentioned stew. I expect a damn good one, they'll have me eating paste over here. If I'm lucky."

"Oh! You meant—oh. I never promised you a concert. But I'll try to nurse you back to health with pearl onions and sirloin."

"Give me some details to last me until then. Do you use sweet peppers or spicy?" Val tightened his grip on the receiver. He hoped she didn't notice his increased tempo.

"Goodbye, Val. You're hopped up on goofballs."

"Come on. Throw me a bone. Do you cook it fast or low and slow?"

"I'm hanging up on you." She stifled a laugh. "Listen…

I'm glad I reached you. But get some rest, seriously. Lunatic."

Val replaced the receiver, somewhat soothed by Sandra's voice, pleased he could quell her fears a bit. He lingered on that, on her. It was easier than trying to remember what happened between unlocking his door and waking up here. The ghosts of the night before, the answers he so desperately wanted, scudded into another dimension. The more he forced himself to figure it out, the more convoluted his thoughts became.

A knock interrupted his ruminations. The strange alignment of the room gave the impression that Graham had materialized in the doorway. Would it be possible to turn the bed to face the hall?

Holding onto the jamb, Graham stared like he hadn't seen Val in years. He leaned back, checking something on the wall outside the door, then took a quiet step in.

"Jesus Christ! You're all ringed up like Saturn!" He shuffled over to the visitor's chairs but didn't sit, pulling off his gloves one finger at a time.

Time for Act Two. "Jupiter, more likely." Val pushed himself out of his sinking posture, using the rails as leverage. The muscles of his neck twinged like guitar strings, and the floor dipped and roiled to one side. "You should see the other guy."

"That so?"

"Yes. If you do, call the cops."

"Very funny."

"Did Sandra call you?"

"No, your neighbor. Raymond?"

Christ.

"Said he saw your front door wide open, no lights on, no sign of you. You're incredibly lucky."

"Exactly what I was thinking!" Val's smile was sloppy and drunken. Lovely stuff, morphine.

"It's a miracle things didn't turn out worse."

"I s'pose you're right about that."

"Who did this to you?"

"Beats me. Think he said he was a fan. Say, maybe it was Andre Wallace."

"Heh. Wouldn't that be something."

"We all want to be the first on the shelves, but wow. Dedication."

Graham sat in one of the plastic chairs on Val's left. "I can't believe there's a fan so obsessed with your book they're willing to resort to this."

"Had I known their intentions I'd have let them read it right there, made them some tea."

"What exactly happened?"

Val shrugged and shook a few more ice chips into his mouth. "Being deprived of oxygen apparently shorts out the wiring." He tapped a finger against his temple. "Oh wait...he used a garrote on me. A garrote! Can you imagine?"

"Where does one pick up a garrote these days?" A ball of lint on Graham's pants had suddenly become a source of great interest.

"I think Wal-Mart put them out at Christmas."

Graham's laugh was unnaturally thin. "Costco's probably sells 'em in bulk. By the way, Anna's downstairs finding a finishing touch for your present."

"You got me a gift?"

"She insisted it needed a bow, since it's impossible to wrap."

"Is it a garrote?"

Anna leaned in, rapping on the door with the brunt of a polished mahogany derby cane. The handle curved into the intimation of a bird's beak, fixed with double brass collars. The bright red bow diminished the cane to a toothpick in her hands.

"Hello Val. How do you feel?"

"Exhausted. Otherwise not bad...this is only a sprain," Val said, gesturing at his ankle propped up on pillows. "Just need to keep it iced and elevated, that sort of thing. Seems I can't elude an attack the way I used to. But now I have that raspy voice chicks dig. Think I'll hit the clubs on the way home."

"You should stay with us, honey."

"No, no, I'll be fine. Think of how much writing I can get done now." Val's right hand tensed against his thigh. A slimy prickling writhed up and down his arms.

"That will be harder for you now, with everything gone," Graham said.

"What?"

"They took everything, didn't the cops tell you? Your manuscript, laptop, all of it."

"They haven't been in to talk to me yet. Shit." Val found himself rolling the sheets between his fingers.

"Don't worry about it, I can send you a copy of the pages you sent me. You've backed up everything in the Cloud, right?"

"That's not the point. And no, I don't use the fucking Cloud."

Graham lowered his eyes. His mouth twitched like he wanted to say something more.

"I'm so sorry, Val," Anna said. She backed into a chair, kicking Graham's foot.

"Guess I'll have to carry on the old-fashioned way until I get a new laptop. Try to recall where I left off. They say the rewrites are always better, right?" Again the feeling that his skin was retracting. He drew the blanket up higher.

"Are you sure you're not afraid to stay out there alone?" Anna asked.

"No, really, I'll be fine. This sort of thing happens all the time."

"To who?" Graham muttered. He and Anna exchanged sideways glances.

"So…you brought me a cane? That's so thoughtful," Val said.

Keeping up appearances was sapping his energy. The weight of sleep pressed in on his temples. The edges of each breath fluttered out of reach, and he laid a hand against his chest as though to capture them.

"What? Oh, yes! I did! I'd hate for you to be stuck with one of those hospital-issue metal things. And look, look what happens when you turn the handle." Anna hesitantly held out the cane, as if she found it discarded and wasn't sure of its rightful owner.

Val struggled with the handle, trying not to dislodge the ribbon. A short cylinder extended into the shaft of the cane. He turned the piece upside-down and twisted off a tiny cap. The familiar comforts of oak and spice rose to greet him and he couldn't help but laugh, a faltering static like the rustle of dry leaves.

"Macallan! I love it, thank you."

"I hoped that would cheer you up."

"This will be great, I can have a slug before getting out of bed now."

An awkward silence passed that Val didn't know how to fill. Their expressions tightened. Graham's eyes blinked left. He slid a hand toward his coat pocket, probably looking for a cigarette.

Maybe I should offer him a drink.

Anna sat forward. "Are you *sure*—"

"Thank you, no. Apparently I have a watchdog next door. Though I'd appreciate a ride home Monday if it's not too much trouble." The idea of the staff calling a cab on his behalf, having a stranger drive him to his secluded home and commit the route to memory, was too much to bear. It would be difficult enough having to put everything back the way he remembered, to recover the words that he lost, to return to a normal way of life without the dread of someone returning when he shut off the lights.

"Of course, honey. One of us will be here for you."

Her voice afforded Val an ounce of serenity. The tension eased out of his hands and he sank against the pillows.

"Where are your keys? We'll bring a change of clothes."

Val pointed at the narrow closet in the corner. "In there. I assume."

Anna stood on tiptoes, digging through his belongings, pulling up short and shooting Graham a quick, flustered glance.

"Need help in there, babe?" Graham asked.

"No." She peered at Val before turning back to the closet.

"Here they are."

Who put my things there, and how long ago? Anyone could've come in, taken the keys, made copies…

That's not possible. Not here. There's enough security in this place to start an army.

"We'll head over by the nurse's station to see when check-out time is," Graham said. "Hey…do you think it's a good idea to keep going? I mean…what if these guys try to—"

"Graham!" Anna whispered.

"What? It's a legitimate—"

"What's the matter with you? Your timing, cripes—"

"I'm serious, Val. Maybe you should back off—"

"*No.* Damn it." It came out as a bark, and had nothing to do with the state of his throat. He swallowed hard in an attempt to soften the rest of it. "Can't sit around twiddling my thumbs. Or my agent will drop me."

"But a little time—"

"We should get *going*, Graham," Anna said. "Rest up, okay, honey? He doesn't mean to upset you, we're just a little shaken, that's all…"

"Ah, forget it. This cocktail is kicking in nicely. Feeling better already!" Val spread his arms wide and burrowed into the mattress. "See?"

"In that case, I still expect you in my office on Monday," Graham mumbled. "Time is money."

"Oh, right. Be there with bells on."

Graham shook Val's hand and pressed it between both of his. "Take it easy."

Anna waved from the doorway and they were gone.

Val forced himself to focus on the faint hospital sounds, his surroundings, familiarizing himself with the normal pulse of the ward.

The stench of latex had permeated his skin. A machine beeped at length, paused, then started up again. Somewhere a baby's cry morphed into the squeal of a dentist's drill. Each drop of precious morphine wobbled in suspended animation, teasing him, before joining its siblings in the vestibule below.

The suspense was still better than reality TV.

Another bang on the door, loud enough to wake aliens in the next solar system. A man in a navy sports jacket strode into the room without waiting for a response.

"Mr. Haverford? Recognize me?" Detective Marczek lifted one corner of his mouth in an awkward half-smile of greeting.

Val centered on the craggy white fang protruding into his lip, snapping to attention when Marczek curtly repeated the question. Val narrowed his eyes and nodded as the detective loomed over the foot of the bed.

"Hate to do this to you now, but I have a few more questions about last night."

"Afraid I don't have much information for you."

"That's fine, let's see how far we get. I'll try to be quick. Are you aware your home was burglarized?" Marczek slapped his notepad onto the overbed table and jotted something. He jangled the change in his right pants pocket, elbow pushing his coat open, revealing his badge.

"I—my friend stopped by a while ago and told me. Sounds like they stole just about everything in my studio."

"We did a thorough sweep of the house and although we can't be sure without your confirmation, it looks like nothing else was disturbed. Your desk supplies were thrown around, but most of your electronics, other than the laptop, were intact. The wall safe in your bedroom was jimmied open. These guys are damn good safecrackers but they weren't interested in the contents. Left the banker bag, all the money."

"I'm under the impression they tried to steal my book." Repeating this fact, however plausible, just didn't sit right.

"That's our best guess as well, right now. You made backups, I hope?"

"Only on USBs, and I stored them in the desk. Guess locking one in the safe wouldn't have done any good."

"Do you plan on continuing your work, under the circumstances?"

Val nodded. "I don't scare that easily, despite my better judgement."

"Hopefully they won't come after you again. We're keeping a lookout for these guys, and we hope to catch them making a mistake sooner or later."

Val was alert now for sure. He pushed himself up, drew his elbows in to stop them from quaking. "What do you mean? Aren't there any leads?"

"Unfortunately, no. Though the front door lock was picked, that doesn't give us the culprit. No fingerprints, no hair fibers. Most of their footprints were covered by the storm, although we got a couple partials under some low-hanging trees. No discernible tire tracks, so we think they were dropped off and picked up on the main road. These guys knew what they were doing, and they did their homework. They must've been watching you for some time."

"Fantastic." Val's IV line was a tether, the bed rails a prison.

"It would help if we had a timeline and a clearer picture of what happened, so why don't we start from the beginning." Marczek leaned onto the overbed table, pushing it over Val's calves, further locking him in.

"I was in the city, dropping off new pages with my agent, my friend, Graham Van Ellis. I realized with the storm it would take forever to get home, so I stopped at a restaurant for a few hours. When I got home, I saw someone in my studio—"

"You saw him in the dark?"

"No, I…turned the light on first. I startled him."

"You're sure it was a man?"

"Well…he seemed too large to be female."

"How do you mean?"

"Tall. Broad-shouldered."

"Go on."

"I tried to run to the bedroom, but I was suddenly—he'd wrapped a wire around my neck—"

"Who? The tall man?"

Val shook his head. "He pulled me down to speak in my ear…I couldn't move—"

"What did he say?"

"Wire ripping my skin…I couldn't—I couldn't breathe. *Christ.*" Nausea tightened like a clamp through his stomach. He pressed his fingers to his eyes. *Be still, be still.* This was humiliation enough without adding one more.

Marczek rapped Val on the shoulder and handed him a cup of water. "Slow down."

The first sip went down like a jagged stone. From behind the rim Val shook his head and said, "I don't remember any more. I don't remember anything after—"

"You told me last night you thought the person who attacked you was shorter than you."

"Why else would he need to break my back to speak in my ear?"

"What did he sound like?"

"Grating. Husky. Like a stage whisper. Trying to avoid being identified."

"You know that for a fact?"

"Unless it was Batman I'd say it's a pretty good guess."

Marczek snorted, raising his eyebrows as he scribbled in the notepad. "Do you recall what he said to you?"

"No. And it's driving me crazy trying to remember."

"And you didn't notice anyone else besides those two guys?"

"No."

"You remember what the tall one looked like?"

"Young. Twenties, early thirties. White kid. He wore one of those hooded sweatshirts that zip up the front. Gray, maybe." *Great. Like about a quarter of the population.* His eyes were pale as his own, but blue, he was sure of it. But did he really have such a bony face? Or was it a trick of the mind? Val shook his head and huffed. All he had were abstract sensations and not one single fact. "That's it, that's all I can come up with."

"Well. Apparently these people wanted to make a big show. Whatever they used on you was meant to tear you up, but not much more. And from the sound of things, it seems they were done with you in about thirty seconds."

Val clenched his teeth at the crude description.

"One more question and I'll let you rest. You're saying you're unable to identify your attackers, correct?"

"*Yes.*"

"Is fear of retaliation the reason you're retracting your implication of Andre Wallace?"

"What?"

"I heard you accuse an Andre Wallace a minute ago—"

"You were eavesdropping on a private conversation?"

"I'd hardly call that eavesdropping." Marczek's lip twitched again, exposing a slim flash of white.

"That was a poor joke I made in confidence. I don't—" *Fuck.* He cringed, quickened his pace to obliterate the twang. "I don't appreciate having my words turned against me."

"Listen, I'm trying to help you by covering all the bases. Are you sure—

"*Yes.* Damn it."

Marczek flipped his notepad shut and pulled a shiny silver case from his back pocket. "Looks like you have some dangerous fans, Mr. Haverford. They're telling you something here; you'll want to be very careful. Have someone check in on you while you recover. Call me if you see something suspicious, or feel threatened." He snapped a business card onto the table. "I'll be in touch."

Val's throat throbbed, the tepid water providing no relief. The re-creations of the attack and Marczek's persistence demolished all the traces of good humor Val so carefully constructed. What exactly about Marczek was so agitating? It was more than aggressiveness and arrogance. Then again, if he'd been waiting around in a hospital corridor for hours in the middle of the night, he'd be in a pretty shitty mood too. Especially when his only witness kept cracking wise.

Avoiding the issue wouldn't work for long.

Start over. The crew came in to set up, and he chatted with Sandra. What about? Couldn't remember. Interview… awkward pauses on his part…typical stage fright bullshit. Cameraman…a little rude, impatient. Sandra…she handed him his ass. Kind of fun to watch. Stayed a while after that… some segue related to that argument.

There.

The email. He showed her that hate mail laden with purple and blue language and they joked about how it came from another writer.

Andre was the type that gave literary prose a bad name, but he was above this level of debasement.

Or was Marczek hinting at something deeper? Did Andre have some kind of past, one he couldn't allude to?

What did Val know about Andre really, except what they broadcast on late-night TV and print in newspapers? Competitiveness ranked high with writers of all kinds; everyone wanted to have that scoop, that next big thing. No matter that 'competition' was just gilded code for 'paranoia,' as though the germination of a premise turned on light bulbs in every other writer's head simultaneously, forcing the originator to race to the final sentence before the idea became obsolete.

But that hate email was sent over a decade ago. That's a long time to hold a grudge, especially when Andre's career was skyrocketing. He'd have no reason to act now, at the height of his popularity, when he hadn't done a thing to Val in the interim. Plus, if Val's calculations were correct, Andre would have been a teenager when it was sent. No teen had a vocabulary that insufferable.

Rationalizing why that accusation didn't hold an ounce of water didn't put Val at ease. He still had the sick feeling that he spaced on an important deadline, an appointment that couldn't be rescheduled, a moment in time lost and unrecoverable.

What about the sound of the attacker's voice, the insistence that he was a fan? But why would anyone plan an attack when they came to steal a manuscript? All they had to do was grab it off the desk. Why wouldn't they both be in the studio to make quick work of it? The shorter man was clearly a lookout, but they didn't run when Val came home. They had plenty of time to hide outside the back door, then sneak around to the front once they saw the lights go on. And why would anyone care that much about an unfinished novel, even a controversial one? If delivering some message was the point of their mission, stealing the manuscript was just insurance. The broken scene played over and over but nothing came together.

And Graham, asking about the Cloud. Nobody saved anything solely to tangible formats anymore; only fellow Luddites would assume he had one source of backup.

Though if he had used the Cloud, he'd only have to download to restore everything. He drowned the wave of nauseous fury with more stale water.

He closed his eyes, trying to picture his front room and seeing only shades of gray. Damp clothing turning to ice. Bitter cold wind slicing his skin, becoming tangible: a thin sliver of metal. This time his fingers scraped over the grooves in the wire, his blood spiraling between them. They were professionals.

The jarring pain, the weightlessness, the jackhammer of his heart returned as he recalled the frenzied conviction that he was about to die in his own home by someone else's hands.

The goddamn phone rang again, for the last goddamn time. The drug-induced numbness had eroded along with his patience. He grabbed the base and yanked with all the strength he had left, ripping the entire jack from the wall with the cord. A flashing red glare lit up the hallway, and a signal droned somewhere down the hall.

Nurses appeared in a flurry of white. Val waved away the oxygen masks. Before he could object, one of them injected beautiful, liquid apathy into the IV. Their stern voices faded into a fizzy rumble, then disappeared altogether.

Chapter Nine

Graham and Anna had little energy left for conversation. A stifling whiff of exhaust filtered through the car vents. He fumbled with the radio dial and for lack of decent music, switched over to the news. Another report of a man in South Loop, shot in a drive-by for unknown reasons, droned on and on. Bent low over a scrap of cardboard box, crouched behind a thick wall of bushes lining the expressway, the victim was killed while lettering a sign begging for change.

Graham reached for the knob. Scanning stations, he caught a familiar voice and paused. Andre Wallace, reading an excerpt of his latest manuscript. The gist sounded eerily similar to Val's. Graham snapped the radio off and tapped the gearshift.

"Can't believe he's going back home," Anna muttered.

"Huh?"

"I'd move right off the bat."

"I can see why he'd want to."

Traffic forced Graham to accelerate in fragmented bursts punctuated by the rubber thudding of pedals. The buzz of neighboring radios vibrated the windows, and a penetrating whine of failing brakes wormed through his ears.

"Something else on my mind," Anna said.

"What is it, babe?"

"He looks at you funny when you talk."

"Hadn't noticed."

"I swear I saw a glasses case in that locker."

"Hm." Graham clicked on the headlights, sprayed the windshield, dug into his coat for a cigarette and came up empty.

"Funny we never saw him wearing glasses."

"He's a grown-up dear, sometimes men buy glasses without telling their friends about it first."

"That doesn't explain the medic-alert bracelet, though. I guess he wanted some bling and decided on a bright red caduceus for laughs?"

"The hell's a caduceus?"

"What's going on?"

"He made me promise not to tell you."

"I'm your wife."

"He doesn't want you to worry."

"Too late for that."

"He didn't even want to tell *me*. He only did so out of professional courtesy."

Anna exhaled slowly through her nose.

"It's something to do with his eyes, some degenerative thing, okay? Starts with an M. I'm no good with medical mumbo-jumbo."

"He's going blind?"

"Actually," Graham said, jabbing the air with his finger, "you don't go completely blind. You gradually lose central vision but peripheral vision stays sharp. He described it as looking at a doughnut, except 'the center is like an infinite black hole in space.' Typical, huh?"

"Oh okay then, everything's fine."

"He's doing all he can. At least it's only on one side. For now, anyway."

"Isn't there some surgery, medication, therapy? Anything?"

"He's already *done* that, babe." Graham rubbed her knee. "That's why he's been giving me chapters piecemeal, why we've been editing as they come. I think he's too proud to admit he's scared shitless."

Graham recalled Val's visit just before Christmas. The way he inched into the office, settling into a chair as if he thought it might collapse beneath him. He'd stared through the towers outside the picture window and delivered the news in the faint, halting way of a man confessing. Graham couldn't remember if Val had ever made eye contact. Only one word described his expression. *Vacant.*

"What'll he do if—"

"Probably have to use dictation software. It's crazy, but I think he hates that idea most. Can you imagine him sitting there talking to himself? And he can forget about working outdoors."

"We have to do something for him. He'll need our support."

"Don't you dare. He doesn't want our help, you know how he is."

"He's all alone out there."

"That's what he *likes*."

"What kind of friend are you?"

"A damn good one. We're not going to do anything, not unless he asks. Until then it's his business."

"I don't know if I can. This must be torture."

"Stay out of it, Anna. I mean it. His career is just getting back on track, he doesn't need you calling attention to this... setback."

"Wow. Nice. The Van Ellis golden goose might stop laying eggs permanently this time. That's the real tragedy here, isn't it?" She grunted, muttering, "Er zijn geen zakken in een doek." There are no pockets in a shroud.

Graham slammed on the brakes just short of ramming a pickup. Anna threw her hand against the dash. His voice came low and steady, squeezing the fury into a tight little ball.

"I'm going to try to forget you said that. When we get home I'm dropping you off. I need a drink, and I sure don't want you with me."

***

A walk in the blistering cold was preferable after the airless traps of the hospital and car. Someone had cleaved a path down the center of the iced-over snow and filled it with purple salt. It crunched under Graham's inappropriate shoes. His legs spasmed at the sudden shortening of his stride.

Only yesterday he'd promised Val dinner and drinks for fucking up their meeting. Yesterday. When everything was normal, publishing rituals progressing as usual.

Poor Lucy was the last to see Val in one piece. She could tell he was pissed about his wasted day, but kept her cheerful attitude intact and smoothed things over so Graham wouldn't lose sleep. He'd called to tell her the news so she wouldn't hear it on TV first, and she'd cried so hard she hyperventilated. Blamed herself for not trying harder to convince him to stay. Silly girl. She nearly broke his heart.

Since locking up last night and trudging home—drifts burying him up to his knees, fur-lined parka like forty-pound sandbags across his shoulders—all he'd wanted to do was run until he was free, break through the whiteout and static.

If only I'd paid more attention to the time. Chased another client out early, made someone else wait. He pushed everything so far out of reach he never caught the end. On the other hand, if their meeting went off as scheduled, Val may have interrupted the break-in. Whether they'd already found the manuscript before he got home or finished ransacking the studio while he was out cold—

And the way they'd left him. Graham curled his toes into fists. He hadn't recognized the man in front of him as his friend. Had to check to make sure he'd read the right room number. He hoped Val was too loopy to notice.

Not wanting to upset him was part of the problem. Anna would have known exactly what to say. But there was that timing thing again.

One minute Graham stood outside Calvyn's, staring into wavy neon imprisoned in the glass block windows, and the next he was stomping off to the agency, gritting his molars into dust. The wrong kind of escape waited at their reserved table.

When he arrived in his suite, he jabbed the security keypad, making a mental note to nag Val to install a system at his place. He reached for the lights but let his hand slide down the textured linen wallpaper instead, walking to his office in the dark.

Fumbling in his desk drawer, he found a crushed pack of Dunhills. The tip and lighter flame wobbled in opposite directions, and he pressed the filter end to the desk to steady his hand. Upending his inbox, Graham rifled through the latest manuscripts until he came to Val's. He read it again, letting every word sink in. The past was evident, pain infusing every line. Must've slaved over those words for weeks to get them that tight. It was nothing if not honest.

Haverford groupies were anticipating this book, the release date circled in red. Anna had a point: Val's latest would turn a profit. Though it would no doubt bring controversy and scores of hate mail, maybe even death threats this time. Real ones.

He cringed. If this attack were anyone's fault, it was Graham's. He'd jumped the gun setting up the interview. More bad timing.

They'd always mocked the haters and posers, dismissed them as full of hot air, when VE&A should have done more to protect him. Those 'empty' rants had mutated into something poisonous, and that stubborn son of a bitch was still writing. He was probably marking up the bedsheets right now for lack of paper.

Graham pictured him sitting across the desk in the guest chair, all ripped to shit, just this side of bloody. He shuddered, turning away to the picture window. Stark white ice floes contrasted with the black of the lake, bouncing on the waves and butting up against the harbor. From that height, they were icebergs, strong enough to float away on, somewhere he wasn't stuck playing a part he had no script for.

They were both too good at this game.

Val spent most of his time alone, snug under a blanket of serenity and peace. Until last night, at least. The tremor returned and with it, another cigarette lit. What must it be like to live without constant observation? Anna never missed a thing. How could Val forget his bracelet was in that locker? Keeping his poker face throughout that whole conversation was Oscar-worthy. And Val answering in that slow way he had, like he needed to consider the weight of every word, softening the ragged edges, trying to make them believe he wasn't being turned inside out.

Whose benefit was it for?

He spun the last cigarette between his fingers. How many has it been now? Facing the desk again, he addressed his invisible client, gnawing the filter as he spoke, his words a rumbly slur.

"Val...how 'bout we work out—"

Sounded like a relationship talk.

"Look, Val—"

Look. Who the hell talked that way? Graham held the stub between two fingers and rubbed his forehead with the knuckle of his thumb, digging so hard he wasn't certain whether the headache existed before or not.

"Listen here, now—"

Fucksake, a lecture? His entire job consisted of client consultations. *Just spit it out. Emulate Dad.*

So true to his roots, so blunt and straightforward, Dad had spooked so many of his clients—some into never returning—insisting if they couldn't handle him, they couldn't handle the rigors of rejection or publication.

Graham's approach netted him more clients than Dad ever had. Out with the imposing desk that dwarfed everything except Dad himself, in with the streamlined, frosted glass table. Gone was the massive desktop, replaced with a silver slimline laptop that made him feel like the captain of a spaceship. He remembered thinking Val would be amused by that. Might as well please the guy who made this place, gave it a name. Always one eye to the future.

Then again, Graham never made anybody. He inherited Val, already a huge success. And every year he had to turn down clients in order to maintain the agency's laser focus and individualized attention. Graham had no interest in terrorizing writers who refused to kill darlings for fear of getting red ink on their hands. Maybe that's why Val had been Dad's favorite. Twice as stubborn, the never-take-no-for-an-answer type, who worked until even the smooth plastic of a keyboard gave him callouses. Dad's keenness for Val was something he and Anna had in common.

Graham's shoulders scrunched around his neck as though they tried to fold over his head and lock him inside. He was stuck in Val's hospital room all over again, growing more and more uncomfortable the more frantic Anna became.

Maybe his frank way of breaking the news—*Looks like somebody attacked Val tonight*—wasn't the best. Couldn't blame her for freaking out. But the way she'd immediately called the hospital for details, wheedling information out of them...

His shoulders did this bunchy thing then too, as she stayed awake all night searching the web, then calling store after store to find the perfect gift. Simple and generic wouldn't do. That cane...such a *personal* thing. And somehow Val wasn't embarrassed. Being high as a kite had its advantages.

It was common courtesy to bring a hospitalized friend a gift. Ice cream for kids getting their tonsils out, flowers for new mothers. A simple gesture made specific because they'd known each other forever. So why did her intense stare, her doleful responses, bother him so much? What did it matter, anyway? It wasn't like Val spent his days like a traveling Great fucking Gatsby.

Out of cigarettes. Graham stalked into the break room hoping to swipe someone's forgotten leftovers. On the counter, circled with dried coffee stains and a dusting of powdered creamer, sat a half-open Frango mints box. Graham scrubbed until the Formica returned to its former avocado green, geometrically patterned, 1970s glory, popping one chocolate after another into his mouth, then wiped down the microwave and coffeemaker until his head swam with chemical fumes. Swirling the pot, he guessed one cup's worth remained. He turned on the machine and stared until steam hissed through the spout.

He should head home. Anna was probably worried. But her gibe still stung, even if there was a thread of truth to it. But it wasn't the money. It was never about the money.

Graham returned to his office, rubbing the glaze off the

mug handle. Val's manuscript presented an unusual voice, something Graham hadn't considered reading it the first time. He'd been expecting the good ol' Val M. Haverford. But things change. Especially after ten years. Graham lacked that artist's finesse, the emotional insight that resonated with a select few. One of many reasons why he'd never be on the other side of the desk. *Right about that too, Anna.*

He snatched a sheet of letterhead out of the printer drawer. He'd pull a Val and jot down his thoughts. Graham uncapped a pen and held it to the paper, a blotch of green ink growing with every second he hesitated. What did they call it, *pantsing*?

Now he understood why his clients worried over the first sentence as though it were life or death.

He poured out every thought in his head, then grabbed another sheet and started over, putting some polish and coherence in place of the rambling mess. Even before he finished, he knew it was a conversation they needed to have in person. Writing his letter lifted the boulder from his shoulders only to dump it into his stomach.

After mulling over whether he needed to sign it, the nib cracked, sending a splatter of ink over the last sliver of white space. He stuffed Val's partial manuscript and the letter into a manila envelope and scribbled *60688* on the back.

The clock crept into double-digits. He should be getting home.

First a few tweets, a post or two. Fans were hungry for updates. As it stood, Val M. Haverford would deliver his next novel as scheduled. But right now they needed to closure, not gossip or teasers. Graham composed a few vague yet positive statements to tide them over.

Heading out two hours later, he paused in the atrium. After a day like this, any reason to put off forwarding his message was valid. Things would seem a lot clearer once he got the chance to talk to Val in person. He flung the envelope onto Lucy's desk. A few days wouldn't hurt anything.

He'd take the long way home. And by the time he got there, if he was lucky, Anna would be asleep.

Chapter Ten

Val mashed his foot into an invisible brake, flattening himself against the seat back. The winding road felt perilously downgraded. Despite Graham driving like an old person, stores and cafés shot past the window in frantic slashes of color. Graham had turned down the radio and the car hummed with faint, unintelligible dialogue and the roar of canned laughter.

"Mind if I turn that up? I could use some noise."

Graham frowned at the road as though peering through smog. "What? Oh. Yeah, yeah, sure."

"Polka would really hit the spot. Do you have the all-polka station?"

"Sure, whatever you need."

"Graham."

"What? I wasn't paying attention."

"No kidding. Something on your mind?"

"Nah. I'm good."

"Bullshit. Something to do with Anna?"

"Funny you should ask."

"Is she okay?"

The leather steering wheel creaked in Graham's fists. He was so tightly wound he'd make rigor mortis look like lounging on a beach. Val shuddered. Was he always this morbid?

Graham sounded robotic, as though he'd been programmed to repeat one sentence. "I think she's seeing someone."

"What, like a therapist?"

"No, not like a therapist," Graham snapped.

"Oh, come on!"

"Things haven't been right lately."

"It happens, or so I'm told. Probably just a rough patch."

"No, there's more to it. She's distant, like she'd rather be with—"

"This is nonsense and you know it."

"I don't think so."

"I'm sure you're misreading something. She's not the type. Why don't you ask her straight out?"

"That'll go over well. Besides, I have an idea who it is, but if I'm wrong I won't be able to look them in the eye again. If I'm right—" He hunched against the car door, braked at a stop light with more force than necessary. Something metallic rattled around inside the glove compartment.

Graham rounded a turn, putting them on the Loop Trail around the lake. Every curve was a nook a car could disappear in. Especially during a storm in the middle of the night.

So many of these houses were set far back on pristine estates, thick Doric columns like sentries guarding alabaster walls, cast iron gates locking out the world. Tiny cameras recorded what their owners couldn't see and intercoms kept them at an unattainable distance. They were as much Val's neighbors as Venus and Mars.

The rough edge of the seatbelt cut into his fingers.

"Listen, I'm the last person to give marital advice. But why don't you take her for a little getaway? Maybe where you went on your honeymoon. Paris, was it? How many years has it been?"

"Going on fourteen. Thirteen. Shit. No wonder she's—anyway, I don't think going away with *me* is what she wants." He shifted a glance at Val.

"What about your party? Everything seemed fine."

"She was distracted."

"Holidays do that to people."

"And now?"

"It's the heart of tax time. She's probably under a lot of stress."

"She's never gotten stressed about that before."

"She never chaired a foundation before either. Maybe she's burned out. If I had to crunch numbers in a cubicle all day I'd be burned out too."

"Mmm-huh."

Val slid his hands over his thighs, drying his palms and scratching some feeling into his fingers. "Speaking of the holidays, I heard the family put a little pressure on her at Christmas."

"What? Oh. She told you about that." Again with the sidelong glance. "Well…Mother can be difficult."

"Maybe ol' Babs put some ideas into her head."

"Oh God."

"She's—forgive me for being indelicate—almost at the point of no return, am I right?"

"I don't know. I don't keep track of that sort of thing."

"Have you thought about it?"

"Not since before we were married. I didn't want her to be the one that got away, you know?" Graham reclined against the headrest, his smile nostalgic and bittersweet. "I guess it's always been in the back of my mind, with the agency and all."

"If you want that, then…"

"No, no, I'm too old now."

"Not necessarily."

"You're crazy." Graham turned to watch a black coupe take its turn at the four-way stop. "You really think that's all this is about?"

Val shrugged. "Just thinking out loud. Maybe she changed her mind and doesn't know how to bring it up. You might be surprised."

Sidewalks narrowed, then disappeared. Brick edging separated lush lawns from a shoulder barely wide enough for a bike. A young woman in a red shirt meandered down the road, thumbing the phone in her hand. She wobbled like a drunk, veering to one side before lurching back, looking up vaguely in the direction of traffic. She'd never know what hit her if she leaned just a little too—

"Has she said anything to you?"

"Sorry?"

"Anna," Graham said, with a wheeze of impatience. "Did she—"

Val laughed. "No. Why would she discuss that with me, of all people?"

"Well, you're...close."

"Not that close. That's a bit intimate, don't you think?"

A huge grin crossed Graham's face. He slapped the center console and nodded to an inaudible beat. "Man, I could kiss you."

"I'd rather you didn't. Save it for Anna. And watch the road."

More people sauntering and trotting while staring at their phones or their iPods. Rarely, if ever, taking note of their surroundings. Aliens could have landed and they'd never know. Anything could happen.

"This is such a load off. Thanks a lot."

"I didn't do anything, but sure."

"You did. You just don't know."

Easing up the driveway felt like the crawl to the crest of a roller coaster before the death-defying plunge. From the safety of the passenger seat, Val inspected his place for some breach. The caution tape had been removed, and everything appeared as intact and unremarkable as any other afternoon, only the windows seemed darker and the door may well have sprouted teeth. The thick rolled neck of the sweater Graham brought pricked Val's skin with thousands of wooly needles.

"I really appreciate this."

"It's just a ride home. It's nothing," Graham said. Yet Val made no move to exit the car. "You don't have to do this now."

"No, I do. I do." His hand inched toward the door handle.

"You want me to come with? I didn't even think to salt the steps."

"No! I mean, that's not necessary. Stay here where it's warm." Val reddened at the thought of Graham witnessing his unfiltered reaction and raised the collar of his coat. "Is it bad?"

"I just went straight to the closet for your clothes. But the frunchroom looked the same to me. Hey...I hate to bring this up again, but—"

"I can take it from here."

Val steadied his weight against the cane, which sank into the snow. He stumbled through the drifts, jostling his way up the stairs, every plodding footfall an effort. One step a gentle hush and the other an ugly, muffled thud from the walking boot.

Each tick of the mantel clock was a report of epic proportions. Turning toward the bedroom, he froze at the flash of movement in the studio. He seized the edge of the entry table and the motion was reproduced. He let out a gush of air at his own image reflected in the windows.

For good measure, he grabbed the iron poker on the hearth and proceeded to cover the room, relying on scenes in bad cop movies. Rolling his booted foot to lessen the noise, he entered the bedroom poker first, waving it around to thwack anything in its path. Bypassing the bathroom, he checked the kitchen, even the cabinets and oven, despite being too small to hide anyone bigger than a toddler. Backtracking, he bashed in the shower curtain before tugging the chain hanging from the ceiling. The light went on with a pop.

His hair frizzed in all directions. Dozens of tiny red pinpoints rimmed his eyes like splattered blood. The corner of his left eye and mouth drooped like a stroke victim's. Turning away from his concave reflection, he chucked the poker into a corner and started up the shower instead. The rest of the inspection could wait.

***

Val was unprepared for the devastation of his studio. A huge dent marred the frame of the northern screen door where the intruder kicked it open. The desk was as bare as the day he finished building it, drawers ripped from their sockets and splintered. CDs lay cracked and warped on the floor, silver shards glinting tiny rainbows under the light, cases flung into every corner.

Sweeping only made a bigger mess. Aluminum from the discs had embedded into the wood grain and had to be pried out with a wire brush. Finding a comfortable position on the floor almost dislocated a hip. Hours passed before things started to look like home again. He righted the desk chair and dropped into it.

He attempted to sort through the few papers left intact, but without consequence or a place to store them, he gave up, resting his elbows on the desk and his face in his hands. He sat that way forever before deciding on a scotch; if he was going to go through this mess, he was going to do it drunk. The phone rang before he could rise.

"Hello?"

"Val, it's me. Is Graham with you?" Anna's vibrato rippled down his spine.

"No, why?"

"He hasn't come home. I can't reach him on his cell or at work; he's not answering."

"What time is it?"

"It's almost eight. He was gone before I woke up this morning. He said something about the pages you dropped off on Friday, how he wanted to prep for some discussion about this book and let the world know you're still on track for release. He said he'd call as soon as he dropped you off."

And the memory of that night broke through his consciousness, a smoky haze parted by a window thrown wide. Val thrashed around in his pockets for his dead cell phone. He stumbled into the kitchen, dragging the landline after him. The charger dangled behind the percolator.

Plugging in the cell, he tried to clear the urgency from his voice. "Stay in the house, Anna."

"What? Why?"

"I mean...in case he comes home soon, you should be there. I'm sure he's on his way. Graham's terrible about keeping track of time." Val forced himself to laugh. The battery icon remained red.

"True..."

"Remember our meeting Friday morning—"

"It never went off, did it?"

"And Christmas—"

"He was so distracted." Anna laughed heartily. "I'm worrying for nothing, aren't I?"

"I bet he forgot all about calling you. Or maybe he's kicking back at Calvyn's."

"You're right, you're right. That idiot."

"We'd better hang up, I don't have call waiting. I'm checking my cell messages. I'll hunt him down for you." The hair stood on his forearms.

"Thank you. Keep me posted? Please?"

"Of course. I'll call later."

A green light.

Val opened each social media app, and immediately his name appeared. More teasers, fans everywhere picking apart each post, trying to decipher the plot from the enigmatic details. Eye-catching banners announced Val M. Haverford and *606/88* were trending news. The phone chirped: a new message. Val prayed it would be Graham.

Static rustled, and at first he thought it was nothing but dead air. A quick succession of clicks threatened a disconnection. Then a disembodied but distinct moan cut through the hissing, followed by a familiar gravelly voice, reproachful now and mocking, as clear as the twang of wire behind Val's ear. "Val Haverford...you are a very...very... stupid man." And the unmistakable sound of ripping paper.

Val slammed through the front door, stomping through his footprints. He forced himself to pull the car out slowly to avoid spinning his wheels in a drift. Graham's building stayed open until nine.

He was miles out before he realized he forgot to turn on his headlights. Bare trees stretched their bony fingers high overhead, turning the road into an ice-black tunnel. Screeching around a turn toward Lake Shore Drive, he gunned the engine and sped into the city, chassis vibrating with the sudden demand.

Time stopped as Val was forced to brake around the

pinched curves. He beat his fist against the steering wheel, wishing he could burst through the barriers and wend a shortcut through the skyline.

Screeching up the exit ramp, he double-parked in front of Graham's tower. Henry, the gray night watchman, stood when he saw Val charge through the glass double doors.

"Good evening, Mr.—"

"Graham Van Ellis. Did you see him come through here?"

"Not yet sir—"

Val bypassed the guard, pressing all the elevator call buttons. Henry stepped into the first car with him, attempting to assuage his confusion with niggling questions Val ignored. The elevator opened into the Van Ellis suite. Before Henry untangled his ring of keys, Val tested the silver handle to the atrium. The door swung open easily.

They followed the endless hallway behind the reception desk, dimly lit by art deco sconces. Graham's office was the last on the right, flanked by rubber trees. Val groped for a light switch. The glass desk, typically amassed with various manuscripts and contracts, was stripped bare. Drawers torn out and shattered, supplies strewn everywhere. A crescent of red mist glistened along the wall. Sitting in the chair in perfect posture, arms resting on the desktop, was Graham, mouth gaping, a single shot to the forehead.

Val turned into the hall, pressing his hand to his mouth. Henry shuffled past and checked for a pulse, then called the police from the phone at his waist. He stepped gingerly around the pool of blood that had diffused around Graham's shoes and soaked the white carpet. He led Val back to the atrium and suggested he sit and wait, pressing a paternal hand against his shoulder. He tried to concentrate on the old man's gentle mutterings, but all he could think was *Anna, Anna*. He promised he'd call. But he needed to think of what to say, and again words betrayed him.

In a matter of minutes, the empty chamber brimmed with officers and emergency personnel. A paper cone of water had appeared in his hand as if by magic. His cane lay at his feet; he didn't remember bringing it with him. His finger scrolled mindlessly on the back of his hand, formulating an invisible script, a collection of words that would devastate her.

Someone called his name through the veil of a dream. A young officer with a kind face spoke to him softly, no doubt attempting to cull information. He heard her say they had sent two officers to inform Mrs. Van Ellis. He shook his head vehemently, patting his sides for his phone. The screen was black; the battery had died again. He wondered if they'd let him use Lucy's desk phone, how he could dial an outside line, when Anna emerged from the elevator, panting in tattered jeans and an unevenly buttoned coat. Her damp hair sparkled from new-fallen snow, random wisps standing around her head. He had not convinced her. She must've run the short distance here, barely dressed, desperate for any information.

"Val?" Anna fought against the officer's considerable attempts to intervene. "Why are you here?"

Every bit of her expression begged him to tell her a lie.

"Who are you people?" She slapped the officer's hands. "Valery? Answer me!"

The officer nudged her into the hall, forcing her to listen. After an insufferable silence, Anna's scream echoed through the suite. Val bent his head low and pressed a shaky hand to his eyes, leaving a uniformed stranger to support her on the opposite side of the glass.

***

A group of officials brought Val downstairs to his car, still double-parked with hazards blazing and keys in the ignition. Anna had already been driven to the station. A cop not much younger than himself sat behind the wheel, staring at him through the open door. Another led him around the by the elbow, called him sir, told him to watch the curb, watch the ice.

"My coat."

"What about it?"

"I need my coat."

105

"Did you have another besides the one you're wearing?"

The passenger side had never been used for anything other than extra cargo space. Sitting in it now, Val had the sensation of being trapped inside a bottle: he was there and not there, filtering everything from a distance, visions and sounds distorted. The second officer followed behind, light bar silently flashing. As the city slid away from the window, beside endless miles of black water and snow like old graves, its benchmarks seemed impossible. He'd seen those skyscrapers only in photographs; the long stretches of private lakefront parks and white-pillared houses only in movies.

"Mr. Haverford? Are you positive we can't take you somewhere else?"

The cop had parked inches from his cabin steps, and stared at him as though he'd been calling his name for hours. Val vaguely remembered rebuffing their recommendations to stay away, at least for one night. He pictured himself in an austere, one-size-fits-all hotel without an ounce of familiarity, just a corporate idea of comfort, all imposing lights and stark sheets and airtight windows.

There was nowhere else.

Val shook his head and turned to exit, but the cop pinched his shoulder with meaty fingers. Delivered some warning that floated past in a fog of condensed air. Exited the car and withdrew his firearm. The slick of black metal rose up, leather holster creaking with its release. Its muzzle rested inside the lip, and Val smiled with one corner of his mouth.

He told himself it was the cold that made his chest raw. The snow that leaked into his shoes is what froze him solid. It was the wind that paralyzed his hands and made him fumble with the keys. The hateful look Anna shot him as he was led away lay waste to whatever remained. He'd never forget that look. He'd seen another like it before, half a century ago, and every day since.

After the cop assured him the place was secure, he sat surrounded by looming shadows, knowing he would not sleep tonight, knowing that Anna was also wide awake staring at the same things and nothing, and all the while he wished that whomever wanted him silent would've been a little less proficient, a little less agile, and had left that wire embedded deep in his neck, so at least one man would be spared.

Chapter Eleven

"Follow the sound of my voice."

Pivoting in a full circle, Val sensed his own property despite the utter lack of markers: no lake, no wall, no cabin. An endless, lush lawn under his shoes and a refreshing gray mist above mixed with Sandra's sweet perfume. A wisp of breeze tickled his skin. There was no harsh sun or glaring moon, just beauty and tranquility beneath benign brightness. Though he saw everything, he knew that he was blind, yet he felt no fear; she was there, and she would lead him.

"Follow the sound of my voice."

He couldn't decipher from which direction it came, but her resonant tone lingered. She giggled, a child playing hide-and-seek. Warmth swelled within him, anticipating her arms wrapping around from behind, lips teasing his ear.

"Follow the sound of my voice!"

Her plea grew more frantic and his heart pounded, worried she had become lost; the fog had grown too thick for them to ever find each other. The sound warped to such a degree it could've originated from anywhere, and the idea that it came from underneath made him split his mouth open and scream her name—but his vocal cords lurched and failed. His strangled gasping turned guttural, woeful, like the baying of an injured animal, and the scene distorted from gray vapor to faintly striped wallpaper like bars of a cold cell.

He knew this place. He'd been here more times than he could count.

But instead of a neat, soot-tinged wound, the top right portion of Graham's head was blown away, revealing a mangled, unrecognizable chaos the color of burning coal.

A forest of fir studs emerged from the papered plaster and

extended across the ceiling. The carpet morphed into an unfinished platform floor scattered with curls of wood shavings and bent nails. A worn sneaker and denim-clad leg drifted into view.

Val was released from the nightmare's grip before he saw Michael, the pool of blood spreading beneath his body. He sat up, clutching the rolled seam of the mattress, but the feeling of being pushed out of the rafters stayed and stayed, live wires jumping through his skin.

Enough. Dreams hadn't ended like that in years. *Enough.*

He didn't wait for reality to settle in. Still floating through anesthesia, he marched to the studio and raised the shades. Stilts elevated the east wall three feet to compensate for the uneven ground. He raised his hand high above his head and rubbed his thumb against a pane of glass. Seven feet, give or take.

Daylight was rapidly fading. And he had the entire wall to get through. All he had were scraps and ripped boards in the shed; they'd never line up, even by the deftest of hands. And there was no time for precision.

By nightfall the loftiness of the room was whisked away along with the view of the beach, the lake; replaced by a ramshackle wall alternating in height from shoulder to a few inches above his head, with wildly erratic gaps to serve as portholes. Boxed up as tight as possible, Val sank into the futon with an arm thrown over his face. Every muscle from neck to knees lamented the unexpected workload.

A faint, high-pitched scratching interrupted his attempt to rest. Two stippled sparrows fought over a clump of soggy bread dropped against the skylight, alternately flittering up to tear it apart and landing for a swallow, beaks and claws striking the glass.

The room clouded into mist. Val pinched the bridge of his nose and pushed his tongue against his teeth: tricks he'd learned as a kid. The birds pecked at the last of their meal and flew off in opposite directions, leaving the stars behind.

Chapter Twelve

Val disconnected the landline and dismantled the doorbell. Hovered over 'accept' whenever Sandra called the cell, swiping 'decline' at the last minute. It took longer than expected for her voicemails to phase from worried to pressing to non-existent.

He turned business cards and brochures collected from security companies into kindling. Assuming the installer would have access to his alarm system, as well as a control center monitoring at all hours from who knows where, he felt safer alone with a fireplace poker and three exits than with an anonymous staff of dozens.

Cloistered in the dimness of the cabin, drowning in the oppressive scent of cedar, scotch doused the inferno that otherwise flared without warning and raged unchecked. Liquid meals sang his lullabies. At some point Anna dropped by, calling his name after her knocks went unanswered, his car sitting outside as bold as a lie. But he couldn't see her this way: sallow, unshaven, clothes limp from his own filth, reeking like the inside of a cask.

One day the knocking was heavier, followed by a thud, and, as Val headed toward the front of the house, the groan of a diesel engine. He opened the door to a large package. Perching on the edge of the coffee table, he tore open the box with his bare hands. His feet were soon lost under a flurry of packing peanuts. Val stared into the box, then abandoned it.

***

Days later he lifted out the smaller box and shook the gift onto the couch. Taped to the lid of the new laptop was a card printed in prefabricated handwriting: 'To Our Dearest Friend.

Here's to your first NBA. Graham & Anna.'

Val had given up on the National Book Award long ago. Those words stung as much like an insult as a compliment.

Setting the laptop on the desk seemed disrespectful, as if nothing had happened. Yet what else could he do, after such a show of faith? Val stuck the note to the upper corner of the screen with a dab of mounting putty. On one hand, he wanted to write something for Graham. Didn't he owe him that much? But.

Val's fingers twitched.

He clicked the lid shut.

***

Anna gave up dropping by unannounced. She sent a terse note along with Graham's funeral announcement, but like everything else it refused to make sense. Val tacked it to the refrigerator among alerts from utility companies.

For a while he ignored it, pretended he'd forgotten and the date was probably past. But on the day of the services, he woke at an ungodly hour as though summoned, suit clothes thrown over a chair, showering in a fury like a prison routine. He slammed around the kitchen—that damn note staring down at him from the freezer door—unable to find a bottle anywhere. He swore he had more wine under the sink, or someplace. He always kept a red and a white on hand. Had he blown through them already? He searched the bedroom closet, under the coffee table and wing-back, kicking at the empties along the hearth to check for dregs. Nothing. *Nothing.* No goddamn Macallan left in the house.

He hobbled into the car and remembered the nearest liquor store was situated ironically beside the expressway. It was a shithole, but they'd have something hard. It didn't have to be his brand as long as he had enough to last the day. But, flying past the dark windows, he realized no liquor store would be open at this hour. Not even in the worst neighborhoods.

There was probably a bar still open. Some people would still consider this night. Instead he gunned the engine and floored it down the on-ramp. Who was he kidding?

The fuel light blinked and he pulled into a gas station barely over the town limits. He paid inside, remembering they always had liquor ready for any time of day. Guzzling from the bottle, the cheap whiskey eroded the tender pulp of his throat, searing a hot trail into his stomach. He sped out of the station, taking a slug every couple of miles, staying just this side of intoxication, slowing only when the hum of the road softened. As time and asphalt stretched, he heard Anna's maternal chiding: *What are you doing, honey?*

It was obvious now where he was headed.

He'd pictured traveling back to Kano many times, wondering if anything was the way he left it. The urge to find Michael constantly pricked at his conscience, but he'd always excused himself the same way. He didn't know where to look. Michael was long gone, just ahead of the wind. And it always seemed a waste of gas to stare at broken landmarks until they started to become fuzzy, like a word repeated ad nauseam until the meaning is foreign.

Funny how, after a certain age and modicum of success, people returned to their pasts via old maps and rubble, stabbing a finger at random structures like intervals on a timeline and exclaiming what used to stand there, fixing a point on the horizon where the old neighborhood was waiting, anticipating the epiphany that marked where it all began.

Shoehorned and forgotten in the center of the state, Kano was pocked with the evidence of annual tornadoes and near-misses. Little more than a fuel station for lost tourists, another dot that disappeared with increasing distance. Hardship in this town touched everyone. But main street's threadbare charms welcomed him back: the weather-worn clapboard storefronts; the tiny pond centered under a lacy white bridge where newlyweds posed for pictures; the single-screen theater that seemed untouched since its erection in '49; the two-story schoolhouse transformed into an antique shop when the population dwindled. He recalled the townspeople's quiet demeanors, the meandering way of life, the subtle accents imperceptible to anyone outside the radius of Chicago's brash timbre.

Every twist and turn, every driveway and mailbox and sign, were etched firmly in his memory. He barely watched the road, focusing more on the houses, the outbuildings, the changing landscape of storefronts and residents, searching for recognition in the faces of people he'd never met yet distantly acknowledged as kin. No one paid him any mind, even when he slowed to get a better look. That severed connection ached like an old bruise.

The main thoroughfare merged from four lanes to two. The structures alongside sat further back, faded and broken. Skeletons of abandoned businesses, nothing more than piles of bricks and plastic signage torn apart, watched him through their empty sockets. He slammed on the brakes before the church, its once-white plaster dingy and peeling, stained glass windows sealed with metal plates. The eight-foot cross in the courtyard, gleaming white drape around its intersection, was surrounded by an iron fence, its gate chained and locked despite being short enough to jump.

Val idled on the shoulder, though his past didn't live on the other side of that fence. His mother had scattered Michael— no, 'dumped,' her words—into the lake one morning before the sun rose, the cloth sack that held him left to rot in the red clay of the bank. Her flat, shapeless shoes slopped its mud onto their back steps.

Val remembered coming home to his answering machine —how many years now? Over a decade yet?—and hearing his mother had passed. Survived his father, by the sound of things. They received the same fate without anyone to claim them. The City did the scattering.

When he pitched his book to Graham, he expected to return here only in his mind. Cementing over any tangible distance allowed his imagination to run without consequence, speculate on the worst scenarios without scars.

Someone else might see such a monument as a symbol of hope, of home, of comfort. The rainbow after the flood. Repeating a message often enough, over enough years, becomes almost tolerable. Like the victim of cannibalism oblivious to being boiled alive as long the fire burns slow. Perhaps this monument was less a tribute than a warning.

A red pickup honked as though he didn't have the entire road otherwise to himself. Val pulled forward, curling his middle finger around the wheel to keep from raising it in the rearview.

Following the road another half mile, he turned at the break between the trees that led to Lake Kano. His parents' old house was one among many lining the rocky shore, façades facing the water. Last he heard, it had been taken over by a sucker for punishment and cozy kitchens.

He saw it in his mind's eye, a fire in the hearth breaking the evening's chill and keeping everyone close, hovering on that warm threshold so two boys could brave the water for a little bit of peace when the storm clouds inside gathered.

They'd never have gone home if their parents hadn't insisted, spending as much time as they could pretending to be Vikings in the little boat they built themselves, camping out along the shoreline. Rowing to the rhythm of locusts thrumming, slowly to keep the sun from sinking, Val wove intricate tales about how Michael would build a house for each of them on the bank of the Gulf of Mexico. How they'd travel back to Kano only for holidays, and they wouldn't have to wait for the tempest to calm before easing into the harbor. If they stayed in the boat, reality couldn't touch them. The longer the story, the longer the summer, every word pinning daylight down. Succumbing to twilight was a small defeat.

During a particularly still, humid evening in August, they stretched beside a grove of pines, knowing in their hearts they'd be camping beneath the stars again simply for the benefit of uninterrupted sleep.

The stone fire pit came to life with a few sharp strikes of flint. Michael lit a cigarette in the flame, took a long drag and perched, resting his wrist on one knee. For a long while, the only sound was the sniffle of burning paper and the smack of his lips off the filter. Flicking away ashes more than he puffed, the cigarette burned itself up between his fingers. He dropped the butt cussing, tossed it in the pit, and lit another. Reclined on his elbows, head thrown back, pretending to search for constellations.

"I'm not going back to school in fall."

"Don't be stupid."

"Pop's getting old," Michael said. "I'll get my schoolin' at the 'yard, pick up where dad leaves off." The space between his eyes creased tightly, fingers clenched around tufts of sandy brown frizz. They spoke to opposite ends of the lake.

"But what about—"

"You know I ain't fit for college."

"It can't be as boring as high school."

"That ain't it. You're the one with the brains. You'll end up rich and famous, and you can have some fancy contractor build your place with an extra room for me."

Val felt the perfect words forming on the tip of his tongue, but they vanished every time he opened his mouth. Instead, he only nodded; it was all talk, he was sure of it. Their parents would never agree to such a thing. Yet Val kept an eye on him, convinced if he fell asleep, Michael would disappear. But he'd been there the next morning, stoking the fire at the first sign of peach sky, flames leaping and crackling in protest.

Without fail, the past stopped at the same place. Val had trained his mind to slice clean across the cue mark before the reel change. Memories always ended on sunup.

He parked at the base of the stone bridge that led over the lake. Walking the rest of the way up, favoring his ankle, a threat scratched his memory and quivered in his stomach. Shells ground under his shoes as he counted: 813. How that number stuck in his head was a mystery. Amazing how such arbitrary things—the bends in the road, a number of steps, the syrupy yellow glow from windows that never opened wide enough—lingered, but—

Val stared down the indistinct tracts to the vanishing point, exhausted furrows like bars on a cage. He must've miscounted. He must've mis-stepped. Failed to properly calculate the length of his stride. Turning on a heel, he looked for the landmarks that marked this path fifty years ago.

The shores had changed. The lake looked broader, not narrower, as things normally do when childhood is long past. But the sharp jut of the pebbled beach that pointed him home: still there. The tree they used as a moor, red-painted stone at its base: still there. The path they wore up the grassy hill to their house was as rough as it was then, blemished with weeds. Yet there was nothing to follow it to. It ended at a gap in the landscape, as though he was peeking through a wormhole and seeing only lies.

Gravel crunched off to the right. An old man, hunched and stumbling, ambled down.

"Sir?" Val cleared his throat and waved.

The man peered up and shaded his eyes from the sun. He trembled, head bobbing as if on a spring.

"Yes?" His voice was as thin and leathery as his skin.

"Do you know what happened to 84?" Val pointed where the house used to be.

"Bungalow, white picket fence?"

"That's the one."

"Oh, she burned some five years ago. Can't nobody afford to rebuild 'round here."

"Burned." The harsh sunlight was making Val dizzy. The black patch laid claim to his right eye, and he squeezed them both tight. "Who lived there at the time, do you remember?"

"Don't reckon so. They got out, moved down the road apiece. Ain't no next of kin. See for yourself, there's still some bits and pieces left up 'ere."

Val rushed past, muttering thanks. Stabbing the ground with his cane, tipping forward to fight gravity, he watched his feet, prepared to take in the entire scene at once instead of chipping away in increments. Dandelion-pocked grass gave way to bare dirt, which his mother never would've abided. The black patch faded to gray, a curtain pulled back for the encore.

The cinder-block foundation was the only thing left intact. The basement had been filled in with earth and black wood, which could've been rotted trees as much as remains of his former home. He passed through a gaping hole in the plastic wood-look fence, bubbled and misshapen from the blaze. The gate hung like strings of melted wax from rusted hinges.

A charred post lay in the front yard. Sharp daggers of wood stabbed out from its broken base, as though someone had kicked it down and tossed it from its anchor. The sun glinted off a sheet of metal bolted to the beveled top. Val stepped over debris to pick it up. A copper plate marked the site:

Childhood home of Val M. Haverford
National Book Award nominee

***

Ghosts of young boys crossed the stone bridge, slapping its arched sides as they raced each other home. As Val passed by, he turned to watch them disappear, then leaned over to glimpse the water flowing beneath for the last time. If he followed it down far enough, would any part of their dragon-headed skiff remain?

Once upon a time, Val had visualized his future the way his father's had been: school, job, wife, kids—grandkids maybe—and finally retirement, spent on an old crumbling porch in a rocking chair he built himself, watching younger generations take their turns at the same existence, each day melting into the next, having traveled no further than he would on this lake. Then he escaped to the coveted big-city zip code and the population he wore like a shroud. After years of determined assimilation his silvery inflection had disappeared, leaving a euphonic lilt that sounded like nowhere. And that was how it should be.

Michael's sketch hung in a polished black frame in the house he'd dreamed of building, over a replica of their skiff. The only remnants, the only proof, that he once existed too.

Three hours before Graham's services. If he hurried, he'd make it before they ended. Val set out with the sun lowering in his rearview.

A canopy of maples painted the endless rows of worn gravestones with a web of shadows. Lettering flabby and pitted, a few were dated over a hundred years old. How many of these were still tended by anyone other than groundskeepers? How many were inhabited by the original occupants and not dug out for a new decedent, the crumbled remains of a former coffin turned to dust? Val bypassed the violated earth and slipped into a pew at the rear of the church.

Other mourners guided Anna along the aisle to the front; better friends patted her hands and supported her sagging shoulders. She sat stiffly, a woman turned to stone, her head jerking intermittently as though she heard distant voices calling. The cloying scent of melted wax clogged the nave. Dozens of tiny flames flickered, sending threads of smoke along the walls.

The congregation raised their voices in song, some vaguely remembered dirge from his forced attendance at Sunday mass as a boy. The pastor, a squinting older gent with a clipped friar's ring, delivered the lengthy eulogy in monotone. Guests took turns speaking at the lectern, but they melded into one irritating buzz Val found too easy to ignore, his mind wandering to the imposing crosses and stained glass saints' condemnation.

Graham would've hated this. I know, he wanted to shout loud enough to reach the nave and back. *I've known him since he was a kid and* I know *this isn't right.* He would've wanted a celebration of his life; a short, sweet service allowing people to remember him in his prime. Which was just a goddamn minute ago. Where were his parents, that cousin, in all this? Or were they too old to speak up? They had to be about…eighty.

Could Val really be only ten years behind?

A familiar sound halted his woolgathering. Sandra had mounted the dais. She plucked a sunburst guitar, singing the same tune she'd serenaded him with at Christmas. Each note was drawn to impossible lengths, swelling over the altar and getting trapped in the rafters like a caged bird.

How much time had passed since he'd seen her, heard her voice, without a computerized filter between them? A month, maybe? He'd spent so much time wallowing in the past he'd forgotten. Yet when they'd hardly known each other, she'd called him in the hospital to check on his welfare.

The seclusion he took such comfort in moments ago left him cold and naked. He gripped his knees, the emptiness between his arms magnified, as he fidgeted to find a comfortable position on the unforgiving bench.

She missed a note, voice hitching.

Val tightened his jaw at her slight.

The song continued, her blunder ebbing under the soaring melody. Her voice plunged at the end of the first verse and rose to meet the second.

Then it happened again, at the same line in the second verse, like a skip in a record.

Without the festivity of Christmas, the rawness of the lyrics were unmistakable: a saga of departure, the specter of a lover soothing the bereft.

He anticipated the skip in the third verse. His heart twinged with the symbolic omission.

A fourth verse was building, racing to run him over. Val shifted, filled his head with static, memorized the grain of the pew before him and the pattern in the carpet runner, and bolted the second it ended.

The cool air refreshed him and he took large heaving gulps of it, grateful for the immeasurable open space, condolences churning into white noise. A thin fog settled among the stones, giving an odd lushness to the neatly cut grass.

The trickle of departing attendees grew, and he pushed out of the crowd. A like-minded guest had taken refuge under a single tree at the top of a rise for a smoke.

"Mind if I have one of those?"

The stranger popped one out of the pack and offered his lighter. Val coughed with his first puff, throat smoldering. After a couple of long drags, the sting lessened, and he hoped he'd adjust to the harsh taste of menthol. He blew lazy streams toward the sky. After a while, he heard the stranger mumble a goodbye and shuffle off.

In the distance, a family of five hung their heads around a gravesite, one stooping to place a bouquet in a lawn vase. They were so far away they resembled a diorama. A shrill laugh cut through the scene and they disbanded. One woman stretched an arm behind her, patting the top of the stone absent-mindedly before trotting after the others.

How uncouth would it be to unscrew the cane handle and drain it?

"Is it all right if I join you?"

He hadn't heard Sandra come up. He smiled weakly, heart swelling with relief. "Please do."

"How you holding up?"

"Been better. You?"

She shrugged and caressed his cheek. "You look exhausted."

"Thanks."

"I didn't mean it that way. I'm worried about you."

He probably looked and smelled like an alcoholic. Since he'd seen her last, gray-red rings had emerged under his eyes and he'd grown thin and pallid. His shirt was a little too loose, the sleeves of the suit a little too long. He'd noticed in the rearview mirror that his eyes were bloodshot. He tossed down the half-smoked cigarette and twisted his toe into it.

"It feels like the air is being sucked out of every room and I'm suffocating, even when I'm asleep. I can't even relax in my own home." He tugged at the knot of his tie, enlarging the sloppy gap between silk and collar, revealing the white bands of new skin.

"I'm so sorry. I know you and Graham were like brothers," Sandra said. "This is terrible timing, but I wanted to let you know I postponed the release of your interview. Out of respect."

Val nodded. "I haven't been working anyway."

"I saw your posts. Does that mean you're scrapping it?"

"I can't think about that now."

Val wrote those posts to prove *they* had nothing left to

worry about, no more threats to eliminate. They were intended for an audience of two; the gossip mill would ensure they were seen, just as Graham's had been. Defeat dripped from every word, the task robotic. *Message received.*

"Sure, of course. I understand." Sandra shifted her feet and cleared her throat.

Val wished she'd leave him alone in this rut, and at the same time wanted to bury his face in her hair and forget where he was, if only for a little while. A passel of clouds swept over the cemetery, threatening rain. The earth tipped and he gripped the tree trunk, dry bark cementing him there. He closed his eyes and leaned his head back. A gentle touch grazed his belly.

"Still getting dizzy spells?"

"It passes."

"How much have you had?"

"Not enough."

"How did you get here?"

Think of a lie, stupid.

"Valery."

Val tossed the cane in the air, fumbling to catch it on its way down. "Walked."

"You can't let Anna see you like this, you need to clean yourself up before—"

"I'm fully sober, Sandra."

"Maybe so, but—"

He laughed without joy. "Fucking cliché. Least I can still identify 'em, right? Bright side to everything."

"Okay, enough." Sandra fanned her fingers as though swatting away a horde of gnats. "She's been asking for you."

"I'm not good with words."

"Is that supposed to be a joke?"

"What am I supposed to do, tell her everything will be all right, don't cry, God took him home because He needed another angel? You're far too young to be anyone's widow, but praise the Lord, Graham walks with Jesus? I can't do that. She's praying to an imaginary friend who could not care less.

121

"And the minister, Christ, droning on about 'our loss,' like Graham was misplaced and all we need to do is remember where we put him. 'My sympathies,' 'my condolences...' they're all worthless euphemisms. There are no words to describe what it's like to reach into yourself and find nothing there."

She rubbed his arm, providing zero comfort.

He stuffed his fists into his pockets. "I found him, did you know that?"

"Oh God. No, I didn't."

"The expression on his face...it wasn't peaceful. He suffered."

He hated himself for being so stolid. Distance kept him from thinking about the details, how Graham's contorted features were a piercing accusation, how his mutilated last words reverberated through his head whenever he was alone. She didn't need to know he died slowly, his killer inches away, laughing. The same man who held him down and warned him this would happen. "When they led me out of the agency she looked at me with such disgust, Sandra, such pure hatred. So what can I say to her? What can I possibly say?"

"I don't know, but you need each other. And you better think of something quick."

Anna was plodding her way up, the squat hill a mountain, lifting her hem to avoid dragging it through the bald patches. Sandra squeezed his hand and headed down, pausing to pay her respects.

She came from old custom. Comforting the bereaved was the polite thing to do.

Impossible.

When he was too drugged to think, too exhausted to fight, he should've quit then. Should've promised to let this go, return to the dusty space on the empty shelf, to the memories and reviews and pictures with his name in lights. That should've been enough.

Yet even now he felt the keys beneath his fingers, pounding out a rhythm only he could create. Not writing was as big an insult as his presence here. There was no answer, none that would satisfy. No matter what support he gave her there would be no pardon, no release of hitting bottom.

A damp chill whistled through Val's clothes as he followed the service drive around the perimeter to his car, newly shined shoes crunching along the gravel, while Sandra gathered Anna into her arms and murmured soft sounds like poetry into her ear.

Chapter Thirteen

Same voicemail message. Same bored, arrogant drone of a detective with better things to do than mollify victims. Marczek was probably just as tired of hearing Val's voice, repeatedly demanding closure. If he changed his outgoing message to reflect that, it would save them both some trouble. But every morning and again before bed, Val dialed anyway. Glutton for punishment. Answers, when he got them, were always the same: there are no leads, no leads, they disappeared without a trace.

Hollywood stuffed chest-beating pissing matches among neighboring police in movies mostly to up the drama. Cops shared information, personnel, whatever it took to form a whole picture. But since Val wasn't blood, his need-to-know status about Graham's case was nearly non-existent. And he didn't have the nerve to call Anna and ask if she found herself at the same dead end.

The fantasy that the attackers left some sloppy clue behind, a subtle calling card dismissed the first time around, infiltrated every thought. That Val and Graham were simply victims of senseless, random violence would bring a sick relief. He hung up after the fourth ring, knowing the fifth would click over and send his hopes plummeting.

Each time Val had completed a novel, Graham carried on his father's tradition of lighting cigars to celebrate. And each time they'd stub them out before they reached the third puff, sending Graham into his bottom drawer for two glasses and a bottle of Macallan to toast and wash out the taste.

This time, Val had planned to pick up candy cigars instead, knowing chocolate had a grip on Graham even more than tobacco. He'd kept a regular stockpile locked in a hidden compartment in the wall, and waggled his fingers over Whitman's Samplers he'd scored at half-price, post-holiday sales, indecisive over the nut cluster or caramel or cherry cordial. Before popping the first of many in his mouth he'd look up guiltily and whisper, "Don't tell Anna. She'll make me do calisthenics or some bullshit." She'd lost the battle against cigarettes, but at least he could humor her regarding trans fats. Graham grinned, making Val his co-conspirator; two children sneaking extra rations from a Halloween stash.

Graham's greeting card was still taped to the frame of the laptop's screen, the words taunting him daily. Yet he couldn't trash it or file it away. He recalled Graham's encouragement, the exhilaration of overcoming a decade-long block, losing all track of time while the growing stack of fine vellum grew beside his left hand. With every paragraph, he'd had a harder time remembering why he stopped in the first place, why he didn't just bang out any old thing for the simple pleasure of it. The worry that this streak wouldn't last had been a nagging force, but he'd planned to enjoy his new burst as long as it lasted.

Val visualized the last chapter, the finished manuscript topped with a lid and sealed like a coffin, and the finality left him hollow. This time there'd be no celebration, no toast.

A niggling memory broke through the bittersweet, plunging him into that night. *You're going to stop writing that book. We have to secure our future.* It echoed as clearly now, even as he forced it out of his head. He'd heard it before, the answer buried deep. If only he could find a way to exhume it without reeling from the dizziness and the turbulence in his stomach, steadying himself on whatever was handy.

Faceless silhouettes no longer invaded his dreams, but had devolved into walking nightmares. After one especially punishing episode, he'd found himself kneeling in the moonlit grass with a letter opener in his hand, dragging it back and forth across his thigh as though wiping it clean. He'd crushed his fist around the hilt to feel something other than half-awake numbness, the fog of insomnia and madness that had consumed the last few weeks.

It's over, it's over.

The pile of newspapers and magazine articles about the violence throughout the Chicago area, the police reports and public records he spent hours thumbing through, now seemed voyeuristic. Nearly fifty years and he'd managed to avoid entire neighborhoods, whole sections of the city he'd never even breezed through. Yet it was in his pure little haven that he was left gasping for air, his skin torn away in the darkness, alive only by some miracle.

The more he researched, the more questions circled over each other until everything was a jumbled mess. Four homeless people in the Loop, two disabled women near O'Hare, three elderly men found far from their nursing homes, three teenagers surrounded by broken syringes in an abandoned house in Chatham.

His hands shook with the panic of writer's block returning, his premise more tin-hatted bullshit than dystopian conspiracy. Crime was on the rise, hopeless statistics the only solid fact. Not enough consistent detail to assume the threat of a serial killer getting his jollies. Even psychopaths liked a good theme.

Val's thoughts refused to connect. Plot lines parched and withered, then rambled onto unrelated tangents. The grisly, torturous scenes he scribbled as catharsis were unlike anything he'd ever written. Their visceral primacy, the bestial destruction, the demand for vengeance had become second nature. The thoughts that used to scare the shit out of him he now welcomed, nestling beneath them each night, craving the vicarious release that followed one bloody scenario after another.

He burst through the studio door hungry for the wide-open space. Puddles of stagnant rainwater made the yard look like a minefield, tornadoes of gnats congregating in the rays of sunlight and brume. The air pressed close and wet as though to drown him, the beach turned to quicksand, the stately homes rolled into the distance like mirages.

A branch snapped, followed by a flash of movement in the trees. A dozen ancient maples towered over the property, wide enough to conceal a person. Even someone tall and broad-shouldered. He ran to the stone wall and bent over it, blood rushing to his head.

No one there. But any number of people could've been squatting behind it, waiting to finish what they started.

It's all over now.

The woodshed beckoned. If anyone was hiding in there, they'd be revealed the second he opened the door. If he focused on carving, he could calm himself. It always worked in the past. He had to believe it would now.

Val grabbed the first block he laid eyes on. He hadn't touched anything since before his eyes started betraying him. He hefted his favorite carving knife to reacquaint himself with the counterweight of the blade versus the handle, rotated the basswood to get the feel of the edges, sizing up how much pressure to give it. Ignoring the tremor in his hand, the images and voices swirling into a vortex, he turned his head until he saw the end of the wood. Brought the blade into view and held its position, forcing muscle memory to take over, reminding him how it felt for everything to fall into place.

An impatient brush of his hand sent the shavings floating down, joining the growing pile of wood curls already on the floor. His marks were just a bit off-center. By following just ahead of the blade, the familiar maneuvers rushed forth, and with it a giddiness to execute each one simultaneously.

Then he lost control and slipped, paring a sliver of skin from the side of his thumb along with a chunk of nail for good measure, springing a line of red beads that sank into the human-like figure and stained it. He whistled through his teeth at the bolt of pain that sparked into his wrist. Wiped the blade on his jeans, wrapped his thumb into the hem of his shirt, and grinned. That was the same spot he'd nicked the first time out, learning woodcarving in the lot of his father's construction business when he was barely thirteen. Creating something of beauty from a hunk of discarded scrap had been a drug to him, a challenge that couldn't be ignored. The scent of wood, the familiar motions, took him home every time.

Born at opposite ends of '52, Val and Michael had been

inseparable since they'd shared a crib. The summer of their sophomore year, Michael thumped Val's shoulder on the first free morning with no schedules, no deadlines, just hot, yawning hours ahead with nothing to fill them.

"Today, little brother," he'd drawled, "we're gonna build us a boat."

Michael led Val to the back of their father's lumberyard and told him to collect scrap. When Val had a pile half his height, he searched for his brother, who'd vanished. He finally found him hunched in the dirt against the showroom wall, brow furrowed, stroking his chin at something in his lap. Val tiptoed closer, and bent over laughing: Michael had been studying a stack of library books with titles like *How to Build Glued-Lapstrake Wooden Boats.*

"Did you just pick those up today?"

Val ducked when Michael faked throwing the hardback tome at his head. He never did get an answer.

"Do you even know what a lapstrake is?"

"Yes, wise-ass. It's overlappin' boards." Michael knocked the clapboard siding at his back. "It'll look real pretty when we're done. Nice cherry hull, natural gunwale and breast hook—like this here." He held out another book with rusty awl marking the place.

Skeptical, Val fanned the pages of the next book in the stack, then a fourth, stopping when he came to a color photograph of a glossy black dinghy with serpentine Celtic knotwork snaking from gunwale to hull, creating patterns he'd only seen in kaleidoscopes. He traced the scrolls and felt the grain against his fingers.

Michael poked him in the knee, huge grin on his face, knowing he'd won.

Building that boat became their shared obsession. Refusing to float around in any simple tub, Val worked discarded balustrades until he'd sculpted an elaborate, menacing figurehead worthy of young men out to conquer the world.

Nostalgia roused the impulse to retest his abilities at that sort of handiwork. He set the little gynoid down in favor of another piece of scrap and reached for his favorite chip carver. Shoes shushing in the shavings as he maneuvered for better light, the beveled edge of the much smaller blade nearly disappeared behind the veil in his eyes. Next time.

He went back to work on the gynoid with the carving knife, gouging out the bloody bit at the figure's waistline. Now it looked more like a fish, but it would do. Considering how far along he'd gotten safely, the crude piece nearly finished, the injury was remarkably minor. He carved until the wood was no longer safe to hold, then reached for another piece, training his eyes to the new technique, looking through to the end of the cut even before he started. Moving on to the chisel, trying more intricate patterns, nimbly skirting out of the way when he lost control or got wildly cocky, he calculated a ratio of times he'd whittled his fingers instead of the wood and estimated an average of three out of ten. Could be worse.

Hours later he had seven increasingly detailed figures and all his digits intact, though cramped, spiked with splinters, and crosshatched with fine lacerations. A fissure in the web between his thumb and forefinger was oddly numb yet buzzing, having been nicked by the tip of a blade. A stream of blood burst forth as through a breached dam. Blisters covered his right hand from having held the tools too tightly in his sweaty grip. Both palms, rough with work and smelling of the grain and the iron of his blood, were quickly drying to a patchy brown.

He'd proven something, but he wasn't sure to whom, or what good it would do; the one who'd be most impressed was not here to give him a slap on the back. But as he held that seventh figure up to the light, just to the left of the bare bulb, he nodded, running a thumb along its (only slightly) lopsided hourglass curves. Not bad. Sanding her to a polish, he smiled at the idea of bringing her to Sandra like some juvenile show of affection. It was a rather decent little figure, but nothing like what she'd already seen. He imagined the flash of pity that would be too hard to mask, and planned on making something more refined, more deserving of her, when he'd fully regained his skill.

As serene as the methodical scrape of iron and scratch of sandpaper against wood could be, he needed some life, some dulcet sound, to fill the void. Music wouldn't cut it.

***

Val entered Calvyn's and squinted into the dank. Hope turned to disappointment when he saw only one patron, the token drunk at the spectator table. Squaring his shoulders, Val headed toward the jukebox. Might as well inject some atmosphere into the place, in case—

"Look at you with that cane, such a fine piece and you don't even know how to hold it properly." Calvyn cuffed Val's shoulder with the back of his hand.

"What do you mean?" Val studied the handle as though expecting it to give him an explanation.

"You're supposed to have it at your side like another leg! Not out in front like a blind man, just pokin' motherfuckers."

"Sorry, Calvyn, I didn't see you. And there you are right in front of me!"

"Must've been a long day. You don't need it anymore if you're holding it that way. Come on over to your spot, I'll set you up." Calvyn clapped Val on the shoulder. "And listen, I was sorry to hear about Mr. Van Ellis. Real sorry."

"Thank you. Me too."

"He was a good man. I'll miss seeing him around here. *He* was satisfied with Ol' Smuggler."

Val laughed. "He was a cheap date, that's for sure."

Calvyn wiped off Val's table with a damp rag. "By the way, you know I named a drink after you?"

"No kidding? What is it?"

"Double Macallan's on the rocks."

"That's not a cocktail, it's just liquor."

"It's what you drink all the damn time. I have to sell more of this fancy stuff to make it worth the price, seeing as you're the only reason I order it. But look here, I serve it in one of these fancy glasses," he said, setting it down. The NASA logo, stamped in pewter, was affixed to it. "And I bought a novelty ice tray just for this. Makes 'em in the shapes of stars."

"That's damn sweet of you, Calvyn."

"Don't go getting all sentimental. Between the two of you, you put my kids through college. The least I can do is make a signature drink for my best regular."

The front door squeaked open and a group of tired, middle-aged guys in Cubs jerseys collapsed into a booth. Calvyn headed over to take their order. Each wanted a different combination of shots and beers, leaving a much needed gap in their conversation.

All the years at this scarred table, people-watching and decompressing with scotch and music, scribbling on an endless stack of rough cocktail napkins, this bar became a second studio. He couldn't admit to Calvyn that he'd given up. The acknowledgement was an insult, an absurdity. An unbroken tradition had died along with the book, in the time it took to order those glasses.

The TV's volume was up for a change, affording Val the treat of yet another interview with Andre Wallace blathering on about his latest work of genius. Not only that, he was conducting a workshop, offering guidance to a hand-picked class of young plebes in the art of fine literature. If Val rolled his eyes any further Calvyn would call the morgue. He skimmed through an old newspaper left on a neighboring table instead, bypassing all the gloom and doom on the front pages and landing on the first-world problems of an advice columnist's readership.

But Andre was unavoidable. A blurb about him, not two inches square, was tucked into the bottom of the page. The date in the header was weeks ago. Val had just touched on the headline, "Local Writer Involved in Skirmish," before Calvyn returned, wringing his hands around a bar towel.

"Want another?"

"Better bring two. I'm meeting a friend." He'd been unsure if Sandra would accept, preparing for a 'no' or an excuse, without any fallback plan. But she'd swept her initial iciness under a sigh and a promise to meet him at six. The minute hand of the Hamm's Scene-o-Rama clock broke into an angle.

Calvyn's worried expression dissolved into a sly grin. "Oh, oh! Got a girl coming, don't you? I know that look."

"Sandra Bayliss of *On the Record*. I thought I'd show her one of my favorite haunts. Pretty sure she'd get a kick out of this," he said, hoisting the glass. They looked up at the sound of the door.

"Oh, oh, this must be your lady." Calvyn nudged Val with his elbow as she approached. "She's a looker. How'd she end up with you?"

"Be nice, Calvyn. You're embarrassing me."

"I'm always nice. Good to see you, Sandra."

"Have we met?" Sandra's voice sounded huskier than usual, the tip of her nose rosy pink.

"No, but you're the only classy female ever to be in this place," Calvyn said, shaking her hand. "I figured you must be with this old coot. Other men would know better!"

Calvyn shuffled off to the bar, chuckling. Val stood to greet her but she turned her head, aiming his kiss at the corner of her mouth instead. A hot, short breath hit his ear, as though she pulled a secret back from the brink.

"Mm. I needed that," she said. She reached down to squeeze Val's hand and he winced. "What happened to you!" She stared wide-eyed at his mummified palm.

"I was carving."

"Aren't you supposed to use wood?"

"I slipped a couple times."

"I'll say you did."

"Everything still works." He stiffly waggled his fingers and attempted a lascivious grin.

She laughed, but it sounded rehearsed.

"Seems like you need this drink more than I do."

"Ugh. It's been a terrible week. Let me tell you, I've about had it with this business. I'm sure you've noticed this?" She swept her hand under her chin. "Gravity's been a real peach. And this? I don't just have crows' feet, I have the whole crow."

Val made a sympathetic click with his tongue.

"Earlier this week I had to smile through a water-cooler discussion of how women of a certain age should start thinking about their legacies and giving back to their alma maters—'and you'd be an asset to yours, Sandra dear'—but today! Today the producers called me in for a 'one-on-one.' That's what they're calling them now, not 'meetings,' despite the fact there were four of us. They suggested I get tucked. I was about to make a similar suggestion to them. And I think Amber Lovejoy is sleeping her way up. She's not helping my mood one bit."

"Amber Lovejoy?"

"She's my Andre. Poor girl should be a secretary so she'd have a desk to rest her massive udders on. You should see these things. On second thought, I'd rather you didn't. I don't need you getting mesmerized by those hypnotits too."

Val tried to compose some romantic sentiment that didn't sound torn from the pages of some schmaltzy, bodice-ripping twaddle. "You're beautiful, and they're idiots for not seeing that." *Christ.*

"You're sweet. But you're blind as a bat."

He had to remind himself that was only an idiom.

"I'm well past the age they like to see in front of a camera and with these…*interesting* looks. I'm lucky I haven't been replaced already. Now if I were a man…"

"They said they were replacing you?"

"Not in those exact words. But it was clear. Get plastic or get out. It's like they're trying to make me disappear, just a little at a time." She groaned and rubbed her temples, then rolled her head in a slow arc. "I could really use something to eat the pain away. Something fried."

"I think Calvyn carries Fritos, Doritos…probably a few other things ending in '-ito'…the tamale guy usually swings by around now." Val's appetite perked up at the thought of Pablo, the diminutive Mexican who wandered the city selling the homemade one-dollar treats to drunks.

"Booze will do nicely 'til then."

"We could both use a laugh. I'll do my best, under the circumstances. I had to suffer this guy until you walked in," Val said, pointing at the TV. "You know he says *lit-tra-chure*?" He made a circle with his fingers and thumb and stuck out his pinkie as though holding tiny cup of tea.

"No he doesn't!"

"He does. He sounds like a three-hundred-year-old English professor. I should know. I had some."

"Stop! You're going to make me say something I'll—um…" Sandra squinted her eyes shut, then rolled them up toward the ceiling, her wide mouth shrinking into a tight little bow.

"What?"

"I guess my head's still at work. You know how it is, when you're stuck in one mindset and *plop!* right into another? My thoughts are bouncing all over the place. By the way, thanks for the drink. Is this that scotch you like? It's so smooth—"

"What were you about to say?"

"Nothin', nothin'."

He'd never seen anyone watch Calvyn refill a garnish tray with such fascination. "Sandra."

She stabbed the cobblestones with her heel. "Something I'll regret."

"In what capacity?"

"Well…you announced you're no longer working on your book…"

"So?"

"So they needed to fill your spot with something…"

"Oh no."

"I know, I know…"

"What is it with this guy! And why does it have to be you?"

"It's not like I want to do it. They're making me feel like I don't have a choice."

"When were you going to tell me?"

"Never? I didn't think you paid much attention to the series."

"Well, I have been lately!" The glass seemed heavier as he

rotated the ridiculous crest outward, then crumpled a limp napkin against it, finally shoving it forward, letting his hand drop onto the tabletop. "This is not how I pictured tonight going."

"I feel terrible. Have you made up your mind entirely? It's dead?"

"I poured myself into it for such a long time."

"I know," she said, petting his arm.

"I think you would've liked it." His brows involuntarily crouched together like they were conferring with each other.

"I'm sure. Can't imagine why this one would be any different."

"You read others? Which did you like?"

"I did interview you, remember. Who do you think I am, Larry King?"

"Of course. Of course you must have. But which—"

"Oh, I can't pick a favorite. I liked all of them."

Sandra tossed her hair off her shoulder with a shrug. Her gaze drifted away to his hand, which she squeezed and then ignored as if uncomfortable touching it. He snapped his fingers closed a second too late.

"I don't feel myself if I'm not working. I never had this much trouble with any of the Battaglias." He couldn't help injecting emphasis into that name. *How hard is it to come up with a goddamn title?* "It's like I lost something and just got it back. But I can't even type without feeling this incredible guilt. No…that's not right. I can use the laptop Graham sent me but not to write. I mean not writing that. Damn it." He sighed and rubbed his face with both hands, the antiseptic stink of gauze filling his nostrils.

Sandra's attention diverted to some sports highlight show on TV. The seconds ticked by like a time bomb. He was convinced their date would end with Sandra fleeing, tired of the verbal equivalent of a toddler banging pots and pans. She'd slipped off her heels at some point and was feeling around for them with her toes, righting them again and slipping inside, the silk of her hose rustling against the leather. He refused to let his thoughts flow after she'd already walked out, leaving him there to imagine how their conversation should've gone, a frustrating replay of their failed first date. The water rings on the table received his initial halting words until a path solidified before him.

"When I was a boy, my parents took me to the tri-county fair. I hated those things; they were overcrowded and sweaty, and you came home with the stench of animals on you even if you never went near the pens. One day a musician, a young fellow with a mandolin, sat outside the entrance. I'd never seen a mandolin before. He had picks on every fingertip of his right hand."

Val flexed his fingers, remembering how the thin steel glinted in the sun, knowing whatever came next would be magic. "I made up a story in my head. He was a prince turned into a dragon by a witch's curse. He taught himself to play the lute in order to woo a princess and break the spell." Sandra smiled, resting her chin in her hand. The old euphoria came rushing back: Val M. Haverford, presiding over the reading room of a bookstore, quoting a favored passage, captivating his audience into silence.

"He was dusty and shabby—maybe a farmhand, maybe a transient—and sat right outside the gates. He slouched on a stool like he had no spine at all, elbows resting on his instrument like he was about to order a Pabst. Yet he had the whole town gathered around him, talking and joking like old pals. Then as if some alarm went off, he straightened up..."

Val lengthened his spine and canted back, raising his hand as though cradling a fretboard, mimicking the carriage of a dancer. "The crowd hushed. He pointed the head at somebody, they named a song and he played it, those metal fingers going all at once, rapid-fire. It was some horrid bluegrass stuff, but I was mesmerized. Never needed sheet music. Never missed a note. His hands moved independently of him. I never saw him again." He smiled and tapped his temple. "At least not in person."

Val sighed, memories flickering like a projector. "I felt like—if I could achieve that level of skill—then it would prove I wasn't just spinning my wheels. Some of the greatest filmmakers of our time optioned my work, and I finally felt like I'd made it. Then one day I lost something—glory? ambition?—I can't name it. So when I started working again, and everything started falling into place..."

The metallic chink of a quarter slipping into the jukebox replaced the reverberation of strings against fretwires, the scent of hay and feed with beer and smoke-infused wood. Val blinked, returning to the present. He had the mortifying suspicion he'd been yammering on for an hour, boring her in the process.

"Well," he said, gulping his scotch. "That was a bit much."

"No." Sandra seemed to glow as though firelight smoldered beneath her and the seething fury at her bosses melted away. Kneading along his shoulder blades, she dug tight circles down his spine. "It was beautiful. Just right."

"I don't usually go on like that." The door squeaked again, and Pablo disappeared, swinging his cooler.

Sandra bit her lip, looked Val over like she was sizing up a subject, her journalist's scrutiny making him squirm in his seat. "I think you should start again."

Val rubbed the back of his neck. His muscles shrank and gnarled into knots. He fought to control his breath, denying the panic that threatened to return. The Cubs diehards were still there, their chatter a little more slurred. They seemed to have cleared out Pablo's entire stash. The token drunk slumped across his table, snoring, as though he'd never leave. Calvyn stuffed his bar towel into freshly washed glasses, swirled once, twice, unfurled and twisted it along the rims, swaddled and turned them upside down on a rack.

"It wouldn't be right."

"None of this is your fault. You couldn't have protected him."

"That brings precious little comfort."

Sandra scooted in closer, cocking her head and lowering her voice. "No one would know. The public thinks it's been scrapped. You can work to your heart's content."

"It's disrespectful. Graham—"

"—wouldn't want you to quit. Don't you think that's true?

He wouldn't want you to abandon your career on account of some psycho."

"That 'psycho' cost him his life, and nearly mine," Val snapped.

"But you're still here. You can't allow those bastards to run your life, not after what you just told me. No one has to know you typed another sentence, and I'll never say a word."

"And what happens after?"

Her jaw clenched the way it had after the interview when she'd stared down Kevin. "Writing is your blood. And I hate that they took that away from you." She tossed back a swig, crushing a chunk of ice in her molars.

Val traced her jawline with his unmarred thumb until it softened under his touch. Her hand roamed down to his chest but this time she wasn't extending an invitation.

"Go home."

"You're killing me, Sandra."

"I just wanted to give you my two cents."

"It was worth more than that."

"That's why you need to go. Figure this out. It's important."

"It'll keep."

She poked him sharply. "No. It won't." She twisted out of her seat and polished off the last of her drink as she stood. "Please think about what I said. Okay? Call me. Tell me what you decided on. And take care of yourself," she added, caressing his injured hand.

"Walk with me." The sound of his need thudded onto the cobblestones. After all the things she trusted him with, she couldn't judge him for speaking so plain. Or maybe he simply no longer cared. "Please. Just for a minute."

She bent at the waist in slow motion and unfurled her purse strap from the back of the chair, then tilted her head from side to side as she consulted with the clock. "It's pretty late."

"That was the longest I'd ever seen anyone contemplate a simple walk around the block. The sun's barely down! A little one."

"You're not hearing me."

"I have ideas brewing all the time. A little fresh air won't blow them away." Val shivered and a cold sweat tingled at his temples. "Writers are night owls." *Or at least I used to be.*

"Val—"

"How about I walk you to your car? This neighborhood's not safe."

It had been a long time since he'd heard her laugh so soundly, head thrown back and red mouth open wide.

"The Gold Coast? Seriously? Anyway, I have mace in my purse."

"It'd take you twenty minutes to find an elephant in there. And it won't do you any good if they grab you from behind." He hoped she didn't notice how tightly he gripped the table.

"You're a pain in the ass." Before he could devise a comeback, she beckoned with mock impatience. "Come on, come on. Short one, got it? Busy day tomorrow." Her expression remained nonchalant but her voice betrayed her. Val chose to ignore it.

The air pressed close and heavy despite the breeze kicking up into a gale. The last of the sun turned her hair mahogany and he caught threads of silver as she tucked her head under his chin. They cooed over the intricate grillwork and nineteenth century stone façades as they approached Lake Shore Drive, making empty plans to ride the new Ferris wheel at the Pier and tour the lighthouse—was it open for tours?—and noting all the changes to the cityscape from when they first came to live here, as though they'd recently immigrated. They counted the sloops bobbing on the choppy waves, losing track as they skimmed past the horizon. Most of her responses were short, vaguely positive hums. The attempts to brush off the weight of her itinerary only spread it like paste on Val's skin.

Was he supposed to make her feel better about taking this assignment? He had no idea where to start, except with a lie. He'd much prefer if some cosmic force sucked Andre into another dimension and took Amber Lovejoy along for the ride.

With one interview, Val faced defeat in a game he didn't sign up for, whose rules he wasn't informed of, by people he didn't want to compete with. How do you hold on to something that doesn't exist? He guessed she felt the same in reverse. If she refused, or they passed her over, they'd consider it equal to forfeiture. The words "forced retirement" swirled inside his head, and for an instant, his thoughts pinged to Graham. He cringed, pushing the correlation aside.

Sandra looked up, brow furrowed, but instead of speaking her mind, she chewed at her bottom lip. She mumbled something that only half-resembled words and kissed his hand, continuing the walk in uncharacteristic silence. He felt her sweeping away even as she pressed against his side, passing cars making it hard to hear the words they weren't speaking. Val clamped up and relaxed, over and over; he had no answer if she apologized. Any response would be a stupid one.

She flitted across the Inner Drive, leaving him to catch up.

Traffic blazed past on the Outer Drive, headlights on before sundown to navigate the serpentine curves. They were confusing even in full daylight, but with shade and sun intermingling, the road resembled an Escher puzzle. Too often cars misjudged and bounced off the concrete barriers, and he pictured one twisting in the air just over Sandra's head, the chain link fence dividing the Drives as useless as a sheet of tin foil. When he reached her he circled her shoulders again, but she barely noticed. She curled her fingers around the wires.

After a long while, she said, "I always wanted to live on the water. Ever since I was a girl. My ex-husband promised me the ocean. He gave me a backyard pool.

"When I left him I came here for this. So I could look across the water and not see the other shore. Paul—my ex—couldn't swim." A wicked grin flickered for a fleeting second.

"Do you talk to him anymore?"

"God no. He found some Stepford type to shack up with. My daughter, Ella, visits him now and then; they're close."

Val waited. Her eyes and mouth danced. There was more, and she was trying to hold it still. "My mortgage isn't paid off yet. It's almost there," she added quickly. "Everything's on track. But little girls from small towns make big plans. One day I had the husband, the house, the baby. Then they started to disappear one by one. I got my life back when I made a career for myself, and then my grandchild came, and then—"

For a second, she looked guilty, gulping down the words. She lifted her head as though to breathe in the view, and her nose glowed pink as it had when she entered Calvyn's. "It will all go away if we just close our eyes."

***

After Sandra drove off, Val considered going back to Calvyn's for another round. Instead, he meandered up and down the side streets until every landmark looked as much like another; if he kept walking in circles, he'd lose himself among the lofts. He imagined riding the waves in one of the little sloops, enjoying the last streaks of color before the stars emerged. The houses facing the lakefront became his parents', his neighbors', from decades ago. He saw the water through his father's eyes, wondering if he'd ever thought about his sons out there on Lake Kano, if he could see them standing up in their skiff plotting adventures.

Again he saw the boat that still burned, the matchbook cutting into his fist. He watched it crumble to ash as the icy water soaked his jeans and stole his breath; the splinters biting into his tender hands as he ripped the bow stem away; the gravelly lake bottom grinding into his knees until all that was left was a single plume of smoke twisting in the breeze.

He shivered. How young he was then, how naïve, believing the water held some magic escape, their puny lake opening to the river and sealing up behind them, providing stealthy passage to the Gulf and better things, their own private paradise free from heartache.

Graham's building was on the Register of Historic Places for a reason. Wrought iron gates and intricate floral reliefs carved into the stone façade spoke of worth and money. Warm red bricks stretched high above the street. Every window had a view to kill for: the lake to the east, Navy Pier and John Hancock to the south, the lush suburbs edging the North Shore, the multifaceted neighborhoods quilting the west. Homey and stately, expertly manicured yet grimy with the grit of city life, a world too rich to savor at once. Tourists stopped once they reached Michigan Avenue, ignoring anything beyond the elite shops and gold trim.

He'd shown up early for meetings with Ed more often than not, claiming he wanted to beat traffic but instead stared into people's windows, indulging in the faint melody of a piano sweeping through the streets clogged with cultured businessmen, with artists and actors, who've slit their wrists for less. Poured out their souls desperate to be understood, stretching to fill their hands with sapphires and silver, only to surround themselves with iron bars and fine whiskey. He arrived daunted yet determined, prepared to sweat and bleed as they have. Dark music thrummed from beneath, a tiger's growl before the pounce.

The horizon melded with the darkening water; towers loomed above, reflecting the changing colors. Dimensions changed and bent as time seemed to dangle over a chasm. Sandra didn't mince words. She seemed ready to battle the men who destroyed so much with her own two hands. A flush of warmth, a gentle ache that followed him to his car, goaded and teased him all the way home until he realized it wasn't Sandra pushing him.

**

He flicked on the lamp, and in the shadows at the rear of the house he saw no one. He headed to his desk and opened the laptop. He didn't rise until dawn.

142

Chapter Fourteen

Someone was watching. There was no escape.

The glowing eye of Raymond's porch light seemed to follow his every move. His watchdog may well be scrutinizing his property on another evening walk, even rubbernecking into the windows. But as Val sat hunched over the laptop, using the coffee table as a makeshift desk, it converted into a talisman as protective and comforting as a child's nightlight.

Wood chips flew out beneath tires skidding to a stop. Val's finger skewed off his track pad as he dove for the wrinkled chapters littering the floor. A car door slammed. He trussed the papers and laptop together with the power cord and darted toward the studio.

The knock at the front door was oddly dull. Once he heard the muttered profanity he grinned, recognizing the voice.

"Coming!" Before opening the door, he set his bundle on the couch and locked up the studio. No point having her see it after the remodeling.

Sandra was leaning against the doorframe, hips thrust forward, balancing a crockpot. She gripped a giant bottle of dark beer by its neck in the opposite hand as though she planned to bean him with it.

"Dinner. You eat yet?"

"No—"

"Join me?" She already stepped over the threshold and out of her heels, scratching the top of one foot with the toes of the other.

"What do you have there?"

"Jambalaya. You do like jambalaya, don't you?" She had the tone of a woman who'd kick him out of his own house at a negative response.

"I meant—" he gestured at the cooker.

"It's a crockpot."

"I'm aware of that, but—"

"I leave it on at work where I can keep an eye on it. I bring it home, dinner's ready to eat."

"But it's still steaming."

"I have an adapter for the car."

"Okay…"

"Can I cook the rice real quick?" She thrust the beer into his hands and carried the machine into the kitchen without waiting for an answer. After a good two minutes of digging, she pulled out a bag of raw white rice. "Got a pot?"

Laughing would be a big mistake, but how she lost an entire pound of rice was a mystery. He wrapped one arm around her waist and reached up to the cabinet above her head, pinching the rims of two pint glasses in his fingers.

"I'll find it. Why don't you go relax? I'll be right in."

"Cook it slow or the texture will be shit. The directions are on the—"

"Yes ma'am." He kissed her temple. "Go get comfortable."

While the rice boiled, he searched every drawer for a decent tablecloth. Coming up empty, he wondered why the hell he thought he had one in the first place. Who would he set a table for? After fretting a little too long over a scratch in the varnish, he maneuvered a pile of napkins over the flaw and hoped they wouldn't reach the bottom.

He paused at the doorway before calling Sandra in. She thumbed through his vinyl collection, peeking at random covers, then selected a pale yellow one. At the touch of the needle, the air crackled and hissed. Languid horns were joined by Claude Thornhill's tinkling piano, a tune as soft as falling snow. Val forgot all about the rice watching her sway to the music, indistinct box step clumsy. Least he could do was wrap her in his arms, so he sidled up to surprise her.

She must have heard his lopsided shuffle and turned. Another plan foiled.

144

He turned up the volume and reached for her hand. "Dinner's ready."

***

With their mouths full, neither could accuse the other for the lack of conversation. Val tried to come up with a decent icebreaker. He turned his plate, pushing everything outward and leaving the center empty, stabbing along the rim. At the periphery, he saw Sandra's fork freeze in midair.

"Um—"

He cleared his throat and cracked open the beer. As he poured for each of them, a stench not unlike motor oil made him sneeze. He nearly rejected the first swallow.

"Shit."

"Yes."

"More?"

"What the hell. It's the weekend," Sandra said.

"No it isn't, it's Tuesday. Rough day at the office?"

She tore a huge chunk of andouille in half with her teeth.

"Oh."

She washed down the mouthful with a swig of beer and grimaced. "Goddamn, that Andre's a pretentious ass. He kept me waiting for *forty* minutes. I was about to go home. Then he breezes in looking like he wants to swallow me whole. When I get back to the studio, I hear from some gopher that our sweet Amber's taking over my next interview to see how she 'connects with fleek audiences.' Or some stupid shit like that." She grumbled a curse into her beer and poured another finger's worth. "All anyone wants is the latest thing."

Val cocked an eyebrow.

"Oh God...I'm—let's talk about something more pleasant. How's the writing going?"

"That's your definition of more pleasant? Don't change the subject."

"Ugh." She drained the second glass. "I feel like I'm running so fast, so hard, and all I'm doing is driving ruts into the dirt. The late hours, the early-morning starts, dealing with

145

these prima donna assholes…once upon a time I was certain I'd retire from there. Now? I'm not even included as part of the team. I'm just filling in, Amber's back-up. When did this happen? And how? I didn't even see it coming, just—" She flung her arm out in a grand sweeping gesture. Flinging her fork into the half-eaten jambalaya, she nudged the plate out of the way of her drooping head. "What are you doing this winter?"

"Sorry?"

She threw up her hands. "We're grown-ups. Let's be frivolous. Your book should be out, you'll have some free time. Let's get a change of venue."

"I don't…" Val took a quick sip of beer, then another. Longer. At his age, trying to play it cool and failing.

Graham, Calvyn, Anna—at various points throughout the years they all told him to get out of his bubble, see the world. With his status he could afford a yearlong holiday. Even exploring his own country seemed foreign. Not too long ago he'd laughed at the idea.

"Am I coming on too strong? This is a lot to take in. Isn't it."

"I haven't given it much thought."

"Neither have I. It was an impulse." But she didn't take it back.

Val waited, giving her a chance to change her mind. It would answer the question for him if she did. Then again, there wasn't a question, per se. *What are you doing this winter?* Not a goddamn thing.

He'd be published, yes, and he'd hire a marketing company if Black Horse didn't do a decent enough job. Writing could be done anywhere they sold paper and pens, if it came to that. But without a single idea in his head, the issue was irrelevant.

Sandra fingered the lip of her glass. Doodled meandering trails in the sweat. "You need a coaster—"

"Where were you thinking?"

"Under the glass."

"You know what I mean."

She screwed up her mouth. "All the places they have me go—feels like I'm never home sometimes, hunting down actors and writers, one interview after another—you remember that job I told you about, don't you?"

Val made some combination of humming, nodding, and shrugging that he never did in his life, a mishmash of vaguely affirmative responses.

"I laughed when the headhunter contacted me, it was so out of the blue. Out of curiosity I told them sure, send me the information." A smile grew from the corner of her mouth all the way across her face, light brimming in her cheeks. "They want me to come out for an interview. Mexico. Can you believe it?"

"Mexico."

"Cancún specifically. They've been following my assignments and thought I'd bring attention to Mexican artists the way they really deserve. I didn't know what to say, so I haven't called back yet. Maybe it's a cliché, but honestly, Cancún sounds like the most beautiful—are you all right?"

"Yes." Val blew on a spoonful of jambalaya. "Yes, of course."

"I said something wrong. What—"

"Don't be silly. I'm just nostalgic, I guess." If you could be nostalgic for something that never happened.

"You've been there?"

"It was a childhood fantasy. We—I never made it there, but if you put me near water I'll be happy." He smiled and gestured toward the tiny kitchen window. "No surprise."

"We can rent a boat. Spend days out there."

"Can you rent a houseboat? Save on a hotel."

"You sail?"

"No. I mean, I used to. A little. A lot of research is needed on this, clearly."

Sandra's mischievous, blooming laugh eased much of the earlier strain. Something inside opened, stretched, failed to wrap around anything tangible. He allowed her to carry him into her fantasy of living free, even if it never left the space between their lips.

147

"Listen to us—houseboats, spontaneous adventures…this is nuts. We're too old to be talking crazy like this, aren't we?" But her eyes sparkled.

The last notes of the album subsided, the needle lisping against its edge.

"You only live once."

***

The beer had grown on them both, as well as the ridiculously high alcohol content. Night hung still and quiet, with just enough of a chill to keep them from falling asleep in each other's arms. Sandra was buried up to her ankles in damp sand, the blanket covering what clothes no longer did. She promised to stay until the stars stopped looking fuzzy. He didn't warn her how long that might be.

The curve of her hip had fit solidly in the palm of his hand. When he'd pushed against her shoulder blades to feel her breasts against him he thought he'd seem crass; burying his face in her neck, inhaling the woodsy scent of her perfume, he'd worried about neglecting everything else for some platonic disappointment. Hit with the memory of their first kiss, he'd considered attempting the wine trick again, this time without the wine; despite the lilt of pleasure it elicited then, she'd probably think he was out of ideas. Which he was. Where the hell was all her brassiness then?

He'd fumbled, muttering about the lack of light, sweating from pure panic and frustration as he slowed to plan the trajectory of every touch, intent on saving every sensation to memory. Her body a maze of outlines, her mouth contradictory, demanding and fierce one minute and soft and subtle the next, she leaned back, offering herself to him. The intricate bow binding her dress seemed to mock his clumsy attempts at romance.

Finally, she'd scraped a fingernail along the front of his jeans, pressing hard against him. Tongues dancing, he inched her skirt up, pausing at an unexpected, satiny band. Her hose stopped mid-thigh, and she wore very little else. He'd pulled back, mind racing. How much of this was expectation? What was the next step at this point, or worse, afterwards?

"What are you waiting for?"

"I'm afraid of moving too fast."

"You're aware you have my ass in your hand?"

"Exactly."

"Do you think I want you to stop?" With her free hand she tugged the ribbon over her breasts, allowing the material to cascade open. She watched him with a wicked expression as he savored the view, pulling his zipper one tooth at a time, enjoying every minute of the torture. He'd been convinced the denim would rip apart by sheer will.

A faint whistle emanated with the gradual hastening of her breath, and he tried to match his rhythm to hers. For the first time in months he felt like he was home, but a static refrain kept sweeping back like the tide. *Make her remember you.*

Now, her mouth made little wet noises as she worked thoughts into words. Did she do that before an interview? She could talk the ears off the deaf and make a sailor sound like an altar boy. At least this time he knew what the questions would be.

All their talk about a trip...such things were important to think about after—this. With her, he remembered normalcy. She reminded him that at one point, the days were gloriously dull, free of the need to look over his shoulder, listen for noises that didn't exist, imagine scenarios in which he outwitted an invisible enemy. But such a commitment...and did she have a date in sight for returning? Would they spend the whole time together, book separate rooms? And that houseboat idea, what then? Those tiny living quarters, not unlike a studio apartment. Quite a leap from this house she deemed 'beautiful' at one point. Fresh air only required jumping ship.

Was she talking about riding off into the sunset? Better rein her in before another one of her impulses ran off to buy tickets without her.

"Maybe we can go someplace closer—like Canada—first."

"Meh, Canada," Sandra said, without looking up. "Hey, I owe you an apology—"

"Nonsense, it was a nice idea."

"Val. I can't think of any other way to say it but I shouldn't have peeked at—I mean, just because you had it out in the open—it wasn't my place."

It took a minute to figure out what she was referring to.

He'd left the manuscript on the couch without giving it a second thought. He noticed the bundle was undone when he'd come out of the kitchen, and a flash of anger had flared and cooled. In its place came another sensation, a calmness built on a foundation of gelatin.

"What did you see? Exactly."

"Snooping doesn't count. Forget I said anything."

Now that she'd brought it to the forefront, it felt like a test. He could have coasted along on the delusion that she hadn't realized what she was thumbing through. Or pretend she'd already dropped it from her mind. Not so long ago he fretted about her wandering around the studio, looking at everything with those eagle eyes. She hadn't even questioned his excuses tonight, accepting 'remodeling' as a reason to exit out the front door in order to head to the beach.

A wall always came down between them when the same trifecta came up: the book, the past, the connection between the two. And this time that tie was painfully obvious.

"You'd have seen it soon enough anyway."

"You remember the conversation we had after your interview? I kept trying to wheedle more information out of you."

"I gave you some good stuff, as I recall."

She adjusted her position, settling her head under his collarbone. If that were a nudge for more, she'd have to dig for it.

"Your dedications. They're beautiful."

He dipped his chin, the smile faltering. "Ah. There it is."

He kissed the crown of her head, more to cement himself than placate her. To fight the sensation of falling into a canyon.

"Anna will treasure Graham's, I'm sure."

Val flicked his hand in a gesture of helplessness. He didn't want to think about Anna's reaction, his doubts that she'd see it the same way as Sandra.

"I didn't know you had a brother. How did he—"

"Accident."

"What happened? Can you talk about it?" Sandra covered his hand with hers, thumbing the dimple of his wrist the way she had during the interview. She tilted her head, likely able to sense the same resistance. The only person left who knew about Michael was Anna. He polished off the last of the beer, swapping one bitterness for another.

He told her about his father, the construction company he built from nothing, his attempt to turn his young sons into apprentices. The desperation that for years was misinterpreted as excitement. How their mother, after her boys were supposedly asleep, rubbed her forehead in the dim light of the kitchen, punching figures into a calculator with the eraser end of a pencil, chewing her lip over the tape stuttering out the back.

"I didn't have a head for the business, any part of it, other than carving. Michael wanted to prove he could do a man's job, earn his education by trade. He talked about dropping out a hundred times. I thought it was all talk, a kid like every other who hated school. He was a natural craftsman, and I resented him for it. So I challenged him. Typical teenage hubris.

"He'd been acting so strangely for weeks—spacey, jittery, staring at nothing. Nowadays people would suspect drugs, but what could he have gotten his hands on then? In a dinky town like Kano? And all I thought was, 'all the better for me.'"

"What was the challenge?"

"There was this fancy new build, three stories, loft... would've been quite a sight. The foreman was like a grandfather to us. Trusted us, having grown up around the place, helping out whenever we could. He said, 'Sure! You boys get into the attic and secure the gusset plates—'"

151

"Um—"

"Metal reinforcements for rafters."

She nodded.

"That foreman." A short bark of laughter escaped Val's throat. "Charles Mulligan. Found him asleep at the desk more often than not. Memory worse than mine. Great with schedules though, army stock. Like a stopwatch. Taught us everything we knew. Until he couldn't anymore. The crew—they were so seasoned—he didn't mind like he used to.

"I bet Michael he couldn't install the plates faster than me, or better. That he'd do a shit job of it. I set the deadline for an hour, before the crew was scheduled to arrive. I took my sweet time, enjoying every second of him fumbling like an amateur. Turned my back on him while he worked himself ragged, trying to do every last one."

He remembered drawing lines between the foreman's office and Michael and back. Calling for help or calling it off would be the same act of chicken-heartedness. He could see this risk playing out full to its end as he scooted on his bottom toward Michael. He hovered a hand toward his belt, crisscrossed his legs tight underneath him.

"It was impossible, but Michael was a stubborn bastard. He was going too fast, lost his footing…" Val flashed his fingers open at the back of his head, then gripped his neck. "I can still hear that sound."

"Jesus. I'm so sorry."

Mulligan's office door had creaked open, the man frozen mid-stride. His protruding eyes seemed cartoonishly macabre, futile prayers rumbling like a volcano into the rafters. Still stooped, he shuffled back toward his office, cheap soles scratching against the gritty floor. There was no reason for him to hurry. A knowledge that struck Val only in hindsight.

"'Come down from there,' he'd called. Never looked up. Not that he'd have seen me anyway. 'Say goodbye before they take him.'"

Val didn't remember descending, didn't understand how dozens of people were suddenly *there,* as though they'd sensed the trouble for miles. He'd retreated on boneless legs, eyes locked on his escape route, shutting out his boss' pleas.

"It seemed the whole town wanted his head on a pike. Letting two precious kids do that kind of work unsupervised..."

Val heard the mob again, angry voices raised, disjointed limbs swinging, another kind of challenge raging through. Like any pack of wolves, they could smell fear. The cyclone of blind hatred—the pure exploding fury—unfolded inches from their spot on this beach, if only in his memory.

Wandering around in a daze, Val had eventually come to a stop at the lake beside the skiff. He fingered a matchbook in his pocket as the stern bobbed stupidly in the sunlight.

"Go on." Sandra's voice stretched thick and tight.

"All my father wanted was a son to carry on his legacy. He knew it wasn't going to be me. The dreamer, always spinning fairy tales. Michael had a brilliant mind, Sandra. Brilliant."

Filtered through murmurings of neighbors, Val learned Mulligan had once done time for possession, had slipped off the wagon at some point after his release.

"They convinced themselves it was Mulligan's idea. Mike couldn't nail two boards together until he taught him the ropes. Could've been an incredible craftsman, if only—"

"What happened to the foreman?"

He shook his head. The man he found in the woods the next day was naked, unrecognizable. "They waited until twilight. A bunch of men banded together to chase him down, torture him. I didn't see who they were. Merely a line of silhouettes. It was never reported in any newspaper. Just rumors...graphic details...but the gleeful retelling, the boastful swagger...those kept me up nights. The shit-eating grins over an act of murder.

With Michael filed away in a steel drawer, Val's mother's grief was punctuated by reminders of premonitions and warnings, layers of hatred and blame painting a pallor over the walls of the house. Overnight, the world had taken on an eerie flatness, a still life depicted in monochrome.

"I learned more from him than anyone else. If only Mike

had gotten his act together. If only they'd had time. From where I sit, we're back in Kano, we just never bothered noticing the signs."

"They're why you're writing this, isn't it."

"That's how it started, yes."

"What's changed?"

"Everything. Nothing. It depends on who you ask."

"I'm asking you."

"Then I have no answer."

Chapter Fifteen

Long after Sandra drifted off, Val slipped out of bed and stood at the windows. Gray wisps of clouds floated past, the discrepant motions hypnotic, and he felt uncertain of his proximity to earth. Moments ago he'd been soothed by the vibrations of Sandra's snoring against his back and he'd fallen into a deep slumber relieved of dreams.

He poked around for a handkerchief to wipe the sweat from his forehead and neck, but it too had wilted in the heat. Each breath was a mouthful of warm, wet sand.

Cancún.

Canada.

Shit.

Those three words chugged along like wheels on a train, hammering a rhythm inside his head. A vacation in paradise shouldn't make his stomach bounce like he was taking a spacewalk. Without having seen his former home levelled Sandra would never understand.

When he'd driven away in a '59 Nu-Klea Starlite with more rust than paint, he'd boxed up Michael and Mexico and lived the tangent. She may well suggest they visit Neptune.

Too much had happened in one night for either of them to make any decisions, the segue about that damn trip and Kano dragging them into silence. They were stuck, unable to separate but needing time apart; Val, at least, naked from the inside out. Two people used to independence somehow trying to move forward together—Sandra's dithering over his invitation to stay proved she grappled with the same disparity. Spending the night was both a great idea and a terrible one.

It could only get better, deserting her wrapped in the

sheets. Why bother writing a note to say he ran out for fresh coffee? He'd be back in a jiff. Didn't want to wake her by starting up the percolator—*don't you know how loud those are?* All perfectly legit excuses for running out the door. Literally. A man his age needed to keep active, maintain his exercise routine, or else risk growing mushy. His ankle needed to be strengthened if it was ever going to return to normal.

Though shouldn't it be by now?

The line at the coffee shop was woefully short, the morning rush over and lunch a long time coming. Would coffee stay hot on the walk home? One of those ten-cup carrier boxes would be an easy solution, if only it didn't suggest he wanted her to spend the day. He speculated how much trouble he'd be in if he dawdled over brunch but proffered a breakfast burrito as atonement. An extra ten minutes wouldn't be such a big—

"Hey!" the counterperson said, flashing a wide smile. "Aren't you that writer, um—"

"Val Haverford." A familiar voice came from behind.

Val spun before he could steady himself.

Marczek leaned back in his chair, one ankle crossed over the opposite knee, blood-red laces decorating gray oxfords. He drank from a massive cup with a thick head of foam, scraping it off his moustache by pulling his bottom teeth over. He held up one hand in greeting. "Join me."

"It really is you. Nice. What can I get you?" the counterperson prodded, clicking her nails against the order screen.

Adrenaline rushed from the pit of Val's stomach and he bounced on his heels. Six feet separated him from the answers he sought for months, eroding the edges of sleep and sanity one raving nightmare at a time.

"Sir? You're holding up the other customers." Beads of sweat from the steamer dampened her brow.

Millennial grumbling worked through the line, impatient for the old man to regain his bearings. He spat out an order of two regular coffees.

The barista placed them on the counter within seconds. No time to form an excuse. Carrying them to the stand for cream and sugar, he blanked on what Sandra took in hers. A genuine reason to stall. After drizzling half-and-half into one and stuffing his pockets with creamer tubs and sugar packets—all five colors—he pasted on a mask of cheerful recognition and headed toward Marczek's table.

One hand rested high on his lap, elbow jutting out, his badge and holstered gun on full display. He probably flashed that damn badge before saying his prayers. He looked Val up and down as though assessing for weaknesses. But these days, Val left his cane tucked between the bed and the nightstand.

"Morning." Val squeezed into a chair between the table and a bookcase stuffed with games and graphic novels. The sooner they got past the courtesy bullshit the better.

Marczek extended his hand. Despite having been wrapped around a mug of cappuccino, it was cool and clammy to the touch, with obnoxiously manicured nails. Clothes too tight, too tailored, stretching to make accommodations. Seeing the man without the haze of morphine, he was nothing more than a hipster past his prime.

"How's things?"

Val sipped his coffee to burn the edge off his tongue and glowered over the rim. He was stuck in a joke without knowing the punchline. *How's things?*

Marczek shook his head and fiddled with the flimsy wooden stirrer drying over a bed of empty sweetener packets. "Sorry, Mr. Haverford, that was glib. You leave the office awhile and forget your manners altogether."

He bent the stick, stressing the tiny fibers. His nail turned white under the pressure, a bead of blood pushing its way to the edge and receding, pushing and receding, as though his body and his ridiculous, misplaced resolve were at odds with each other. Marczek's voice was softer, slower, than Val remembered. But that Southern accent was the same kind of greasy.

"Let me start again. How is your health?"

"I'm managing."

"The ankle then, you're—"

"Fine. Right as rain."

"Good, good to hear." Marczek swirled his mug to wash down the foam, a metallic tang of fake sugar rising between them. He stared out the picture window as he drank and brightened as a cluster of kids exited a car, but his expression fell as they ran in the opposite direction.

Val removed his cup lid and blew on the coffee simply for something to do. Was it too soon to leave?

"Awkward, huh? I'm a little distracted." Turning from the window, Marczek stared straight on. "I got your messages, Mr. Haverford."

Val sputtered. "The hell do you mean? What have you been doing? Anna and I—"

"I know." Marczek bounced his hand up and down.

The hazy memory of that maneuver came rushing back, and heat flooded Val's face. The cup creased under his grip, his strength to remain impassive collapsing along with it.

"It's been hell, for both you and Miss Van Ellis, I'm sure. You want to see these people caught. So do we."

Miss. Val's stomach flipped.

"Problem is, things don't seem to be working in our favor."

"The hell does that mean?"

"Keep your voice down." The gentle tone vanished. Marczek may have been apologetic, but he was damn sure still in charge. "Let me remind you there's a statute of limitations on aggravated assault. We have three years—"

"You still don't have leads, is what you're telling me."

"There's no statute for your colleague."

"I'm aware of that. But you can't help him anymore, can you?"

"I won't pretend I know what this feels like. But we have nothing to report. They were good, Mr. Hav—Val—"

"Mr. Haverford."

"They knew what they were doing. They've been leaving you alone, and that's great, just what we predicted would happen. It also means they're not making themselves known. We don't have enough to go on to make an arrest or obtain a search warrant. We can't even be sure they're still in the area."

No matter how fast he drove that night, they were faster. They could've been lingering outside Graham's tower, lurking in the trees to watch the ambulance take Val away, could be here right now. A man in a hood would blend in like any other if he wore different clothes.

"Is there any other information you can give us?" Marczek asked.

"Such as?"

"Are you still working?"

It was Val's turn to stare out the window.

"I'll take that as a yes. Was there anyone else in your home around the time the crimes took place?"

"No." *Yes.* "Wait. Sandra Bayliss. She conducted an interview with me the week before it happened."

"I think I've heard of her. *On the Record?*"

"Yes."

"She's definitely memorable." The stirrer splintered in his hands. His stare never wavered.

"If you're trying to tie her in to this—"

"Not at all. I'm covering the bases, finding out who knows what, and when. She may have seen someone of interest, someone who seemed inconsequential at the time. A nosy neighbor perhaps, a deliveryman—"

"Nosy neighbor?" Val snorted. "That's putting it mildly."

Marczek whipped his little notepad from his jacket pocket and flipped the cover, a smooth, practiced procedure.

"Do you think he witnessed anything?"

"He lives too far away to see anything from his property. But he's always around, one way or another. I understand he called 911 for me. But he would've talked to you if he knew anything." Val raised the cup, resting his teeth against the wax lip before drinking. "Boy, he would've talked."

"Sorry, what—"

"He would've talked your ear off if he'd heard so much as

159

a sneeze."

Marczek put away the notepad and looked outside again, weaving for a better view around a charter bus. Bored or impatient? "I'll be sure to check him out."

"I can't believe you haven't already."

"Sorry? You'll have to—"

"Nothing. Mouth and brain don't always get along before breakfast," Val said, raising his cup.

"Okay, sure, sure. Look, V—Mr. Haverford, take my advice. These guys might not be causing you trouble but that doesn't mean they're not watching. I suggest leaving town for a while. Take a vacation, maybe with Ms. Bayliss. Have someone check on the place. Before you return, call me and I'll make sure everything looks fine, and you should be golden." He stuck out his hand again and waited for a response. Val anticipated the sentence would end with 'capice?' Instead, "We always look out for one of ours."

"Living in the same goddamn town doesn't make us partners. I'm not 'one of yours.' Or are you extending that camaraderie to Graham as well? Does everyone qualify or just the unlucky stiffs in your jurisdiction?"

Marczek's shrank a little inside his sports coat as he smoothed down his hair. "I don't mean to upset you. Like I said, I'll keep you posted. These boys could be anywhere, searching for a chink in the armor. Of any kind."

Empathy cracked Val's temper. If they both were in the dark, they each had equal stakes. It couldn't look good to lose a high-profile case like this, have your suspects vanish in your own community, especially where the worst crime was joyriding. At least Val had made him equally uncomfortable. Any success at this point, however petty, counted as a victory.

"Listen, I'm—"

Marczek flicked his hand and tucked a stray thread inside his sleeve. "Don't worry about it. I hate to call it PTSD or some new-age snowflake shit like that, but—" His expression brightened as he followed the paths of two bright pink patches coming around the corner.

Two little girls tumbled through the door in a flurry of sparkles and feathers. The blonde led the other—a chubby brunette buried under huge Coke-bottle glasses—by the hand. He turned quickly toward the window again and nodded at a woman with silver-white hair in an ivory suit slamming the back door of her BMW, a puff of glitter wafting into the gutter. She adjusted the silk scarf at her neck and crossed her arms, drumming her fingers against her elbow.

"Hey! How's my little Munchkin?" Marczek hoisted the blonde girl on a bouncing knee. "What happened in school today, huh? Learn anything cool?"

"We talked about what we wanted to be when we grew up! Right, Deirdre?"

Her companion didn't respond.

"Hello, Deirdre," Marczek prompted.

Deirdre grinned and waved, a joyful sound replacing a greeting. Marczek's face clouded over and he nodded, returning his attentions to his daughter as soon as Deirdre's eyes wandered.

"And what did you tell them?"

He dipped his head to hear his daughter's whispered secret. A hint of a bald spot was revealed by a wisp of black hair flopping forward. Like a widow's peak.

A man with a child, discussing the future.

Val stood abruptly, the wire chair screeching against the floor and banging against the bookshelf. "I'll leave you to—"

Marczek addressed his daughter as though Val hadn't spoken, his high-pitched tone unnerving at best. "Do you have homework, Sammie?"

"Yes daddy, coloring."

"*Coloring,*" he mouthed to Val. He pulled the wrinkled pages and box of crayons from her backpack and set them up at a table across from them. Handing his daughter a few dollars, he sent the girls to the counter for a treat.

Again, Deirdre was led by the hand, stomping more than running.

Marczek shook his head and swore under his breath.

161

"Coloring. You believe that?"

Val sighed, hoping the point would make itself known so he could escape. "Sounds typical for a child her age."

"She's almost seven. What does coloring teach you? Not a thing. Do you have children, Mr. Haverford?"

Val coughed. "Never married."

"Our greatest asset, kids."

"Guess I can't argue with you."

"Doesn't it bother you, paying taxes on schools, yet all they're teaching is *coloring*?"

"I'm sure there's more to it than—"

"Merit badges for showing up, perfect attendance…too many kids are being forgotten and lost, and learning… nothing…" He jerked his hand toward Deidre, who inched over, peering around a tower of whipped cream. He lifted her cup onto their table by the rim and shook the cream from his hand.

"I'm sorry, I think I must have gotten distracted somewhere—"

"Consider what I'm telling you, Mr. Haverford," Marczek said, the steely focus returning, a soldier for his cause. "Don't chase something that can only cause trouble. An—Miss Van Ellis' foundation is seeking to help kids—the *right* kids, *good* kids—get ahead in life, give back to society. She needs to focus on positive things, and so do you. We get ours, and we send the elevator back down. We can make sure the next generation has things even better.

"They're what's important, Mr. Haverford. Not some freak show. Isn't that what your novels are about? The fearless hero, jetting through space and time, to make the future a better place? You and I have a lot in common."

Val's stomach threatened to empty itself right into Marczek's mug.

"Since the perps are still at large, you need to watch yourself. There's no room in this world for people who take more than their fair share." His fist flexed and closed around the mug handle, eyes hardening into little black bearings. His voice had the insistent bite that comes with warnings instead of advice. "We're on the same side. Now, now, I'm not saying that to piss you off. But we both believe the same things, don't we?" The question rose sharply, as though Val's understanding meant everything. The last piece that would solve the mystery if only they had that common bond.

Shit. Val bit his lip to keep it from curling. Criminals skulked as close to Marczek's backyard—and his daughter's —as his own. The woman outside untied the silk scarf from around her neck and fanned herself with it, muttering. Her gold watch flashed as she checked how much longer their mandated visit was going to last. If Marczek was estranged from his kid, it was only natural he'd be overanxious.

"Good to have neighbors looking out for each other, I guess." Val said.

"Like the old guy to the south of you." His words were clipped, dropping as if under pressure. The boss was watching him too.

"Raymond Fellows, yes."

"Quite a fan there. Could be dangerous. You never know what people are up to when they flock to a celebrity. What was he doing there, so late at night?"

Did Marczek really believe Raymond was an accomplice? He was a frail old coot, gentle and genial and quiet. Generally speaking. Comfortable in his own right, having climbed the ranks of some banking empire back in the day, he didn't need a piece of Val's fortune.

"He stops by now and then—"

"For what reason?"

"Just to say hello, I guess. He's a little needy, tends to drive me nuts, but—"

"Don't you think that's a little weird?"

"I think it's lonely."

"You seem to have a lot keeping you busy. Reading, writing…research must take a lot of your time. Am I right? You're looking into quite a few dark corners with that project of yours."

"There's an understatement."

"But this man interrupts you a lot."

Some days were more balanced than others. Sometimes even the ill-timed chirp of a bird would send Val into a tirade, and he'd have to read entire chapters' worth of material to get back in sync. Other days he wouldn't even notice a thunderstorm passed through until he opened the door to a quarter acre of puddles. Raymond still lived in the same tiny Bible-Belt town he grew up in, where it was perfectly acceptable to appear unannounced on your neighbor's porch and stay for hours.

"Like I said, sometimes he drives me nuts. He clearly wants to sit and chat but I'm not that sort. I think he was offended I never invited him in."

"I get you. Last thing I want is someone sticking his nose where it doesn't belong."

"Daddy, no more work talk, you promised."

The little girl's voice drew an invisible curtain over their conversation. As if her mother agreed, she leaned on the horn through the driver's side window. Val's problems forgotten, the spotlight returned to this broken family and the children Marczek had an unnatural fervor to protect.

"I should get going." Val said, inching from the scene as though he'd intruded. "Be careful."

"I'm not the one who caught the eye of extremists," Marczek sneered, white fang splitting his mouth. "It's you who needs to be careful."

Hot air pushed against him as Val stepped outside. His body swung oddly as he walked home, shifting like a cheap suit that he'd thrown on and crookedly buttoned.

We can make sure the next generation has things even better.

His feet were no longer attached to his legs, but passively followed his brain's instructions.

What the hell just happened?

Marczek was failing, out of his league. He may be a good actor, but Val's attackers likely knew that's all it was: bravado. Smoke and mirrors.

Anna's foundation, Sandra's show—Val went incognito for a reason, turned away from his fans for a reason. The whole point was to change the world, at least his little corner of it. Disappearing to a foreign country would be career suicide. Marczek had him there. What message would leaving send?

At the corner, Val looked back at the coffee shop before crossing. Sunlight streaked over the windows, concealing the interior. He whipped his head around, examining everything that moved. A man across the street clipped his shrubbery into perfect domes. Clusters of women in athletic gear power-walked around teens tapping at their phones. No sign of Marczek, no telling if he was still inside or tailing him. And at this point, neither provided much solace.

Sandra was still young, whether she believed it or not. Except for the job she seemed to hate, she had no ties whatsoever. His publishing contract was the life preserver holding his head above water, the anchor holding her beneath it.

He stared at his front door, two cups in hand—now cold—contemplating a strategy for getting back in without setting them on the ground. The puzzle solved itself when the door flung open, slamming against the railing and bouncing back. Sandra held it with one hand, the crockpot balanced in the other, and glowered at him from the threshold. Her cheeks blazed.

Without a word, she clicked her key fob and stalked to her car, snatching one of the coffees as she passed.

"San—"

"Nope." Balancing the cup on the overturned pot lid, she loaded herself behind the wheel. After a second of readjustment, she threw the car into reverse.

Val hopped to the side to avoid getting flattened, and found himself standing between her headlights. He searched for a response that wouldn't make her gun the engine, and instead relied on a single shake of the head. When she didn't mow him down, he leaned a hand on the hood.

She lowered the window and folded her elbow on the sill, rolling her head enough to look him in the eye.

"I'm really bad at this."

"Tell me more."

He moved to her open window. Miles separated one word from the next, and he winced along with every stumble and hesitation. Sandra wouldn't offer many more chances, if any. Whether he deserved one now was questionable.

"It's...been...a long time..."

"I need more than you're giving."

"Listen..."

"About that job in Cancún." She looked down at the gearbox and eased into drive. A shift, a moment suspended. "I accepted the interview this morning." She grasped his hand and gave it a little shake. "Take the hint. Figure this out." Then she raised the window and peeled out onto the road, spraying wood chips against his legs.

Back inside, Val's world collapsed. Another door slamming shut, erasing sunlight with the turn of the key. The absence of her voice, the floorboards without the rhythmic tap of her shoes, the life that she stole from the house when she left it made the walls expand into a warehouse. Regret that he couldn't form an explanation before she left him for good, that it would be too late regardless and he couldn't blame her if she did, echoed off the ceiling beams. But none weighed more than the fact that he had nothing to say. Frustration mounted as Sandra's last words filled the dead air, in a quiet, halting platitude that wasn't quite her own.

Chapter Sixteen

"Thank you for coming on short notice." Anna's hair was tucked into a gray bandana, her compact body tethered in spandex. A light sheen of sweat moistened her cheeks. The scent of bottled pine wafted into Val's nose.

He wasn't sure what he expected after keeping away since the funeral. A punch to the gut, a tearful tirade—either would have been deserved. But she grinned as though it were any other afternoon. And after yesterday's fiasco with Sandra, it was a relief to see a friendly face.

"No problem, I wasn't that busy." No sense ruining it with the truth.

As she rose up on her toes for a kiss, he had to stop himself from shrinking back. Without Graham, the fine line between platonic affection and respectful aloofness blurred. At this range, he noticed her cheeks were pink from a dusting of rouge, her lips an unnatural tinge of red. She walked down the hall, beckoning him forward. He peeked over his shoulder to check if her neighbors were watching. The tacky smear of lipstick clung to his face, yet when he wiped it away his fingers came back clean.

"Want some iced tea?"

"Sure."

"Go sit, I'll get it." Her voice echoed from the kitchen. "I've been rattling around this place forever, it seems like."

The condo was littered with boxes. Some of the furniture was gone and others were arranged in new configurations. Half the artwork was propped against the walls, leaving a spray of tiny holes across the plaster. The framed photo of her and Graham on their wedding day, which used to hang in the breakfast nook on the other side of the galley, gone. Vines from hanging plants stretched across the space instead.

"I hardly know what to do with myself. I'm up 'til all hours, culling stuff from closets…it's amazing what you find when you sort through old junk." Anna placed a tray of refreshments on the coffee table. "I made enough krentenbollen to last a few years; there's no way I can eat all of it before it goes stale. Take some with you when you go? Don't let me forget."

"Sure. But I'm guessing you want to talk about something besides sweet rolls."

"I'm afraid of what you'll say. Not to mention what you'll think of me."

Val slathered a roll with butter.

"I've been in a bit of a bind since the agency was broken into."

"Do you need money?"

"No, honey, that's not why I called you here." She tapped her fingernails against her glass. "This is hard. Saying it out loud…they say when God closes a door, he opens a window, but I feel like he's slammed everything shut and left me alone."

"I'm here, Anna. And I'm in no hurry."

She took a deep breath and plowed forward. "I'm in the process of liquidating the agency. I wouldn't know how to run it, and none of us feel comfortable going back there, carrying on in that office like nothing's happened. So I'm afraid when you start writing again, you'll have to find a new agency altogether. I'm sorry, honey."

He should've seen it coming, it made perfect sense. But the fact that she'd already kicked off the process, her calmness at odds with yet another loss, gave liquidation a new meaning. His stomach turned to water as he tried to devise ways to turn back time, to grab hold of something that had already dissolved.

"Ed is behind me, as much as he can be, I suppose. Pretending everything's fine when it isn't. Babs, as usual, blames me. There's something I don't need."

"She's always been such a delight."

"I can't believe I'm going through with this. It seems any choice I make is wrong. The agency was his baby, his pride and joy. And this is how I choose to honor his legacy."

"He would do the same," Val said, so quietly he wasn't sure she'd heard.

"Leg-Up?" She frowned. "All my work, gone…like that?"

No response seemed appropriate. He had no idea what Graham would do.

"People always talk about the little details they miss, the changes in routine, after their loved ones pass on." She stirred her tea, ice clinking like wind chimes. "Have you ever built another boat?"

How dare she bring that up now. How fucking dare she. He reminded himself that the grieving didn't have much of a filter. "Never had the desire for another one."

"Sometimes this place reminds me of the helm of a ship. Remember that scene in *Titanic,* when all the water's leaking into the ballroom and everything is weightless? That's what it feels like all the time now. I think it hurt Babs to realize she'd never have that grandchild, that last thread. The anchor to keep us from feeling like we'd all just float away."

Goddamn it. Graham had brightened at the idea of a child, the mere possibility. Clearly he hadn't broached the subject with her. Timing was never the issue. But Anna couldn't have been having an affair. She wasn't the type, Val was sure of it.

He bent forward, knitting his fingers between his knees. The thick piping of the cushions pressed into his thighs. He sped through his recollections of the Christmas party like a videotape. She hadn't flirted with anyone. She played a perfect hostess: friendly, warm, just distant enough. Somewhere in his memory discordant strings crashed.

Anna tugged at his shoulder. "Listen to me. You have to let go or grief will eat you alive."

"You don't quite understand."

"I know all too well, unfortunately. Graham and I had a terrible fight the day before, and I said some unforgivable things."

"About—never mind. That's none of my business."

169

"About you, actually."

"Me? Why?"

Anna squinted like she was trying to calculate how much information to divulge. "After we visited you in the hospital, I accused him of caring more about your fiscal worth than your health. I can't believe I did that, even now. I apologized later, and I meant every word. But you can tell when you're not truly forgiven. The next few days he left at dawn. And he went to his grave thinking I had such a low opinion of him."

"He loved you too much to believe that."

"I know that now. It took a long time, some very good friends, but I pulled myself out of the hole I was lying in. Otherwise I'd never have had the strength to let go of the agency." A light flush colored her cheeks and she stared at her hands.

"I should've been there for you more. What do you need from me now?"

"Just don't disappear on me again, okay?" she asked, her voice in bad need of an oiling. Tears welled up and she clutched him around the waist.

He raised his hands in surrender before limply enclosing her in an embrace. The simplest touch a dishonorable, covetous gesture, he stiffened as she conformed to the soft contours of his body.

Before he could protest, she flinched with a pained "Oof." She extracted a fountain pen from her pants pocket and foisted it in his direction.

"You left this here at Christmas. I kept forgetting to return it to you."

Val rolled it around in his fingers as if it were made of onyx. "Guess who gave this to me."

"No way. It looks…"

"Ancient? It is. After the first film deal, Ed invited me to an impromptu celebration at their place that same night. You can guess how Babs felt about that."

"Oh, I'm sure she was ecstatic."

"Ed passed cigars to everybody, even Graham. Naturally after one quick puff Babs smacked it right out of his mouth.

Ed caught it midair, and then, I think, smoked both together."

Anna giggled, nodding, no doubt picturing a younger Ed, his grandiose personality at once obtrusive and charismatic.

"Graham was over the moon, full of admiration for these two successful businessmen, and talked about having that for himself one day." Val paused, clearing his throat. "The best part is, he was too shy to give it to me directly. Ed was the middleman."

Anna's eyes disappeared into creases. "Baloney. Graham was never shy."

"Oh yes he was, painfully so. I'm glad he finally got the nerve to talk to girls or he may never have met you. I don't think he had a date until grad school."

"You're terrible."

"I exaggerate. But only a little bit." He hefted the pen, admiring how well the inscription had held up after all this time, and clipped it into his shirt pocket.

"Why is the 'M' the largest letter?"

"He didn't understand how monograms worked, then." Val smiled widely at the memory. "He figured the middle initial should go in the middle, why not? That still makes me laugh; it's one of many reasons I can't get rid of this old thing, beat up as it is."

"He would've loved hearing that story." She held a hand to Val's face, tracing his cheekbone with her thumb. "Thank you for these memories. It's good to share them with you."

Val fiddled with his cuffs, unbuttoning and refastening.

"You know, whenever he was down, he'd call you for a drink. He knew you'd make him feel better."

Val nearly choked. "He was the most upbeat person I knew!"

"To you, maybe. I saw what you didn't see. He was jealous of you."

"Nonsense." Val furrowed his brow, unexplained anger rasping his memories. "I never saw Graham read a book, much less write one."

"Not you specifically. All of you. Artists. He spent his whole life fostering the talents of other people, he never had time to work on his own. And none of them seemed to take, God rest his soul. He took up piano, painting, sculpture, poetry, even crochet, if you can picture that. See that spot over there, above the bar?" An uneven, whitish patch disturbed the beige paint.

"Never noticed it before."

She deepened her voice in imitation of Graham. "'Anna,' he said, 'I'm going to sketch your likeness for the world to see.' When he made a mistake he'd scrub it away with one of those fat pink erasers. He took off a layer of paint, trying over and over to get it right."

"I had no idea." Anger sank out of his body like air from a balloon, shame sinking into its place.

"My goodness, all those endless hours spent at Calvyn's— what did you talk about all that time?"

"Apparently nothing worth keeping." *Probably me, my problems, my books.*

"Those years you weren't writing, he never gave up on you."

Val rubbed his stubbled face, suddenly exhausted.

"You know what? I never refilled your drink."

"Oh no, I should be on my way. I'm the designated driver." He whipped a skinny eyeglass case from his shirt pocket and slipped on a pair of distinguished copper frames. "My night vision isn't quite what it used to be."

"By the way, how's your—" Anna balled the spent napkins in her fist. "Shit."

Val laughed so hard his shoulders shook. Anna sputtered, but soon joined in until the two of them giggled like children sharing a dirty joke.

"If it makes you feel any better, I did have to drag it out of him," Anna said.

"Ah, I knew he'd tell you eventually. He couldn't keep a secret if I'd doubled his commission."

"I can't help worrying about you. You're out there in the woods, all by yourself—"

"I'm a big boy."

"I always thought that rough old place could use a

woman's touch." She reminded Val of Babs, the lilt at the end of her words hinting at a life unfulfilled.

"Mail-order brides aren't as easy to come by these days." And he'd be lucky if Sandra still wanted to speak to him.

Anna rolled her eyes. "Truthfully. How are you?"

"I'm not bad yet."

"Are you in pain?"

"No, no, nothing like that. There's just a big damn black spot in the center of everything. Lefty's not giving me much trouble."

"Is it safe for you to keep driving?"

"Well, I keep passing the test…"

"Val!" Anna punched his shoulder.

"What? If you have decent peripheral vision and thirty dollars, they send you through."

"Your jokes…I swear…"

"My doctor is leaving it up to my best judgement."

"You're not making me feel any better." She held his hand in hers, doodling in his palm like an amateur fortune teller. It felt like mosquitoes had hatched under his skin.

"I'll behave myself, I promise. Now I believe you owe me some krentenbollen."

Anna paused, then exhaled sharply through the nose and sprang off the sofa. Seconds later came the impatient zip of the roll-top bread box and the sharp snap of a paper bag. "How many do you want?"

"Did I say something?"

"No. Give me a second."

Val rose unsteadily and meandered toward the kitchen, unsure if it would be better to help or stay out of the way.

Anna jumped at his sudden presence. Her eyes darted every which way, as though he caught her putting together a package of illicit drugs.

"Oh! I didn't hear you coming. It's a mess in here. Don't look at anything." She thrust the bag into his arms, attempting unsuccessfully to prod him out of the kitchen.

"Don't be silly—"

"I'm glad you're able to take such bad news so well.

173

About the liquidation, I mean. It makes the most sense. I can channel the money into the Foundation in his memory. We can't keep holding our breath on this investigation. We need to move on. Okay?" Her smile compressed into a tight line and stabbed into her cheekbones.

"Are you sure you're okay? If I said something—"

She scratched her head, flicking out a puff of lint. "No, no, I just hate having anyone see such a pigsty. I was cleaning up before Ton—I mean, right before you came. I hadn't gotten around to this yet."

"Tony?" Val stepped into the kitchen and she obstructed his path, stowing the rolls that had tumbled out of the breadbox. She stared at the residue on her fingers left by sticky raisins, but licked it off rather than reach for the towel on the rim of the sink.

"This batch could've used a bit more butter. Next time you come I'll bake a fresh—"

"Anna? Who's Tony?" Val had the odd sensation of silt sieving through his grasp.

"Anthony. Anthony. Marczek."

Val grit his teeth. "I *knew* he was an unprofessional scumbag. *Tony.* How cozy."

Anna shifted her weight and inched along the counter, but not before Val spied the extra coffee mug and egg-stained plate resting in the basin.

"Jesus fucking Christ, Anna! What's it been? Two, three months?"

"Six. Six months, Val."

"That bastard is the special friend you were talking about?"

"You don't understand—"

"You're damn right I don't. How long did he wait? Or did he move in on you as soon as the services were over?"

"He's not like that." The music in her voice blasted the last remaining scrap of Val's sanity. "He reminds me a little of—"

"*Don't.* Stop right there."

"What do you expect me to do? The walls are closing in on me. You don't know what it's like to be alone!"

"You're right, I have no idea."

"You're a committed bachelor and always will be. That's not my fault."

"At least I didn't hop into bed with the first person who offered me a shoulder to cry on. Of all the people—talk about honoring his memory." He regretted that comment even before it left his mouth.

"I needed someone to help me through this, and God knows it wasn't going to be you. He's the one who convinced me to liquidate, donate the money. Graham will have a wing named after him! He looked out for me. As usual you weren't around when I needed you most. But then you had a lot of practice."

Val inhaled through his teeth. "Wow, that was low."

He focused instead on her pink and gray running shoes, one foot tapping the linoleum. He wasn't sure whose shaky breath filled the space where there should've been reparations. He let Graham down, again. Over the ringing in his ears, the broken tin of her voice, he heard her next comment very clearly.

"Get out of my sight."

The door closed and the deadbolt clicked into place. Despite the cavern she gouged into his chest, it hurt more to know she needed a barricade between them. Val stabbed the elevator call button, growing angrier every second he stood there like a fool. The doors gaped open, waiting to give him the bum's rush.

Slamming the bag across the passenger seat, he peeled out of his tight parking spot, weaving through the side streets until he hit Lake Shore Drive. The lights from dozens of skyscrapers dispersed, one becoming indistinguishable from the next.

The day swirled into an incoherent blur, fracturing into bits and pieces. Who threw the first barb? An hour earlier they were laughing, trading bittersweet stories, and somewhere it all turned to shit. Trying to figure out the exact moment was impossible. It was something he did, or failed to do. He wasn't sure who he was angrier at.

175

He had a vague obligation to return home, but the desire to put distance between himself and it was stronger. He'd rather be hypnotized by white lines flashing beneath his wheels, preferred to drown his thoughts with the hum of the motor. No torch singer could fill the silence this time.

Before he could orient himself he was crossing the Skyway, without any recollection of exiting the Drive. The stately elegance and personality of Chicago was replaced by imposing smokestacks and skeletons of architecture and industry, a burning crematorium even at this hour of twilight. Panoramic postcards he'd tacked up in his childhood bedroom may have loaned him part of his dream, but being here, a footnote among the giants, was more stunning of a piece than he'd imagined then. Graham understood that more than Ed ever had, his heart powered by that same churning, terrified it would stop if no one was there to listen. Ed never understood what it felt like to drown.

Val turned toward home in the wee hours. He barely gathered enough momentum to drag himself from the car. Rounding the cabin, he shambled through the sand and splash of turgid waves, and pitched the bag of krentenbollen in, turning his back as it slowly disintegrated.

Chapter Seventeen

Anna's leg twitched at every noise, from the chafe of shoes against the berber carpet to the clatter of the communal coffee pot. Sounds she never noticed on any other day.

Idle hands are the devil's workshop...

But every word she typed came out gobbledy-gook, spell check squiggles making a mess of the page.

Policy wasn't her job, but at that moment, she wished she had some experience. With any luck, Tony would set the tone of their conversation. She felt the weight of the angel and devil on her shoulders, only she didn't know which was which. Her minister offered no help, although she omitted more details than she gave when she asked for guidance. Advance directives contradicted with the teachings, in a way, but what about charity? One could not exist without the other in Leg-Up. Then again, offering charity to only a select few...where did that fall on the sin scale?

She sensed Sammie's voice before she heard it, the quick patter of inexpensive sandals giving the child away. Before Anna could stand up to greet them, Sammie's pigtailed head bounced into her office, her little arms reaching out for hugs.

"Miss Annie!"

Always irritated that the girl never learned her name properly, Anna didn't let it show. They only saw each other every few weeks when Tony had custody, sometimes less. He tended to drop by the condo after his hours with her were over.

Tony shrugged at Sammie's error, his grin guilty. Anna lifted the child onto one knee with an exaggerated grunt, overplaying how big the little girl had gotten since the last time.

"You're almost old enough for college."

Sammie tipped her head back against Anna's collarbone. "Silly. I'm graduating second grade this summer."

Tony rolled his eyes. How he hated awards for being a kid. She'd heard it a thousand times. Graduation parties for each grade, trophies for participation, telling everyone they're amazing and beautiful when that simply wasn't true. Unique, certainly. Cute, often. But five-star compliments on a thoroughly average child set them up for disappointment down the line, when overly opinionated in-laws, slave-driving bosses, and nonstop social media commentary told you otherwise.

Her thoughts drifted to Val and their *discussion* a few days ago. How critical acclaim caused so much pain, followed by and endless chase for more. An addiction. And Graham, who never chased a darn thing, yet—

"Anyway." Anna interrupted Tony, his mouth puckered mid-sentence, but she hadn't been listening. "Your daddy tells me you want to be a nurse when you grow up."

Sammie nodded so hard her pigtails flailed like broken blades of a windmill.

"Do you know I work for a program to help kids get jobs like that?"

"Some kind of special ed."

"Right. Your grades are pretty good, and since you know what you want to be already, you're further along than a lot of other kids your age. If you're accepted into the Leg-Up program, when it's your turn to get a job, you'll be ahead of the game."

"Isn't that like cheating?"

Tony looked away to hide his annoyance, but his moustache twitched with amusement. Sammie might not be the best at schoolwork, but she was sharp, quick. Other kids might just go along, while Sammie used her brain. You don't let that kind drift away.

"Not at all, Munchkin. Think of it more like a gift. Mommy and I give you gifts sometimes when it's not your birthday or Christmas, right? This is the same. Only this present will help you when you grow up, so people will see just how valuable you are, and the world will be a better place. You'll be giving to people instead of taking."

"Okay." Sammie shrugged in an exaggerated way. "Now what?"

"We fill out some papers for you, and after school three days a week you come here to learn some advanced things. About what it's like to be a nurse. We'll—"

Anna wasn't sure how much information to give. She sounded less guiding than pushing, living someone else's life for them. Tony's divorce darkened his view, always talking about the security of Sammie's future as if the break-up spelled disaster for her, their rift a literal chasm she'd fall into. "Plenty of bums on Wall Street used to work at the board of trade," he'd mutter, getting wheezy deep down in his chest.

But he cleared his throat at Anna's hesitation, raised his chin in a gesture suggesting she continue. If his ex hadn't quit Leg-Up months after training, maybe she'd be stuck having this conversation instead.

"We'll teach you a little bit about how to make your dream come true, and what that means for you when you're *all* grown up."

"Don't I just become a nurse and that's it?"

"We mean…after that."

"After?"

Language, that was the problem. Not the plan, the explanation. They didn't invent good words for this sort of thing, not for kids. How to explain the way grandparents signed papers giving up their chance to go home?

Tony should have waited until she was older, started college, when this would be explained during the natural course of study. No one needed to think about it at seven years old. He had some weird ideas of what was important.

Or was Anna's fumbling based solely on the strained look on Tony's face confirming that she failed?

"We—hope you'll be a good nurse for many years—"

Anna's parents had waited too long, left her sorting

179

through papers and red tape after their car accident, having no advance directives to reference. She'd watched life slowly slough away from her old man's brittle hands, lingering on the precipice of death for months. Watched money drizzle from their account like water down a drain. If he'd only worked things out beforehand, talked about it so she'd know what to do. Yet for years after they were finally dead and gone, Anna stalled the same way about her own future, convinced Death hovered greedily, ready to swoop down and collect her as soon as she signed the papers. As though she were giving God permission. Such thinking went against all tenets of her faith but she couldn't get away from the feeling that her skin was a size too big.

Tony, speaking as plainly as he'd list his weekend errands, explained this process was as natural as filling out tax forms. More, even, since God didn't create taxes. There were only two things certain in life, after all; at least one you could control. No raping of your dignity by the government, no overextended hospitals keeping the generator going. Until they decreed euthanasia as an acceptable practice—

"Can Deidre come too?"

"Who?" Anna didn't remember hearing that name before. It brought unnecessary discomfort, a fear she couldn't define.

"No, Munchkin, she can't," Tony answered.

"Why not?"

"She's not as smart as you," he said curtly. At her downcast expression, he got down on one knee so he could look both of them in the eye. "Only a few kids can get in every year. We can't get greedy or that wouldn't be fair to kids who've earned it, right?"

"Guess so."

"Fantastic! It's settled then." He rubbed his hands together like warming them before a fire. Holding Anna's arm, he bounced onto his heels before straightening, favoring his good side. The left hip did not appreciate certain positions, but he'd die before letting anyone else find out.

"Anna will sign you up. It's like a special club. It lasts all the way until you're no longer able to work. And when that happens, your future will be all taken care of, sweet and easy, just like a good girl deserves."

Anna swallowed. She set Sammie on her feet and fanned the pages on her desk that told her short little life story. Her better-than-mediocre grades, her general interest in nursing, her empathy toward those that Tony called 'needy.'

Anna's mother, merely a shell after the accident, doing menial tasks in the dayroom; the nurses fawning over every sorted paperclip as though she were categorizing rare gemstones. As she sat smiling at everything and nothing, empty head spinning lies.

That would not happen to Sammie, not while they could help it, not while they had this society to make sure people lived a life full of worth and meaning. Nurses could actually *nurse* instead of babysit. So families could say goodbye when there was time, instead of waiting for life to take it from you, leaving everyone else to foot the bill.

This was the Lord's work, every minute of it, seeing that a young member of his flock was looked after so early. No scary waivers signed by proxy, nothing explained now that didn't need to be. And once Sammie was taught, in pure scientific terminology, just what those end years would look like, she'd have the peace Anna did not.

Chapter Eighteen

Val tugged at his suit. The thinnest shirt he owned was imprisoned beneath it, the wool coat already a burden. Sweat beaded around the over-starched collar. The sleeves had been shortened to fit properly again, but now the whole costume felt a size too small. He bounced his shoulders up and down and shook out his arms, trying to straighten the seams and creases. And after tying and retying the silk millstone half a dozen times, it resembled a dirty pile of leaves.

"Fuck this."

Ripping the tie off, he unfastened the neck and next two buttons. Life was too damn short.

If only he could persuade his stomach to settle. Three days ago, he'd pored over every word of the last chapter in a caffeine-fueled frenzy, tweaking until he could hum its tune, from the top notes down to the bass vibrating the floorboards.

The familiar satisfaction of completing a manuscript comingled with the melancholy of having the journey nearly over with and, as he suspected, nothing more in his head than a period at the end of a sentence. He'd forgotten what this brand of uncertainty was like. He'd always had some other project to immerse himself in, mind exploding with plots, keeping the anxiety at bay. Torture couched in madness.

After way too much procrastination, he'd mustered enough courage to call his publisher cold, hoping it wouldn't seem completely unexpected. Though they were accommodating enough, they didn't understand that 'trust' no longer existed in his vocabulary. He ignored the attitude, the obvious infringement on their time. No way in hell he was signing a new contract electronically, or even entrusting the post office to deliver a hard copy. He was going to meet the people who would hold his manuscript in his hands, memorize what they looked and sounded like, no matter how precious it made him seem.

But flying out to Manhattan, even for an afternoon, was also an excuse to stall. These characters were resurrections, a farewell he wasn't ready for. Until this small reprieve, he didn't realize how much weight had sardined into his chest. He itched to call Sandra and tell her the good news, but he had another meeting to deal with first, and he'd rather use her as a reward. Assuming he could produce an adequate apology first, and the span of a few days was enough time to cool off...

This was going to be a long couple of days.

The article about Andre Wallace wouldn't leave him alone. It was so immaculately worded the depth of meaning was scrubbed clean, and the incident seemed to have been erased from the city's collective memory. He stared at a photo of the man until he could stop sneering in distaste.

***

"A visit from Val M. Haverford. Well I'll be damned. I thought that phone call was a prank. I was reading you when I was a kid!" Andre stood barefoot in the doorway, squinting up at him.

"Is that right?" Pride had a chalky, bitter taste.

Andre led him down a creaky hallway lined with family portraits into a little garden at the rear of the house. He sat in one of two white, cast iron chairs beside a matching table holding a sweating pitcher and glass of lemonade. Shrubs and bushes in various states of bloom choked the courtyard. The oppressive scent of flowers surrounded them, the individual perfumes impossible to recognize. The musty funk of an oncoming storm hung in the air. Andre gestured impatiently toward the other chair.

"I loved your classic style of writing. Old-school. You were a real mage of the English language; made me want to be an astronaut when I was coming up. Imagine what it felt like to be named the next you in the *Chicago Lit Review*! Did you see that?" His coarse guffaw chopped through the warm air like an axe. "I suppose I owe you a debt of thanks." Andre took a large sip of his drink and poured Val half a glass.

"I appreciate it but—"

"Your call came as a surprise. What do you need?" He pitched his head and bottom lip forward, flicking his hand, eyebrows peaking. He was the master of subtlety in his novels but that trait didn't come naturally in life.

"I was having problems with a project, and I think it's because of—"

"What kind of problems?" Andre grinned and lounged back.

"Honestly, I hadn't had so much trouble with a novel since my college days. Before I decided to stop, I sometimes wondered if I knew what I was doing anymore, if any of it made a lick of sense," Val said, the words lumbering through an obstacle course.

"We all feel that ennui sometimes. But you have to push past it, write every day, whether you're in the zone or not. You can't wait for the muse to come to you."

"Yes. Right. Not quite what I'm getting at." The lemonade went down like duct tape. "I heard about your unfortunate conflict recently."

"Got out of that neighborhood real fast. Should've done it long before, but now that I can afford it…" He swept an arm outward as if preparing to gather up his recent good fortune for an embrace.

"Do you mind if I ask you a few questions about that night? You're probably aware I experienced—"

"Right, somebody nearly choked the life out of you too!" Again with that laugh. "Is that what fans are doing these days? Used to just hide in the bushes to take a picture of you coming out of the shower."

"I have some theories. What's most upsetting is there are no leads on my case. My friend was killed and though all signs point to the same perpetrator, the detective in charge insists they have no hard proof."

184

Andre twisted at the curly hair spiraling from his loosely buttoned shirt.

Val continued, "All I know about what happened to *you* is what I read in the newspapers, and they print very few details these days."

"That all depends on where you live. But let's not get into aberrations. What do you want to know?"

"I heard it happened here, while you were alone—"

"Well, not *here,* at my former place." He punctuated the sentence with a sharp rap of the glass on the armrest. "People get violent there more often than they change clothes. And I wasn't alone. My wife and older kid went visiting and I stayed home with my baby. They weren't gone more than ten minutes before somebody tried to strangle me with a wire."

Val sat forward, knitting his fingers together.

"He was going on about the novel I was writing. I'm sure you've read about it in the *Trib*, the *Sun-Times*, the *Reader*..." Andre rotated his wrist, two fingers drawing circles in the air. "Told me to shut it down, destroy it. Didn't need to tell me twice. I know how to play the game." His intense stare softened and drifted to a wilting peony bush. The set in his jaw said he'd learned the rules far too young.

Val realized he was staring slack-jawed at the complete nonchalance of that admission. "You didn't have a problem deleting—"

"You ever get an idea while you're in the middle of an inchoate work, Mr. Haverford? Another one enters your subconscious, just like that, when you least expect it. Happens to me *all* the time. So I write it down. Another and another, again and again, I write them all down. At the end of a week I have a notebook brimming with ideas, more places my imagination will take me. I didn't need a book like the one you're writing." He turned his head slowly back in Val's direction, maneuvered his hand into a C shape, and volleyed it back and forth. "I had a stack this thick."

Blinking usually takes a fraction of a second, but in this case Val made an exception. He wished the lemonade had a shot in it.

"Family is everything to me," Andre continued. "When you have a wife like I have and kids like mine, none of that other stuff matters. My baby even saved my life. Can't wait to tell him that story when he's grown."

Val couldn't help raising an eyebrow. "Your *baby* saved you?"

"Right. I could barely breathe. Had that wire wound tight…" He took a swig of lemonade, drawing his lip back from his teeth. He mumbled the next line, seemingly in disbelief. "Short little man, too. Saw his reflection in the window—"

"You saw him?" Val sprang forward. "What did he look like?"

"No, I saw his *reflection*" —another clank of the glass— "and it wasn't clear enough. Just a short, white man with dark hair. If it wasn't for my baby squalling—anyway, he took off running, but not before cracking my skull with a bat."

"I'm glad you weren't seriously injured." Val picked up his glass and set it down again.

"Something else on your mind." Andre twisted the wrist with the watch as though burdened by its heft.

"There's a pattern…something's off."

Andre's brows creased above thoughtful eyes, but his mouth ticked up, bemused. The concerned look given to men deep in their dotage, telling stories that may or may not have happened.

"What sort of pattern?"

Humor the coot; get on with the day. Val pretended not to notice. "We were both attacked, over similar novels, with the same type of weapon, and the police have no idea who did it. Don't you think it's odd?"

"Another ersatz conspiracy theory? Violence and reason are rarely bedfellows."

Val shook his head, sick of the dismissiveness, sick of his inability to see clear. Another question, another push, would drive a wedge between them where none existed beyond the one in his mind. "What about the results of your case? Did they find who—"

186

"No. Just like yours." Andre gripped the clawed ends of the armrests and his sturdy, neckless frame seemed to stiffen and expand. "Really want to know what I think? There is no pattern. There was no blizzard the night I was attacked. In fact, it was early evening in springtime. And I lived in a shack off a busy strip, not in some secluded suburban beach house. Yet not a shred of evidence anywhere. One meticulous deranged fan, wouldn't you say? Only I wonder what would've happened if I refused to stop writing *my* book. Would that degenerate have gone so easy on me? Waited for me to make up my mind?"

Val stood to go. "If I made you uncomfortable with these questions, I apologize—"

"If?" Andre chuckled, but there was no joy in it. "You enjoy reliving it all those nights alone in the woods?"

***

Val fumbled with his car keys, scraping the paint on the door before getting it open. He no longer recognized the world around him, the Wright-inspired homes as surreal as any Martian habitat dreamed up after a night of wild sketching. He slumped, defeated, behind the wheel. The mid-morning heat had roasted the interior.

His skin crawled the way it had as a boy when he sensed an imminent beating, trouble he couldn't pin down and couldn't predict. He felt raw, hyperaware of every crease in his suit, the angle of every bone, every muscle, the hair on his neck bristling. The answers blinked red outside his line of vision, and when he glanced in their direction, they disappeared. At one point he'd twisted himself into knots over being left in Wallace's dust. What he wouldn't do to erase their conversation and return to that position, clammy with anxiety over extraterrestrial unknowns and simple fusions of words.

He blasted the air conditioner and snatched the map from the glove compartment, figuring the best route to Midway Airport. He was as confident about his internal compass as anything else these days. Spreading the map against the steering wheel, tracing with one taut finger, its thin lines bounced and twisted every which way.

Idiot. This is what smart phones are for.

Before he could open the app, his phone trilled with the riff he assigned to Sandra's numbers.

"Val! You busy?"

Not long ago, he would've jumped at the chance to talk to her, be with her, but there was no time, not now.

"Actually—can it wait a little bit?"

He thought he heard her swear under her breath. "What's 'a little bit?'"

"I have a meeting with Black Horse. And I have you to thank. But I can be—" The phone clicked. *This again?* Fat clouds threatened to eclipse the sun but only a light breeze ruffled the bushes. "Sandra? Are you there?"

"I'm here."

"You sound like you're in a cellar."

"That's not far from the truth. I need to see you right away. How long will you be?"

"Everything all right?"

"I came across something odd and I want your take on it."

Another click. "Are you hearing that?"

"What?"

"Never mind, forget it. If all goes well, I should be back in town around seven."

"Come straight to my place, okay?"

"Sure. I'll call after we land." After the third click he had half a mind to throw the damn thing out the window. *How could a two-year-old phone be obsolete?* He shut it down and tossed it into his portfolio instead.

He peeled onto the street. Pieces of the puzzle floated in and out of the ether until he couldn't see which ones were missing, and he couldn't make sense of the rest. About a month ago, he saw that article at Calvyn's. Two seasons had gone by since Graham was taken. No one had laid a hand on Val in that time. *It's over.* Sandra was in his life. Somewhat. Anna was getting hers back on track, however recklessly. *It's over now.* Those words had a beautiful ring. Yet he didn't quite believe them.

Anna. He wanted to shake her until she came to her senses. That manipulative prick must be quite the guy if she could look past everything and—

The very idea made him nauseous.

Six months had passed in a blink.

The circuitous main road ended at a T-junction. All he had to do was make a U-turn and race to her condo. He could figure out how to fix things on the way. But the chance *he* would be there, alone with Graham's wife—and her cheap shot stuck like a dagger in his side, tearing a new fissure every time he breathed.

A black coupe approached from behind, pulling up close. Val turned right. Anna could wait. This meeting—and Sandra —could not.

Midway Staffing Agents—a sandy brick box halved by a layer of grimy windows—emerged meekly behind a wide lawn. He must've tapped the wrong entry on the map.

Looking up through the windshield at a roar over his head, he caught sight of the underbelly of a plane. Considering its proximity to the ground and the name of the agency, the airport must be close.

The road narrowed to one lane, leaving no place to turn around. Grim, outmoded houses, relics of a bygone era of pensions and war bonds, defined the neighborhood. Towering oaks lurched with intensifying wind. The sky and clouds melded into a dense mat, so heavy he felt he could wrap his fingers around the edge and peel it back, revealing an unpolluted blue that went on for miles.

Overgrown branches swept at the road, which rose sharply to a splintered wooden bridge. A single traffic light dictated which direction was allowed over at one time. Beneath the eroding asphalt and ash-gray beams, four rusted train tracks stretched along a gravel bed. At the green light, Val inched over the bridge. A freight train bore down underneath, whistle screeching at nothing, its speed and weight rattling the ancient structure. Raindrops pounded one by one, each a dramatic swan dive, before collectively bombing the neighborhood. Val swung wide at the first intersection and headed the way he came, hoping the rain wouldn't delay his flight.

The light on this side blazed red. He modified his directions while he waited. Three miles away. Still enough time. He tossed the phone in the cup holder.

Closing his bad eye, he massaged with his thumb until it watered, pleading *just this once*. This was not a good time or place to get stuck navigating around a black disc. But the more he tried to ignore the splotch, the more it elbowed for attention.

The black car from the T-junction crested the bridge. Slowing to a near stop, the driver's smoke-tinted window lined up with Val's.

The outline of a gray hood flashed under a bolt of lightning.

No face.

Val's heart stopped.

The driver surged ahead.

Val checked the rearview at the sound of tires squealing. The coupe made a U-turn and gunned the engine. Val slammed the gas, undercarriage scuffing the asphalt. The coupe rammed him at the summit, sending him airborne.

The impact brought his chin into the steering wheel. His cell phone bumped out of the cup holder. Crashing into the wheel well on the rear passenger side, Val fishtailed, overcompensating. He lifted his foot off the gas as the coupe skidded into Midway's lawn and spun its tires in the mud. Stomping the gas again, Val hydroplaned for hours before shooting forward.

The neighborhood was backwards. Nothing looked familiar.

He heard the gunning engine again and veered right at the junction, hand slipping on the slick of blood on leather.

A motorcyclist approached the intersection from the right, bent against the rain, missing the stop sign.

No time to hit the brakes.

He punched the horn. The motorcyclist raised her head. Jerked the handlebars.

Val swerved, clipping the opposite curb, missing her by inches.

Another squeal of tires skidded sharply, followed by a piercing scrape of metal as the two vehicles collided.

Bought a couple seconds.

His stomach twisted, horrified at that affirmation.

Checking the rearview, a jumble of detritus trailed down the road and into the trees. The coupe had only slowed, careful not to do more damage to its own tires, and steadily picked up speed. Val couldn't see the motorcyclist.

A quick glance told him his phone hadn't landed on the floorboards. Probably got stuck between the passenger seat and door. Couldn't remember the name of the street he was on anyway, even if he could dial 911 without taking his eyes off the road.

She was probably fine. Someone had to have seen that.

Forgive me.

The expressway ramp came into view and he floored it. Weaving between cars on either side, he shoved guilt beneath the wheels. A blue sign pointed out the exit to the airport. An ocean of rain poured down.

Rush hour was just getting underway. The road ahead yawned open for a good half mile with a tangle of red lights beyond.

High beams of the other car winked in and out of his rearview. A van in the far left lane pulled nearly even with Val's, only a few feet from a Mack truck. Yanking the wheel, Val flew across the road and cut in front of the van, causing the poor bastard to slam on the brakes. Relief lasted until the driver lay on his horn for a full ten seconds, broadcasting Val's location. He whipped his head around to check every angle, convinced the black car could miraculously squeeze between the lanes and crush him between its wide metal grille and the concrete barrier.

He jumped at a fat drop of blood hitting the back of his hand. Pressing his handkerchief against his chin, the pain brought three truths into focus: his logic was fucking ridiculous, his Evel Knievel antics very nearly made him a permanent a fixture to the truck's cargo doors, and catching his flight was out of the question. If they spotted him on the off-ramp, they'd just follow him to the airport parking lot. All those empty cars, very few witnesses...and even if he ditched the car at the nearest gate and somehow avoided security, there's no way he could outrun the man in the hood.

Traffic came to a complete stop. Val's stomach vanished. He joggled his hand against gearshift. He couldn't distinguish the face behind the wheel. Never got a license number.

The hooded man would expect him to head home. Calvyn's was out; anyone who knew him knew how often he dropped in, drinking until inspiration hit.

He'd have to find somewhere bustling with the life of the city, loud and ancient and gritty, where no one would expect him to be. Someplace where if he shouted for help, the entire block would hear it. The opposite of home.

There used to be a B&B on the South Side. After bouncing from blues bar to blues bar in his college days, he stayed overnight when he was too far gone to navigate the train lines.

Tailgating at top speed, stiff and refusing to blink and fighting the urge to get out and run, punished him as though he'd been beaten. Heat and tension threatened to knock him out, but the tremors pinballing through his body felt like they'd keep him awake for days. He eased off the gas as a massive underpass swallowed the gridlock. Crawling through the dim tunnel was both a nightmare and a blessing as each car became an indistinguishable part of the creeping mass.

Traffic spread past a stall on the narrow shoulder. Switching lanes, he flew across the widening road to the first exit and whisked through the South Side, rain battering his windshield and roof like machine-gun fire.

The tract wasn't nearly as colorful as his memory insisted. No more music clubs, no more vibrant nightlife. Abandoned stores stood amid gutted gothic fortresses, windows long ago destroyed. Bare lawns glittered with shattered glass. Rickety structures struck out of vast lots of overgrown weeds and rubble. Children darted up the sagging porches, ducking under broken eaves and graffitied doors. Doorways shrank behind gates secured with padlocks bigger than fists.

Handmade markers hung from lampposts and chain link fences, shouting tearful epitaphs that would soon be torn off by officials hell bent on keeping the city pristine. The rust-brown stains on the sidewalk would never be erased by rain.

Dangling from corroded hooks, Lucille's B&B still advertised vacancy in flickering red lights. A slanting carport ran the length of the building, and Val pulled in as quickly as the narrow passageway allowed, clicking his door quietly shut. He stared out from the shadows, crouched at his front bumper, trying to come up with an escape plan if the black coupe spotted his license plate from within the depths.

He had none.

The cooling engine ticked down seconds, then minutes. His joints seemed to freeze in place.

Convinced he'd lost the coupe, he squeezed around his car and onto the sidewalk, listening for screeching tires. The hangdog expression of a man about his age stared at him from a memorial poster twist-tied to a support post. The carport's corrugated plastic roof lent an eerie, greenish cast to the poster's loose cellophane wrapping, but Val could still read the messages of love and of fury at a life cut short.

Rain buzzed off the carport in hard streams, drilling holes in the mud. Cold water sluiced into Val's collar. Struck by the thought that this man died right *here,* on this corner, Val glanced down the block looking for others. The picket fence enclosing the B&B's yard was lined with posters; a vigil for a neighborhood of lost souls.

Val dragged up the B&B's splintered, rotting steps bolstered by braces and chipped, uneven bricks. Flanked with scaffolding from the second floor to the roof, the wood siding faded to a yellowed gray like week-old bruises.

He had no problem getting a room. Night settled quicker on this part of town.

The door stuttered open, metal hinges pealing. Water-damaged wallpaper, rank with humidity and age, bubbled and hung from the plaster. A dingy floral canopy sagged over the four-poster bed.

After locking himself in, he remembered his phone lost somewhere in the car. He picked up the vintage handset on the nightstand and was relieved for the chance to apologize to a nameless Black Horse receptionist, agreeing to whatever rescheduling she suggested.

He treaded new paths in the bare floor, every muscle wound to capacity. Fact and fiction contorted into one massive beast, feeding off his ignorance and incompetence.

At least one of the men who attacked him and Graham was still in town, watching his every move. Graham's office was destroyed in exactly the same way as the studio. Whoever murdered him called to make sure the extent of his determination was fully understood. Val was certain the gravelly inflection belonged to the same man who attacked him. They gave him a chance to stop writing but he refused. But they had no reason to go to Graham's office to finish the job; killing Val in his own home would've eliminated the risk of witnesses. They'd broken in before without the neighbors noticing, why not try again? With his injuries and that damn walking boot, it would've been no contest. They must've known he'd be at Graham's, but how? Graham was always so discreet. He never disclosed—

That goddamn intern. He leaked all those spoilers in December. Was he divulging notable visitors like some amateur paparazzo? Graham refused to reveal the kid's name. Loyal to the end.

The internet was populated by sick people. Somebody got the wrong idea, like Marczek said, and decided to take their obsession a little too far. Stories like that were reported all the time, especially by young fools who believed the web made them anonymous.

Val had to find out the intern's identity. But what if security refused to let him in the Van Ellis suite? Could a guard be bribed? He tried to recall the name of that sweet receptionist. If she still had a key—

They had a keypad security system. And Graham had given him the code, saved on his voicemail from months ago.

But he couldn't risk opening his car door at this hour, lighting up the carport like a beacon. It would have to wait until morning, when he was just another guy going about his business. When every car slowing past didn't make him jump, every tick and scrape didn't signal a faceless, hooded man popping up in the unlit hallway.

The next morning couldn't come soon enough.

Chapter Nineteen

Gambling that his car was more recognizable than himself, he walked toward the Red Line platform two blocks away. On first glance, Val looked like another businessman on his way to a meeting. But the unsteady feeling stayed with him, his body and mind off-kilter, sound and picture out of sync. Heat and adrenaline had woven into the dank folds of his suit.

Remembering Sandra far too late, he'd left a message on her cell during one of the many times he jerked awake. He sputtered some sleep-laden excuse and a vague promise to see her. The rest was lost to exhaustion and defeat.

Nothing mattered but finding out the truth, even if it meant he was crazy. The answer was tucked among Graham's old files. Assuming Anna's crew hadn't emptied Van Ellis & Associates by now.

From his vantage point outside the tower, Val saw the daytime security guard at her front desk post, the glut of morning traffic impeding her senses. She waved to everybody, paying little attention to the masses racing in and out. Tucking into the throng, Val slipped into the first elevator, breathing only after the doors banged shut.

When the last person stepped out at the eighth floor, Val tapped 12. The doors remained open. He pushed and held the button. Nothing. Jabbing at hummingbird speed, the doors slid closed, but the car descended. He quickly pressed 11, and at the seventh floor, the car paused and climbed.

Of course. The building owners must've locked the control panel to prevent random people from exiting on the floor of a crime scene. The only option was to walk up and hope no one locked the stairwell door.

Every step echoed off the walls like beats on a tin drum. When he reached 12, he stopped before turning the knob. What if Anna was on the other side, packing up? Would she trust a moving company to deal with everything unsupervised? Was it against the law to enter a building you had a code for? He had no explanation for being here. Blood pounded in his ears. He cracked the door wide enough for a peek.

Empty.

Perfect.

Opposing picture windows plunged the suite in ethereal blue light. The keypad glowed yellow beside the glass doors. Val pulled out his phone. Slipped it back in his pocket.

He didn't need to listen again, just a minute to think.

8-5-1-2. He'd have bet good money.

The alarm system droned, flashed red and held, along with Val's breath, before returning to yellow.

Wrong.

Risking exposure and detainment, one pane of glass away from a breakthrough, and he was defeated by a four-digit number. One Graham had trusted him so implicitly with, tossing it in his direction without a second thought. Yet within the span of only six months' time—

He pattered the keypad's rubber-sheathed buttons, prodding his memory. Random numbers bounced around his head, refusing to be caught. He weighed whether to attempt a different combination, but too many false attempts might lock the thing down permanently, alert security.

Val clawed the alarm system's casing, clammy fingers slipping off the curved plastic.

Idiot. What are you going to do, hot-wire it?

That voicemail was the only way in, the only solution.

He pulled out his phone and scratched at the power button.

What was the last thing they said to each other? He just needed a little something—anything—to brace himself with. A spoonful of sugar before the bitter pill. Time heals all wounds.

After fumbling in the password to his voicemail, he

switched to speakerphone. That little bit of distance would make all the difference, the code drifting up loud and clear while the rest of the message remained blissfully incoherent.

This is no time to be sentimental.

He didn't remember Graham's initial frustrated sigh, a hiss through ether. Val's throat collapsed and stuck like a wet balloon. Graham's rasping "Hey…" echoed through the hall, and he spun, dropping the phone, expecting to see that crooked shit-eating grin one last time. But Val was alone, wandering, killing time before a meeting that would never take place. Searching for a place he'd never find. A museum that vanished behind an eruption of high-rises. A boy with a nebulous warning and a broken, swaying street performer tapped a hole into his chest, wide enough to fall through as if a linchpin had been pulled.

A robotic female voice drop-kicked him back to reality.

He missed the code.

Leaning against the wall for support, its corded paper concrete and comforting, he bent to retrieve the phone. Still squatting, he cautiously selected "replay" before holding it to his ear. On that first word, he was transported to Graham's office, in that streamlined, state-of-the-art, completely uncomfortable Marcel Breuer chair that did nothing but cripple his back while Graham made plans to orbit the moon. The rest of that day, and all that followed, sped through his memory in full color and sound. Graham's clear voice dissolved into the wordless warning of a man beyond saving.

"Fantastic, am I right?"

Val pressed "save" before the automated voice could interrupt the silence. He struggled to swallow. Quaking, he inched his way up, slid the phone back in his pocket, and keyed in 4-8-1-2.

The door unlocked with a *thonk* and stuttered as though startled awake. He pushed the cold handle with his free hand, wrapping his fingers tight around it before pushing off the wall. The suite looked altogether different and the same, welcoming and austere. The furniture was draped with white painter's tarps layered with dust. Boxes sealed with duct tape were scattered haphazardly as though waiting for a trip down the incinerator. Decades of work left unfinished, a legacy severed. Graham must have kept every manuscript he read, every contract. Val doubted if Anna had even given the contents a second glance.

All the little touches collected over the years had been removed: the fat glass ashtray Graham insisted stay at the reception desk as an homage to Ed, the colorful works of art and fake vining plants that had once been everywhere. Bright, bounteous, hopeful. It was Graham's, without a trace of inheritance or obligation. His youthful exuberance had bounced off the walls.

The thin steel lettering behind the reception desk had been erased like so much pencil lead. In its place, a swath of paint untouched by grime, a ghost peeking out through the decades. A little scrub to assure new tenants everything was fine. The spray of holes in the plaster filled in and forgotten.

Val was the only thing living, half an image reflected in the door, a lateral slice of a whole person. Some sound—a whistle in the air system, the squeal of a cleaning machine a floor down—tightened through the walls.

He saw Anna here again, shredded. She'd spent hours as a widow and had no idea. *And all you could do was watch.*

Grabbing a flashlight off the receptionist's desk, Val started down the hall toward Graham's office, once Ed's. The same path he'd taken since signing his first contract as a young man. He swept the flashlight in a shaky line up, up, where the rubber trees once stood. The carpet ended, the edge of a tiny cliff, all feathered pile and rough fringe before a stripe of filth on concrete.

Grab what you came for and get out. You don't belong here anymore.

The intern's office across the hall had no window. It was so narrow, it may once have been a supply closet. Val opened each drawer, rifled through endless scraps, looking for a name, a check stub. An unmarked red folder contained a year's worth of insurance updates, memos, and other minutiae left over from the first day on the job. Something heavy rattled among the papers.

A photo ID.

Val ripped at his collar, unbuttoned three buttons, wheezed against the phantom wire digging into his throat. The same pale face stared from its plastic prison, hovering above a shirt and tie instead of beneath a hood. Blue eyes, clear as blown glass.

Travis Gorski.

The man who insisted Val was taking too long to die.

Looking at the photo was like hearing a stranger tell a story about himself. Travis must've known every move Graham made—deals with the publisher, interviews—but who was the other attacker? That idiot cameraman? Graceless, rough, blotched with tattoos—he would've been an obvious outsider in Val's neighborhood.

His mind raced through one violent scenario to another, landing fists into flesh and bone until they exploded with color. This bastard released the spoilers, intended to ruin his career. But the man had no ties other than access to some manuscripts. He wouldn't have needed to break in; he had everything funneling through him at work.

Though none of the answers filled in like he'd expected, proving one of the attackers was connected, in however convoluted a way, imparted an odd lift in the despair that abraded his thoughts for months.

He wandered to the atrium in a daze and swung the flashlight back onto Lucy's desk. Before shutting it off, he caught a familiar number scrawled on a manila envelope in green ink: *60688.*

There was no such zip code, not really. It was exclusive to a single postal facility near O'Hare. He checked a thousand times before using it.

A shirring came from the hallway, a blaze of red light blinding him in the near-darkness. The elevator, heading to this floor. He must've alerted security through the surveillance cameras.

Cameras.

Of course there had to be some sort of surveillance system

with so much confidential information around. Cops would've discovered as much. They would've taken the feed as evidence.

Val grabbed the envelope and lifted the flashlight beam to the ceiling. Two tiny brown domes bulged down.

Three more were embedded in the hallway outside the elevator.

Graham's killer was on video somewhere. How could cops take so long to find a man if they had his picture?

The flashlight slipped and bounced off Val's shoe. It couldn't be.

The spoilers. Graham. It all happened too quickly.

Marczek insisted it was a fan.

Click. The elevator was rising: second floor, third.

Marczek...he'd accused him of eavesdropping.

Click.

The digital readout glowed four, five, in beautiful, flourishing script.

Click. Like on his phone, time after time, and he had no fucking clue. They heard the plans to meet at Graham's office the night he was killed. And the message with the code.

But not just anybody can arrange a wiretap.

His brain scrambled in a dozen different directions. How extensive was a bug? If they recorded GPS, maybe that's how they tracked him to Midway.

Idiot. You'd told Sandra your whereabouts, your plans.

Leaving nothing to chance, he ripped the battery out and ground it beneath his heel, tossing the phone in the trash.

Six, seven, eight...no time for anything but a quick reset of the alarm. He fumbled with the buttons. Hands shaking twice as hard as before, he dropped the envelope.

Fuck.

Nine. *Faster.*

Ten. The yellow light of the keypad blinked brighter.

Thonk. No time to make sure it held. He darted into the stairwell.

Chapter Twenty

Were there cameras here too?

No time to check.

Twice he nearly dropped the envelope while trying to stuff it into his jacket, pleading for his heart to keep pace. The air hung thick and oily, clogging his throat and lungs. His ankle grated with every flight.

Bursting through the lobby doors, he wobbled onto the street before anyone caught him and hailed the first cab he saw.

"The Drake."

The gothic hotel was close enough to Anna's; he'd run the rest of the way. An extra dose of paranoia couldn't hurt.

***

One civilized knock on her door was all he had patience for. When it went unanswered, he stopped himself from bellowing her name. Neighbors would ease their doors open, snoop through the crack afforded by the chain guards, and call the cops.

And there very well may be one inside.

Trying the knob, it turned easily. He barged in and sprinted down the hall.

Afternoon sunlight streamed through the grubby picture window. One steaming cup of coffee sat on an end table, but the place smelled of apathy and smoke. Piano music trilled through unseen speakers, just loud enough distinguish an earful of haphazard, discordant notes. A tie was thrown over the back of Graham's overstuffed recliner, which had been dragged to the center of the room. Tread marks left by the casters rutted the carpet.

Anna's size ensured her robe—Graham's—enveloped her, but any other time she'd have bunched it up at the breast. Surrounded by bare walls and dim track lighting, she looked sickly and used, staring through muddied mascara at the apparition on the wall. She held a Dunhill like a pro, flicking it with a shaky thumb over an ashtray perched on the arm.

"Anna?"

She sniffed in greeting, chipped at a crusty patch on the skirt of the robe.

"What are you doing?"

She raised the cigarette and dragged it. "Smoking."

"No, I mean—"

"Want one?" She still refused to look at him.

"Listen—"

"No? Then get out. Nobody asked you here."

"Anna, listen to me now. Mar—Tony—isn't who you think he is."

"You don't say."

"Anna. Get out of that chair and come with me. I'm not playing a game with you."

"He left me, you know that?"

"Who?"

"*Tony*. Who else is left who isn't dead or…you?"

"I don't have time for this. Grab a few things and—"

"All because of you," she said, tipping her head in Val's direction but only looking out the corner of her eye. She twirled the cigarette in the air. A long tuft of ashes tumbled onto her lap but she didn't brush them away.

"Me?"

"He was using me to keep an eye on you. Couldn't exactly rent a room at your place, right? He thought if the people who—" Her voice broke, but before Val interrupted, she held up a hand and stared daggers over her fingers. "He worried if Graham stored your work here, they'd hurt me too. Even though I told him a hundred times Graham never brought his work home. But he wanted to make extra sure because he's such a *huge* fan! Isn't that great?"

Shards of ice scissored up Val's spine.

"Never wanted me at all. Getting to be a real broken record around here."

"I'm sorry, Anna, but none of that matters—"

She laughed, a brittle, sobbing bleat that erupted from depths he couldn't reach. "Still making yourself the center, I see. What about the Foundation?"

"The Foundation?"

Anna rolled her eyes. "Figures you wouldn't remember. Tony was our biggest donor. Wanted to help me construct a place for kids to really *be* something, grab their dreams and make them come true. Him and his brat. Just like Graham failed to do. Remember when we talked about that and you nearly lost it?" She snorted. "By the look of things, you're well on your way."

Looking out for the kids. The right kind *of kids, naturally.*

She pointed to the blank splotch on the wall. "At least I got that out of him. Got that great big donation. The first and last."

Graham's last act was promoting Val's book. He wasn't just a casualty.

"You writers, I swear. Life isn't just what you research, Val. And yet you kept writing, didn't you?" As she stared at the smoldering filter, the knots of anger in her face melted, comprehension illuminating the hollows and combusting. "It was never about Michael," she whispered.

She was right about him. Every word.

"All this time you could've written anything else, anything at all."

"Anna. That's simply not true."

Her response was a tightening of her fist around the stub, a wisp of smoke snuffed between her fingers. The faint tinkling of the piano reached a harried crescendo, still too tinny to decipher the piece. Anna pointed a remote at the wall and the sound cut off mid-note, the frenzy still resounding in his ears.

"This is all I have," he said.

"You had a lot more before you started."

"I can't stay here. I don't have my phone, I don't know

when I'll be able to contact—"

"How 'bout you don't contact me?" She flicked the spent butt in Val's direction, missing by several feet. "You think the usual shout-out on the acknowledgements page is going to make up for capitalizing on my husband's murder? Enjoy the spotlight while you can, honey."

Chapter Twenty-One

The L sighed to a stop. Val collapsed into the first empty seat.

Sparks raked the windows as the train's metal cages whined around curves. His nerves shredded with every impatient shriek of the whistle. Did it serve to warn potential jumpers or improve their timing?

Covering over a dozen miles in excruciating three-minute increments gave him unwanted time to think. Anna had looked away, red-faced, their friendship dissipating in the air between his faltering words. Walking past him like a ghost, she locked herself away in the bedroom, waiting for him to leave. Without Graham's collection of splashy art, it was another basic condo under renovation. There was nothing left to say goodbye to.

His cheek itched with the kiss he never received.

The L doors opened to a burger wrapper skittering across concrete. A long, yellow puddle seemed to ooze out from the wall. Despite the harsh lights and fresh white paint, shadows lurked under arched tunnels and around metal girders. A canned voice announced the name of the station, but no one entered the car. The train eased forward, the rhythmic rattling of the doors like the chattering of teeth.

Seconds ago the seats were filled with people, but somehow their eyes never met. They stared at shoes, spaces between heads, gave their full attention to the posters advertising catering, colleges, festivals. All things they couldn't afford yet were teased with during their entire trip. No matter how hard they worked, how much they salted away, they'd never be welcome.

Every time the doors opened, they whisked away another thought until logic turned to vapor. He searched for a reason to head back to the B&B in the first place. What did he have to collect? A portfolio with the laptop and a manuscript, a couple of USBs, and a publishing contract. An extra shirt, toothbrush and expired toothpaste. Another night of rented sleep. His tattered car, with nothing to prove ownership other than a smear of blood on the wheel, was free to whoever picked the lock. He'd be back on these trains again tomorrow, heading toward the airport. Without Sandra.

Too many variables swirled in his head. Calling from his room to say goodbye seemed like tempting fate. Calling after he landed was safer.

Or would it be better to pull his famous disappearing act one last time?

Knowing Anna wasn't on Marczek's hit list didn't make it any easier to leave her behind.

How much did he owe the dead?

Regardless of his destination, he needed his passport. And a change of clothes. For once his home at the edge of the world felt like a burden. How would he get from there to either O'Hare or Midway airport without being noticed? They already tailed him once. Like the outlaw in Westerns from his youth, he needed to cross enemy territory without earning an arrow in his back. If he were smart, he'd have gone home directly after seeing Anna, instead of riding the rails for hours, trying to purge the last few days from his mind.

Reaching up to rub his face, the envelope in his jacket poked him in the chin. He'd forgotten he had it.

He pulled out the pages he'd brought Graham at Christmas. But there wasn't a single mark on them.

The last page had a grainy texture. Letterhead. Val squinted to decipher Graham's handwriting, the green ink bleak against the white paper.

It was dated February third; Graham had gone back to the office after visiting hours were over and penned this letter. Did he never mean to send it or had he just not gotten the chance?

He skimmed it, mouth flapping open and shut with no

sound, and pulled on his glasses. Held the letter up to the light to check the watermark. Read it twice more, trying to find a different message in it, a brighter interpretation. But Graham's diplomatic technique was never anything but direct. Val's heart cringed into a lead ball.

When had he lost his touch? Once he stopped releasing novels within his traditional two-year timeframe? Or worse, long before then, while *Vanishing Desert* was still a new release? Was this latest effort merely to satisfy the completists? Graham had dropped enough hints, interest waning even as they discussed the interview at Christmas. Even left the *Chicago Lit Review* on the edge of his desk. Was it coincidence, or was he just like everyone else, relying on the old Haverford light to flare one last time before the supernova?

Anna's warning about having to find a new agent…if she let slip that she knew about Val's failing sight, she'd never have held on to information this juicy. If it wasn't for him playing detective, the termination of Graham's contract would've remained a secret.

The canned voice called out again: end of the line. A security guard strolled past with a German shepherd muzzled into a wire cage. The guard's lead vest stuck out at odd angles; the black pants, shirt, and boots turning him into a solid figure. One color, one shape, one purpose. He banged on the car's windows with his nightstick.

Val's knees pushed into his calves. His hand wrapped around the tacky stanchion, hoisted him up. Every joint jiggled loose; any second his limbs would clatter to the floor and down the gap between car and platform.

The train squealed down the tracks. It would turn in a circle half a mile south and continue, over and over, in a giant endless loop. Val ascended the elevator to street level rather than wait for the inbound. Used side streets off State guide him back to the B&B.

If only Graham had waited to post that next batch of announcements. If only he'd sent this letter. *If only you'd listened when he warned you to quit.*

Residents propped against doorways and lounged on stoops. The tiny orange lights of their cigarettes glowed and dimmed, smoke punctuating hushed conversations and loud laughter. Gossip followed by the cozy humor of familiarity.

When was the last time he and Graham shot the shit at the pub, talked trash into the wee hours? A drink at Calvyn's would be perfect right now, even one of Graham's favorite shitty beers.

Especially one of Graham's shitty beers.

Val crept up the front steps of the B&B hours later and clicked the door gently behind him. The entrance table held a bowl of matchbooks with an outline of the building in its heyday stamped in gold foil. He cradled one in his palm as though it would break.

After fastening the deadbolt to his room, he unplugged the phone. Peeled off his clothes and recoiled at his own ripeness. Stood naked on the bathroom tile, the chill locking into his bones.

He dumped the manuscript into the tub and struck a match. Lit the entire book ablaze and held it until it singed his fingers. Dropped it and watched the papers go up, let the smoke burn his eyes, memorized the way this looked: the curling pages, the blackening edges, the ink molting into lead, the flakes of ash flying up like tiny birds before gravity jerked them back down.

A smoldering pile of confetti filled the bottom of the tub. Val turned on the showerhead and rinsed the pieces down the drain, gray rivulets staining the porcelain like a poor-man's Pollock. Kneeling on the floor, he ran the water until every last trace of color disappeared and nothing was left; no sign of it, of him.

But the letter, Graham's letter, he kept.

Chapter Twenty-Two

The evening passed in a surreal haze.

The swish of wind through the trees, the lapping of the lake against the sand, the faint grind of tires on the road had composed the soundtrack of home. Here, with half the community swept away, an unearthly silence hung like a threat along the eaves. Sleep had seemed ridiculous until he'd tried to go without.

As second-shifters stirred, sound amplified through the barren alleyways. A driver unfamiliar with the patchwork streets bounced through one pothole after another. Voices echoed off deserted buildings and found each other again. What at first seemed like a typical conversation turned clipped, two curs snarling at the ends of their ropes. Grumbling, Val rolled off the bed and stared down through the torn window screen. One of the men weaved in and out of sight: a wave of oversized clothes, a scruff of blond hair, right leg slagging along behind. He pushed off with the side of the dead foot and pulled himself forward, lurching down the sidewalk. Somewhere a bottle shattered. Another man, gray either from age or hardship, loomed into view. Cheeks blotched with rage, he looked demented as he followed his companion into the shadows. He shoved the younger man off the curb and wandered across the street, continuing the argument as they stumbled. The last remaining transients finding a shred of solidarity.

Silence again. Val turned to go back to bed, but the dull thudding of fists against flesh nagged at the edges of consciousness. He turned on the prehistoric fan in the corner, hoping to drown everything out with the grating snore of the blades. Collapsing onto the sagging mattress, he counted the popcorn in the ceiling instead of sheep.

Minutes later, Val startled at some blast, a shout, some howling emergency, from the direction the vagrants disappeared.

Another, more feverish. Euphoric. Val flicked off the fan.

A sharp crack followed, electric. Some otherworldly sound heard only in movies. A woman screamed a man's name, demanding he get up, stop playing.

Again: an explosion too abbreviated to be thunder. A third time, then a fourth, a fifth, reverberating through the walls.

It could've been a car backfiring. Or idiot kids testing noisemakers a few days before the Fourth of July.

It was neither.

The shrug of indifference resounded of "or."

Wood scraped against wood as Val threw the window open. The urge to witness the scene for himself, force the conspiracy out of his head, pulled him over the sill.

Standing over the bodies, slapping his companion on the back, was a young man in a gray hooded sweatshirt. Val waited, willing him to turn. The woman's sobbing drowned out their voices.

The second man talked into a cell phone held in front of his mouth like a recorder. They ran back the way they came and out of sight, but not before Val caught the face beneath the hood. Travis. Thumping his boy on the chest, both of them grinning, swinging their arms like champions. Val ducked back in, his breath a roar in his ears.

Oscillating red shadows leapt from doorways. A whole fleet of emergency vehicles arrived within seconds. Lights spinning, sirens off, like they knew there'd be nothing to save.

An unexpected flash of movement across the street made him flatten against the wall. A sliver of a woman appeared in a gaping window and shook her head. Two floors down, a man crossed himself. Then they readjusted the darkness and vanished. Far from abandoned, these buildings were full of people who had seen it all before, who prayed to the same God his mother had, who received no comfort other than the fictions they manufactured themselves. A population of people one level away.

In the distance, a pitiful wail uncoiled and slithered into every crevice. Incoherent terror held the only proof these two men existed.

Within the hour, the resolute hush returned.

Chapter Twenty-Three

A bang at the door propelled Val like a cannonball, leaving his skin behind in a heap.

He froze. The dusty fringes of sleep clogged his mind.

"Val? Are you in there?"

Sandra.

He leapt out of the armchair, wrenched open the swollen door. She dropped a valise as he yanked her into the room, letting go just long enough to ram it shut and re-secure the deadbolt. The tendons in her arms skewed beneath his grip.

"How did you find me?"

"I searched the number on my caller ID," she said, tearing up.

"Anyone see you come in here?"

"Probably a dozen people—"

Val shook her, hard. She whimpered like a puppy kicked in its side. "Were you followed?"

"I don't know—"

"Think!"

"You're hurting me!"

He released her and she retreated, rubbing at the bruises blooming like blood spilled in water. The short space between them seemed to grow into a chasm. He stood on the precipice, unsure of how to cross.

The yip of a siren made them both jump. Val peeked out from behind the curtain. A police cruiser snaked around some jaywalkers and headed east, its lights still. The world was awash in dead air, hovering on the edge of some weird hour, the crime scene clear as though nothing had happened.

"What is going on with you?"

"Where to begin."

"You're scaring me. What happened to you? You never showed up, and look at you, your face…"

He stared at the ceiling, pulling his mouth and eyes wide. Blinking ground like sandpaper. His lungs refused any more air. Another siren, louder this time, a frantic whine that built to a crescendo and cut off abruptly.

"Valery!"

"Did anyone contact you, looking for me?"

"Yes. How did you know?"

Val's muscles tensed. His hands curled, the edges of the windowsill digging into his palms. He welcomed the pain of it, imagined the wood splitting in his grip, the newly broken ends at the ready.

"Tell me what he said."

She shrugged. "He asked to speak to you, but I told him you weren't there. Did he catch you?"

Val laughed at her choice of words. "You didn't tell him I was coming over?"

"No, why would I? And why did you give him my number instead of yours?"

"I had no idea what was happening. I wouldn't have let things get this far."

"You're not making sense. And you look like you haven't slept in weeks. I needed to talk to you, Val. It was urgent, at least I thought it was. Is. I called your cell a thousand times, and I find you hunkered down in this—place…"

"Tell me now."

"Let me get my cell phone. Okay?" She had to ask permission, like a hostage. Val nodded at the floor and pulled on his glasses.

She dug around in her purse, then held the phone so they could both see the screen. Forced to stand close enough that they breathed the same air, she leaned back, one leg angled like a kickstand, as though preparing a head start.

He immediately recognized the fabric of his couch. The camera panned in a deliberate, smooth arc past the veiled window, paused briefly on the front door, and swept past Val and Sandra talking at the edge of the room. The lens zoomed

214

in at the threshold of his studio. From that vantage point, the southern door and Raymond's porch light were visible. Two fingers popped up, then pointed north. The camera continued to pan until it had turned almost 360 degrees, then stopped between the fireplace and the window, pulled back slightly, and took in the full width of the space.

The same place where his attacker had been waiting.

The screen went black. "Just a second," Sandra said.

When the light returned, the lens zoomed in for a tight close-up of Sandra, then Val. The camera paused, waiting, until he stared directly into it. Kevin had captured a perfect recording, so detailed the viewer would never make a mistake.

"I thought Kevin was acting weird that day. When I asked him about this video, he said he was doing a lighting test. But it looks like—"

"That son of a bitch. He's one of them."

"One of *who*. Valery, I swear to God—"

He unhooked his reading glasses and rubbed a thumb and forefinger into his eyes. "It was all just a goddamn story."

Sandra replaced her phone and dropped the purse at her feet. "Valery." She tugged at his wrist, forcing him to look at her. "What kind of trouble are you in? What was 'just a story?'"

"Where did you find that video?"

"In the archive. After you told me you were writing again, I got excited about the book's release and how much publicity it would generate. I wanted to see if we could recycle any of the footage from your interview." She made those twisting motions with her mouth as she tapped her fingernails on a bedpost. "They took wild offense to my digging in there. They talked to me like child, Val, with her hand in the fucking cookie jar."

"So they fired you."

"Considering my response I guess you can say I quit."

"Does Kevin know you have this?"

"He's the one who called security."

Marczek was sure to write down her name on his little

notepad. He knew her show. Labeled her 'memorable.'

"I don't think I'm writing fiction."

"What's that supposed to mean?"

"I think I stumbled onto something I was never meant to know. When I was attacked, they warned me to stop writing. The only thing they stole was my work, all of it, not just the manuscript but notes, research, everything.

"Right before I passed out, they said, 'We have to secure our future.' *Ours*. You know what that's from? A supremacist slogan coined by David Lane."

"Who?"

"Aryan leader, founder of a sect called The Order. There was an article about Andre in the paper not long ago. Did you see it? Exactly the same situation as mine. He was strangled with the same type of wire, and warned to stop writing his book. He did, and they left him alone. They didn't want to kill me, they wanted to silence me. Until now."

"Now?"

Until I refused to obey. "I got lost in residential corridor when a car with tinted windows started chasing after me—"

"Chasing you!"

He waved away her obvious next question. "I didn't tell anyone where I was going except you, over the phone. It was tapped, and has been for months. I never told anyone your number, or that I was coming. They're after anyone who doesn't fit. And the man who called you tonight—they wanted to make sure they didn't make another mistake. It was never a fan, Sandra. And now they're watching you." Acid poured from that statement, the foul taste burning his mouth.

Sandra paled and eased onto the edge of the bed. "Start from the beginning."

He told her about how every pattern crumbled the further he dug; the details he refused to acknowledge; the parts of the narrative that he only noticed once they went missing. Truth hidden between the lines of articles and reports melted into one ceaseless roar.

The link wasn't crime, but need. Affliction and

circumstances eroded the city's economy the way the wound attacked the leg of that boy on the bus. It wasn't swift politics that cleaned up the city, it wasn't taxpayer dollars that reduced poverty and diminished the gangs, no reduction in unemployment that saved the homeless from sleeping on cement mattresses. There was a reason for everything, a plan in place, the witnesses mute.

The next level had been reached, the next victim offering himself up like a goddamn volunteer.

"'I don't know how you found out about us.'" Val massaged his throat. "They think I'm on to them. They're not done with me, or anyone else they think outlived their worth."

"I still have contacts, I can release—"

"Release what? That video?" Val grabbed her purse and shook it before throwing it back down. "There's nothing on there. No one will understand what it means, there's no obvious connection."

"There has to be a way—"

"Remember when I disappeared after Graham's murder?"

Val turned to the distorted window and stared into inky blackness. The moon reflected twin discs like the eyes of a predator stalking. He was uncertain what animal waited on the opposite side of the glass. It would skitter in and out of the shadows tonight, waiting.

He heard her swallow.

"I couldn't sleep. I couldn't work. So I veered off course. Wrote a manifesto. Torture, right down to the last detail. To this day I feel like someone else. I haven't dug myself out, but further in. I can't see the other side of this."

Something in him twisted, something he couldn't put words to. He turned halfway, not able to tear himself from the window.

No cars were parked anywhere near the B&B. Her Caddy was nowhere to be seen.

"That man who called—did he say anything else?"

"I thought it was your publisher." She rubbed a slow line back and forth across her stomach. "He said he...*they*...are no longer interested in just the manuscript."

"It was a mistake, you coming here."

She opened her mouth to speak but nothing came. Looked over her shoulder, guilty. Like she couldn't wait to run from this insanity, from him.

He followed her line of sight to a small leather valise near the door.

She didn't come here to simply show him a video that she could have shared in an email.

"Good timing." With any luck, she'd be gone before they find out she's unemployed. *Undesirable.* "Did you tell anyone you're leaving?"

She shook her head. "Not yet. Ella's out of town."

"Find a good spot where you can watch the sun rise."

Chapter Twenty-Four

The last-ditch edit on Graham's laptop was so much sweeter than any dedication. Though he'd never have approved of changing the antagonists' identities. 'All names used within this text are purely coincidental' disappeared in a rush of euphoria.

Val saved the latest incarnation on a USB and dug the publishing contract from his portfolio. He pulled out Graham's pen and uncapped it, but hesitated before signing. Novelists don't write exposés. Then again, that designation no longer seemed to apply to him.

Tears threatening, Sandra had straightened her back and walked away without a kiss goodbye, a touch...no hint whether he qualified as a hero or villain in her eyes.

Too late for indecision, reparations. There was only point A, point B, and the path to last chances. They'd have to find him to sue for libel, and he wasn't planning to send anyone a change of address card. Tucking Graham's pen into his shirt pocket, he scribbled his name with the cheap ballpoint clipped to a stack of takeout menus in the desk drawer.

***

A few blocks east, curbside mailboxes lined the grounds outside the post office. Val eased his car into the narrow pathway between them and the sidewalk. Envelopes of all shapes and sizes crammed the maw of one. The others appeared to be empty, but there was no telling whether his package would descend to the bottom or get stuck part way, leaving a corner poking out for anyone to grab. It was a holiday weekend, after all. No pickup for the next three days.

He'd only made one copy, stuffing the blank USB in his pocket. Foolish or genius? If they caught up with him, they'd destroy any other copies as well as the laptop. Jitters had coursed through his wrist as he'd held that second USB up to the port. Metal scraped against metal as he'd tried to fit it in, distracted by racing images of where he might leave it. The desk drawer was too common. Windowsill, next to the phone, too obvious. Under his pillow, ledge of the bathroom sink, tucked inside the Bible? The shaking worsened until he dropped it with a clatter, breathing through the bile threatening to rise. If they ever got wind of where he'd been hiding, identified his car and searched the room, Lucille would be at risk too. He'd just have to make sure nothing went wrong. Mail it in, head home, get in and get out. Drive to the nearest L stop and ditch the car there instead.

Val pulled the envelope out of the portfolio and twisted the edge in his fingers. Checked the address for the hundredth time against the business card in his wallet. The USB, the contract, and the eight-page disclosure inside would do the talking, assuming the package made it past Black Horse's mailroom in the first place. Assuming they didn't have the same reaction as Graham and toss it in the shredder.

And who sent manuscripts via snail mail these days? There was no internet service at the B&B, at least until renovations were complete. And by Lucille's gaunt expression, she wasn't expecting it come Monday.

She'd swayed inside her colorless dress, hands clasped as though preparing a chant, as she asked if he'd needed anything else before he moved on, the hopeful hitch in her voice begging him to say no. He'd smiled with half his mouth, staring at those calloused hands, wanting to squeeze her creased fingers. Instead, he'd answered with a simple "no, ma'am," glad he'd tossed every dollar he had onto nightstand before checking out.

He held the envelope onto the lip of the chute, fingers clamped white around the metal. More than sixty years ago he'd lit cherry bombs with his delinquent friends, threw them into mailboxes, then waited around bends in the roads until they bulged with muffled explosions, the doors tearing open and spewing confetti onto the gravel shoulders.

Kids were still kids. He should have made another copy.

Releasing his grip, he tossed the envelope on the dash and pulled out the laptop. Still plenty of battery left; he could take care of it right there. He fumbled with the bunched-up lining of his pants pocket, panicking over the USB just out of reach.

In the distance, a handful of quick pops followed by the bristle of a Roman candle made him look up. Not six feet away, a chiseled tower of a man stared through his windshield, wife-beater pulled up at the hip. He bent, squinting, winding his dog's leash around the boulder of his fist.

"Hey." He jerked his chin up, rubbed the fine line of stubble that edged his mouth and jaw. "You."

Had Lucille recognized him at some point, gossiped to her friends? Or maybe his hiding spot was discovered and she'd given him up to save herself. Like an idiot, he'd chosen a mailbox within walking distance. These wide streets concealed nothing.

Val chucked the envelope down the chute. It didn't make a sound.

***

Dusk had fallen by the time he arrived home, the erratic route giving him a sense of cover and Sandra a bigger head start. On its face, the township was a ghost town every Fourth, streets and front porches abandoned in favor of backyard barbecue pits and neighborhood parks. Restless energy murmured from somewhere unseen. Faint voices hovered on a waft of charcoal and grilled meat.

The spirit of his cabin had shifted, its cedar scent soured. Nothing was displaced, not a speck of dust unsettled. Yet the span of one day felt like years, mustiness lingering over the threshold. Silence carpeted the floor and knotholes ogled from the walls.

All he needed was in the bedroom safe and closet. But.

Crouched between the bed and the wall, leaving the safe unlocked, he mentally searched the house. The sketch, the miniatures, the bow stem. How long would it take to grab all that? Five minutes? Everything else could be bought. Pricking his ears, he rose up slowly and made his way back to the front room.

He sensed the threat before he saw it. As he unfurled his handkerchief on the mantel to lay the bow stem inside, the absence of light hit him in the stomach. He'd purposely left a gap in his patchwork boarding of the studio to allow safe passage for Raymond's nightlight.

The studio was black. Impossible shapes lay beyond.

He gripped the bow stem and wound the handkerchief until it was secure in his fist. The wood was thin, dry. But it was better than nothing.

He rocked forward on the balls of his feet. Electricity sizzled along the walls and intensified as he moved catlike toward the studio.

At the threshold he tried to adapt to the darkness, listen for the other man's breathing. He couldn't be certain, no matter which way he turned his head, whether the odd shape in front of him was his desk with the new drawers pulled out or a trick of the mind.

Inching his left hand along the wall, he found the light switch and flicked up.

Nothing.

Jerked forward by the collar, a sledgehammer force collided with his face, sending him reeling. Grasping for anything solid, he latched onto a bookshelf to regain his footing.

The taste of salt and rust trickled into his mouth. The intruder came at him again, shoving him sideways for another blow. Val bent inwards and started to raise the bow stem. But if this bastard could see him well enough to kick his ass in near darkness, he'd have to be patient, wait for a better opportunity. Hope to Christ one presented itself.

Val pressed the bow stem against the back of his thigh and inched toward the southern door. Gears clicked, the metallic crunch unmistakable. A thin shaft of shifting moonlight broke between the boards and illuminated the intruder's silver pistol. Glassy blue eyes, set into a ghastly white face, stared at him with wolfish ferocity.

"Remember me?"

Val nodded at the pistol. This time Travis was clearly in control. There was no novice with a garrote giving him a chance to form alliances.

Light traveled much faster than sound. Would Val ever hear the discharge or would the flash be the last thing he saw? Even if he moved lightning fast, the bow stem would be about as helpful as frisbee. Numbness tingled the palm of his hand. He twitched the muscles in his fingers.

"Looks like you cleared the place out yourself this time," Travis said. "Where's it hiding now?"

Think. For Christ's sake, think.

"Answer me, old man." Travis took a step closer.

"Shed." Val swallowed. "There's a copy in the shed."

"Bullshit. You think I didn't look there first?"

"I make boxes to hide valuables in. See that pencil case there?" He tipped his head toward the desk. "There's a hidden compartment to stash a few bucks, a note, what have you. There's a bigger one in the shed where I keep the manuscript."

Travis seemed to mull that over, unsure of whether he preferred to look sloppy or stupid. "Take me to it."

Val rushed toward the southern door, pulling his right arm in front of him.

Travis closed in, running the gun up Val's spine. He recoiled at the touch.

"Slow down, old man. I'm not chasing you." Travis rapped the gun between Val's shoulder blades.

His neighbors to the north were bathed in the soft yellow of patio floodlights. Patriotic music tinkled from a stereo. Did that mean they could hear noise coming from his property? Or was their music loud enough to drown everything else out?

No difference. One shout and he'd be dead before it registered.

As they neared the stone wall, Val saw his opportunity.

He hovered over the railing at the top of the stairs, unsteady on his feet. The punch to the face made this truth.

Tensing his hand for effect, he watched Travis from the corner of his good eye as he descended.

Travis stepped down after him, skimming the rail.

With his left foot braced one step above, Val turned his right foot outward, faking a slip. As Travis grabbed the handrail, Val shoved hard with all his weight. The wood splintered, breaking away from the posts. The loose post popped out from between the stones, dry mortar flying in a spray of dust and jagged shards. Travis pitched over, losing his grip on the pistol.

Val twisted his heel between the bones of Travis' wrist, driving it down, and kicked the gun away with the opposite foot. Travis growled and swung a leg around. Too slow to dodge it completely, it caught Val in the chin, opening up the scar and pushing him back.

Travis gained the momentum he needed to roll over and rise up, teetering to regain his footing on the shifting sand. Keeping between Travis and the gun, Val waited for the next punch.

When it came, Val swung the bow stem in a wide arc. Missed. Travis' brow wrinkled with confused laughter as he tried to glimpse the weapon. He lunged, one arm thrust forward to force Val into the wall.

Turning his hand outward, Val gouged the air as though mowing with a scythe. A rip of fabric was quickly followed by a gnarled cry of pain. Travis bent at the waist, scooping and clutching at his midsection as he crumpled to the ground, wadding his shirt. Val ignored the keening that seemed to pour from the air itself.

Quite a performance.

Val kicked at the sand to uncover the gun, watching him out the corner of his eye. Travis would drop the act the second Val let down his guard.

Moaning turned to muttering. A frantic, gasping whine like a child lost in the dark. Travis was curled into a tight ball, hands against his sweaty head as though saying a bedtime prayer.

Val snorted. Good luck, kid.

High overhead, an explosion of light and sound died with a fizzle and shower of sparks. His neighbors leaned over the balcony and pointed at the streams of pink and yellow.

Another pop of firecrackers.

Pause. Pop. Pause.

Testing for duds.

The nose of the gun shone under the flare. Val flicked at his handkerchief to find the end of the knot. Gasped at the sodden squish. The next flare illuminated the paste of blood and viscera staining the wood of the bow stem, now quite a bit shorter.

Travis' white shirt was crimson, the gash in the center glistening. His attempt to hold his intestines in was impeded by the splintered ends of the bow stem stabbing into his torso.

Val fixed on the wood as it quivered with every ragged breath. Squatted, favoring his good ankle. Traced a finger through the sand to relocate the gun so he wouldn't have to tear his eyes away.

How slowly blood soaked into sand, the slick sheen sparkling under the champagne starbursts. The color never really fading. Rubies on a bed of white gold. Val's panting slowed until it was as even and tranquil as the cycle of waves. He fought with the contradiction of wanting to put the boy out of his misery and causing so much more.

The sound of a car door slamming broke the spell.

Travis' eyes widened as Val loomed over his trembling body. "They're coming, old man." He eased onto his back.

"Who? Who's coming?"

"You're fucked," he spat, thick and wet. Smiled, his mouth bright with blood and frothy bubbles.

And by his ear a cell phone.

Chapter Twenty-Five

Val tamped the remainder of the bow stem into the sand and ran into the studio. Pacing before the east wall, the wood slats a cage, he tracked a man in an ill-fitting sports coat covering every possible vantage point.

Marczek squatted to check for Travis' pulse. Picked up the cell phone and stalked toward the lake, waded ankle-deep, and hurled it in.

He stared at the sky, waiting.

Val tried to match his gaze, unsure what he was looking for, holding his breath to avoid fogging the glass. A moth beat its wings against the screen.

At the next starburst, Marczek pointed his pistol and fired. One shot was all he needed. Travis' head bounced and rolled with the impact and was still.

Marczek marched toward the cabin, tensed and ready. He had the bearing of a man whose experience with guns far outmatched that of wires.

"You know what I hate even more than nosy neighbors and deadbeats, Haverford? Arrogant fucking writers who can't take a hint."

Other than the southern door, the studio was soundly boarded. Would Marczek enter a pitch-black room without knowing exactly where his target was? Or whether he was armed?

"How you figured this one out, we'll never know. We've been keeping an eye on you since '74, and you just ain't that clever."

Paralysis crept over Val in a heavy wave as that inconsequential number mutated into cognizance. His feet turned to stone, the weight rising until he was numb. Ice flowed where blood should be.

How many people misread "Green Skies and Blue Fields" as propaganda? And his brilliant evolution of levels, of prescribed gentrification, came to Val through newscasts, articles, eavesdropping on conversations at Calvyn's; speculating on history's atrocities, the sick imaginations of maniacs, turning fragments of the city over in his mind and wondering what would happen if society crumbled beneath his feet.

All the times he toyed with scrapping this project. But it was great, it was genius.

Marczek swore and spat into the sand. "We liked you a lot better when you blamed everything on aliens." He laughed, a mocking trill that grew into a gasping, hardy chuckle.

Val heard the voice again, a door to the past slamming behind him. *You're a very…very…stupid man.*

"Come on out. Hands up. I can make this quick and painless."

A few boyhood hunting trips aside, Val had never touched a firearm in his life. He held Travis' pistol so the hammer was in line with his good eye. The handle was hot, crosshatching gritty. Colored lights glinted off the front sight. Unable to find the rear, he stuck the muzzle through a random gap in the boards. The barrel knocked against the window. Wouldn't the glass explode in his face?

"You come out or I come in, that's the last decision you get to make."

Two possible escape routes remained: through the unboarded studio door—with Marczek pacing outside—or through the front. Starting up his car's ignition without sending him running and shooting out the tires was a gamble, but Val's only option.

Black blotches battered his eyes with every beat of his heart. Val cranked open a window. Wind whistled through the boards like screams through nightmares.

Ten thousand explosions pierced the sky with light. The full fireworks show had started.

A short *thwip* was followed by a hot flash near Val's ear.

One of the books in the west wall caught the bullet that was meant for him.

Opening the window gave away his position.

Val fired back without thinking. He staggered at the blast reverberating from shoulder to hip.

"Wrong choice, Haverford."

Val darted to the opposite end of the studio as Marczek raised his weapon again. *Let muscle memory take over.* Where was the position of his hand? How high was his arm? *There's no time to think...*

Glass shattered, followed by the high-pitched chime of the bullet ricocheting off metal, as Marczek got off another shot. A third, splintering a wood slat. Shards seared through Val's thigh.

Weight, counterweight. The muzzle eclipsed Marczek's body, an angular silhouette against the blitz of light. *By following along just ahead...*

Stalking to the door, Marczek squeezed his arms in, pistol pointing at the ground, ready to raise and strike.

Aim between the elbows. He's doing the work for you.

Lightheaded, Val pictured that son-of-a-bitch doubling over as his stomach exploded under a sky full of fire.

He forced himself to swallow around his shit-eating grin.

And he understood.

He prepared for the kickback and fired. Fired. Fired until the gun was empty.

A scream cut through the noise, clear and clean like music.

Caught between a laugh and a sob, Val tore off a slat for a better view, leaning a hand against the glass.

Marczek was half-sitting in the grass, veins in his neck popping as he gripped his inner thigh. Blood welled through his fingers.

Val rocked back on his heels and watched his handprint fade.

He'd shot an officer. Attempted murder.

No matter the kind of monster Marczek was, no matter the extent of the wound or if he lived through it, no one would see it any other way. And he'd never deny it.

Wisconsin was just over an hour north this time of night. He might have a chance to make it across the state line if he bolted before the fireworks ended. As much as he'd like to finish what he started. But Marczek had the last loaded gun.

Pain lashed through Val's leg. His right side ran warm, heavy. *What a shit time for exhaustion to set in.*

Sandra was in Cancún, or should be. The shoreline of the Gulf was a million miles long with plenty of other places to choose. He'd finally see it in reality, feel the sand between his toes, stare across the water to the States through the eyes of an old man. The way the plan was supposed to have gone.

Snatching randomly at the figures over the sketch table, his trembling hand knocked most of them to the floor. *Leave them. Grab the banker bag and* go. He tossed the gun aside as he lurched down the hallway. No sense wasting time wiping it down.

Marczek had pulled his car along the side of the cabin. Nothing blocked the driveway. If Val's limbs cooperated he'd be out of there in seconds. But it seemed even his face dragged along the ground.

He folded himself into his car and threw it into reverse. Stomped the gas and collided with the steps. Wiped the sweat from his eyes before hitting the main road. It was completely empty except for the splotches of light teasing him forward. Somewhere he swore he heard a siren but it sank under the breaking waves of the Gulf.

The lake.

Trees morphed from birches to palms. He swallowed, his mouth so very wet, the taste of adrenaline a sweet cocktail. The empty shell of his cabin a souvenir bobbing in the distance, shadows claiming the whole of it, until it was nothing more than a skiff he'd sail away on. He'd have a home built from the sketch based on memories and incessant dreaming, tucked under the sun on a white, warm beach on the bank of the Gulf of Mexico.

END

Fantastic Books
Great Authors

darkstroke is
an imprint of
Crooked Cat Books

- Gripping Thrillers
- Cosy Mysteries
- Romantic Chick-Lit
- Fascinating Historicals
- Exciting Fantasy
- Young Adult
- Non-Fiction

Discover us online
www.darkstroke.com

Find us on instagram:
www.instagram.com/darkstrokebooks